Cont

Chapter One

Jerome Decarie clutched his duffle bag in his left hand with his ticket in his right as he waited at the local bus stop. Soon he'd be returning to New Orleans. He'd only been there briefly in a failed attempt to get hired on with a band. He glanced over at his mother who had given him an attempt at a hug while his sister was wiping her eyes. How fast he'd moved from playing saxophone in small bars and concert halls in Jackson, Florida, to being in one of the lead groups for the Jazz Festival. That was where he met Lewis, band leader for The Spirits. Now he finally had an offer to join his band in New Orleans. It was a great next step for him. They had a regular gig at the main bar in the Royal George Hotel. He watched as the bus pulled in and gave his mother a quick kiss on the cheek.

"I'm off to the big city."

He grabbed Janice close before he ran up the steps into the bus.

"Love you." He had a moment of regret as he left them standing alone. Since his Dad took off back when he had turned thirteen, Jerome took on the man in the family role. But, his mother relied on him far too much.

Tired from a last night of partying with old friends, he'd had little time to rummage through his few possessions to decide what to take with him. After they left the station and pulled onto the highway, he'd fallen into a deep sleep, his head against the hard vinyl back. He woke at early dusk with commotion surrounding him. Passengers around him yawned and rubbed their eyes while they pulled themselves to their feet in the aisle of the bus, carry-on bags in hand. The man seated next to him shook his shoulder.

"We're here in The Big Easy. You awake?"

Jerome pulled himself upright and stretched. "Yeah. I've waited a long time to play in this city, the birthplace of jazz." He glanced out the window and watched dirty cardboard and newspapers blow down the street.

"Well, right now it's just survived one of the worst hurricanes ever seen in these parts. Be careful when you travel around."

"What should I see first?"

"Most tourists hit the Riverwalk down along the Mississippi first thing. Waters down some now and you can usually find some street musicians there."

"Good idea. I'll give it a try once I'm settled. I was only here for a few days last time and never left the French Quarter." Jerome recalled the packed streets of tourists mingled with locals on Bourbon Street at night, many with drinks in hand. He felt a catch in his throat as he recalled the music from the open windows of restaurants and bars, the smell of southern cooking. It was the vibrant culture of the city that attracted him to come back to stay, at least for a while.

The stranger hurried down the aisle and left the bus with a small wave. Jerome followed him out the door, circled around the mud, and stood by the underbelly of the bus as he waited for his only suitcase to be found. After a quick look at a city map, he headed towards Canal Street to check in at the Royal George. At least six inches of silt had covered parts of the lot when the bus pulled in but there was no evidence of it in front of this solid mid-town structure. Jerome went straight to the desk clerk. "I'm checking in to join the band. Lewis okayed it." He looked down at the brand new mahogany desk. "Didn't it flood this part of town?"

The desk clerk glanced up. "The French Quarter drained as soon as the water level went down. But, we still had some damage." He directed Jerome to the bus usually used for tours, parked in the back lot, where band members were housed. He soon found the only empty bunk and a rack for his suitcase. He scrunched up his nose at the stale odor of smoke and mildew and headed back out for fresh air, only to find the smell had followed him.

During the stroll down to the Riverwalk, he passed a few men in dirty clothes cigarettes in hand, and watched another man break a shop window. He decided not to get involved and looked away. Too much risk with him a recent arrival in town. Soon he stared out over the choppy blue-grey waters of the river with the Greater New Orleans Bridge clearly visible in the distance. The cement wall in front of him was broken in places and the walkway covered in dried mud. Shredded cardboard boxes stunk with an odour he couldn't quite identify. Not dead bodies he hoped. He'd heard they were still finding bodies in some of the houses along the waterfront which were now marked with a red "x". Over 100,000 people had been evacuated to Atlanta, before and after Katrina. He shuddered and pulled his thin jacket over his chest as some protection from the ever present winds. Jerome found his hands shaking and his throat tight as he continued to walk away back to the security of his hotel. He'd need a few hours of sleep before he joined this new crew for practice.

*   *   *

Several nights later, Jerome brushed back his long blond hair from his face, feeling disoriented as he followed the brothers from his new band across the parking lot and into the Royal George Hotel. Lewis played trombone so they had something in common since Jerome loved the sax but he was still uncomfortable with the other two musicians. The double bass player, Clarence, sported tight black curls and a loud tangerine satin shirt. And what a jerk the piano player was. Simon constantly reeked with cheap cologne. Lewis had told him it was mostly locals showing up for music now with the lack of tourists. He held back when they burst through the front doors of the hotel and strode across the lobby, with Leo dragging his black music case behind him.

He watched them cross the floor until they huddled around the chair of a young black woman who was alone in the lobby. She sat rigid against the chair and tried to ignore them. As he got closer, Jerome admired her small breasts, visible through the green dress stretched tight to her body.

Clarence was smiling at her. "Which way is the bar, honey? Why don't you join us? We're the regular jazz band here and we're good."

The young woman slumped forward in her chair, her shoulders drooping. From the back of her head he studied the corn rows with their small tight braids.

He watched Simon move closer to the woman and cringed as he towered over her crouched form. "Now, girl, we're here to entertain you, not to scare you." She sat up straight and stared at him but gave no response. Jerome could see the girl was still nervous as he came closer.

Then Lewis put his arm on Clarence's shoulder and nodded to the piano player. "Okay guys." He said, "Follow me. You know the bar is this way. Leave the young woman alone."

Jerome tucked the tails of his white cotton shirt into his loose beige trousers. He wished he'd taken more time to dress in the bus. Then he picked up his saxophone before he approached her. A smile lit up his face as he raised the sax to his lips and blew a few appreciative notes in the girl's direction.

The girl appeared to ignore him.

He walked over to stand beside her. "Oh, come on now. Since you're in New Orleans, you must dig music."

She looked up at him. "You with that band, just arrived?"

Since he could tell she was still nervous, he made a quick decision to lower his tone. He offered his hand. "I'm Jerome Decarie, the sax player with that group who caused all the commotion. I joined the band a few days ago. You like jazz?"

His approach worked as he watched her straighten her shoulders still holding her head high. She glanced at him again and hesitated before she spoke. "That's a co-incidence. That's one thing we have in common. Music, that is."

He smiled. "Good. What are you into?"

"I'm a singer from over in Atlanta. Got my start with the Baptist Church choir. Last year we travelled by bus to Nashville for a concert."

He nodded with enthusiasm. "That's great. I love all types of music. You sing solo or just with the chorus?"

"Our director, she's giving me a tryout with a few solos when I get back."

"Then you've got to listen to us play tonight. Why don't you come?" Jerome asked. "We're good."

She shook her head. "No. I've got personal problems to deal with. I'm here in the city to find my family. It seems they've been evacuated. But I don't know where. I'm worried. I'm hoping someone in the hotel might know where local people went."

Jerome shook his head. He'd been shocked by the destruction evident on his journey from the hotel to the Riverwalk. "I know. On my walk, I saw some of the silt from the waters, broken porches and roof tops and trash littering the streets." He paused. "You haven't heard from them at all since the hurricane hit?"

She held her head in her hands and shook it back and forth. "Our house was on LaSalle Street which got flooded. I just arrived in town on the bus last night. It's worse than I expected. I couldn't find any streetcars or taxis and very few cars are moving on these streets. I'd tried to phone home from Atlanta dozens of times with no luck. There's still no telephone service except for the hotels.

Both land lines and the wireless networks are down. I want to walk there tomorrow."

"Have you talked to the city about that area? I noticed their office is open. They'll know if the house is still standing. I hear some houses are condemned."

She dropped her hands. "That's just it. The streets aren't safe. I walked up Canal Street yesterday asked the local people if they knew where my Aunt Noreen and Uncle Henry might have gone. No one seemed to know and then I was followed by two drunks. They tried to pick me up, and I was scared to death I'd be attacked."

Jerome dropped to one knee beside her. "Tell me what happened."

"I hurried the rest of the way back to the hotel with them trailing behind and ran into the lobby. When they saw the doorman, they didn't try to go any farther." He could see even now how she trembled and her eyes stared at him with fear and revulsion.

He could feel his face turn hot with anger. He breathed deeply. "No wonder you don't want to go out alone again."

She continued. "But I need to find my Aunt and Uncle. I have to go to the house tomorrow. It's the only place I have to start the search. They may have left a note or some clue as to where they went."

"I don't think it's a good idea for you to do that?" Close up, Jerome liked her smooth heart-shaped face and deep dark eyes. He had to admit, she'd grabbed his attention from the beginning. He'd like to know her better, but knew he should take it slowly. "Maybe I can help you tomorrow since the band doesn't start practice until four. That's if you want company?"

He could tell his offer impressed her but her hesitation suggested she was cautious about men. She watched him carefully as if ready to flee. She must have weighed the alternative of wandering around the deserted city alone because she didn't leave. He waited for her to decide.

"I'm glad I met you Jerome as I could sure use a friend. By the way, I'm Lara Jackson." She sat in silence. "Let's wait to see what tomorrow brings. I've been hoping to talk to other guests here in the hotel who might be going in that direction. I'll see what I can find out. I don't want to walk these sidewalks alone again."

He took her hand and felt a tingling sensation crawl up his arm which left him feeling foolish. "Okay, Lara. "I'll be up and in this lobby here early tomorrow." He saluted her with his saxophone before he strolled down the hallway towards the sound of his band as they warmed up.

* * *

When Jerome woke the next morning, the sun streamed through the window of the tour bus where he'd been told all the new members of the band were temporarily housed. The other members all lived locally. Until he earned some more cash, he couldn't afford a regular room and, who knew if he could even find one now after this flood. He pulled on worn jeans and tucked in a denim shirt before leaving the bus for the hotel where they had showers for the staff. After Jerome took off his clothes and stepped onto the cold ceramic floor, he shivered. What would his sister be doing now? He'd never been so far away from home before. Would his mother miss him? She'd been so short with him this past year with him out so late most nights. When the warm water hit his cool skin he watched the streams of soap run down his lean body and relaxed. It felt great to wash off the sweat.

As he wandered into the hotel coffee shop, next door to the bar, he recognized Lara dressed in tight jeans and a sleeveless tee shirt, with a denim jacket thrown over her shoulders. She was seated with a man and woman, engrossed in conversation. Before he could reach the table, the couple got up and left.

Jerome took the empty chair across from Lara. "So, what's your decision about today? Did I get up early for nothing?"

Lara's smile reached her eyes. "Maybe not."

He watched her take a deep breath, her face turning serious. Did this mean she had decided to trust him?

"Actually, my friends rented a car to drive up to Baton Rouge where people in the disaster centre suggested they might find her brother. It's good news for them, but they won't be free to go with me today." She sat back and checked his reaction carefully. "So, I'm inviting you to come along. I have no desire to pass that same group of men on the sidewalk today without a friend by my side. It's not safe, a woman alone in this God forsaken city."

Jerome breathed a sigh of relief. He'd have another chance with her after all. "Well, pretty lady. I'm still available. When do you want to get started?"

She blushed and smiled at him. "Thanks. That's kind of you. But why would you want to give up your free time to help me. You don't even know me."

He brushed a tuft of hair back off his forehead. "You look like you could use a friend." And I want to be the friend you'll remember.

Lara finished her coffee. "I'll accept that. Now grab some breakfast before we go. There are croissants over on the counter and the coffee is self-serve."

"It's okay. I ate already. The band gets to eat with the staff in the back kitchen."

Back in the lobby, things seemed normal. The marble floors gleamed against the walnut wainscoting. They stood at the tour desk, studying the map on the wall waiting for the bell captain. When he'd listened to what they needed, he took a red pen, and marked out the best route to get to LaSalle which bypassed the lower areas of the city which were still pretty much under water. "Avoid the Lakeview area, in particular. It was hit hard by the storm surge from Lake Pontchartrain."

After the couple left the hotel, they found the central business district of New Orleans deserted. Although Jerome could see Lara was very tense, she seemed to know the way, so he followed along, his eyes alert, street after street. She stopped abruptly, turning onto LaSalle Street. Was this it? He gazed into her face. Her face was tight and hands clenched.

"I can't believe how much the Tulane district has changed. Back when I went to school, all those porches would have been filled with women dressed in bright striped and polka-dotted dresses. My neighbours would wave at me and call, Hey, Lara. Where have they all gone?"

Jerome looked around at the houses and streets now empty. Most of the people would have been evacuated by the flood. He couldn't see any cars and trucks on the streets. The odor of dead animals and putrid mud hit him.

"Like I told you, before I left Atlanta, I tried dozens of times to phone home. I couldn't reach them. That's why I came here myself. I had to see what happened to them."

"Yeah." Jerome agreed. "That must have been awful. The desk clerk told me the destruction in the French Quarter was fixed quickly. Many of the journalists and construction workers are still housed at the Royal George. He told me even the bottom of the reception desk had been warped by the water."

As they continued down the street, he discovered fallen oak trees and downed hydro lines. Jerome knew the danger from those had passed, since the power was still off in this part of the city. "We're lucky to have running water in the hotel. I've heard that many houses don't have anything coming from their taps. Lewis told me it's sporadic at his home even after two attempts by the city to get it flowing again."

As they walked on, they passed lawns and gardens covered with sand and mud; shredded cardboard and plastic bags blew across their feet. Trash and muck was left behind everywhere by the hurricane winds and the receding flood waters. Their sneakers were soon covered in silt even though they tried to step over the spilled garbage and broken branches.

He watched the sadness carve deep lines into Lara's pretty face as they proceeded. Her shoulders trembled.

"I couldn't come back to look for Noreen and Henry until Mayor Nagin lifted the ban on visitors. But, why hasn't he done more to help the people who evacuated?" Her anger returned in a flash. "People say he should have called in the National Guard sooner to deal with this disaster."

Jerome put his arm around her shoulders. They continued to walk. Then she stopped in front of one small bungalow. This one wasn't as bad as some of the others on this street. The blue siding was stained and dingy, but the shingled roof looked intact.

He watched her bound up the weathered front steps and onto the rickety porch. She tried the door. When he joined her, she tried again, knocking loudly. Nothing. It appeared to be locked which was a good sign. The two of them stood on tiptoe to peek in the window next to the door.

The ruin inside was sobering. Moldy walls, buckled wallboard in the kitchen left by the water which must have seeped into everything. The floors were wavy, covered in silt and didn't look like they would hold anyone's weight. Her aunt and uncle couldn't be living here. But, he could tell she was disappointed.

"I guess I should have expected this. Where could they have gone? She slumped into one of the old teak porch chairs, and buried her face in her hands. "My aunt and uncle are the most important people in my life. I have to find them."

"Are you okay?" He took her hand before they walked around to the back of the house to check if there was more damage. Any holes in the roof. When the two of them returned to the porch, they saw two young thugs dressed in tattered jeans and fishnet tank tops with their fists bashed at the front door.

He raced up the stairs in time to hear the skinny one exclaim to his buddy. "I wouldn't go in. The floors don't look too good."

When the guy realized Jerome's presence, he turned to stare at him, his face covered in a sinister smirk. "Don't you get too excited. We're just wantin to help those inside." He gave a short laugh.

Jerome stared at his bulging muscles. From below him on the sidewalk, he heard Lara scream. "Jerome be careful."

Jerome grabbed the shoulder of the closest one to turn him around but instead he was shoved aside while the two men charged off the porch and ran down the street. He heard the skinny one yell at his partner.

"Let's go. We don't want no trouble."

He'd heard from the other musicians about petty criminals who were preying on the victims of the storm. Just as Jerome had thought, they were usually cowards at heart. He'd seen some of the looting of shops and homes since the storm. He gave Lara a hug. "We'll be all right. They're long gone. Take your time to catch your breath." He'd been relieved there was no "x" marked on the door with the number of bodies inside. That's what the National Guard was using to mark where they needed to return later.

Lara grasped his arm. "Let's go. At the hotel, I heard the Superdome was the major evacuation centre."

The trip to the Superdome was unsuccessful. Jerome's apprehension grew when they were the only passengers to get off the bus in front of it. They soon knew why. When they opened the large front doors, the sight to greet them wasn't pleasant. Hundreds of people in dirty and damp clothing lay on the cement floors with only the blankets they'd been given when they arrived. When they walked through the rows of people looking for Noreen and Henry, he heard children begging for food and water. The guards shook their heads and said they were still waiting for the city to drop off supplies.

Jerome's shoulders drooped. "This situation has gotten out of control."

Lara clenched her hands. "How shameful. Well, they were mainly black people, so why should the city care."

Jerome watched her face and kept silent. From what he'd seen on the TV in the hotel, there were long lineups for the few working toilets. Small children were crying while mothers went from place to place seeking medicine. But the worst was when several of the older people died there and officials just covered them with blankets. This centre was only supposed to be open for three days. The city is still trying to put together plans for evacuation to other centres in the area.

Jerome took her hand, as he helped Lara down the stairs and onto the sidewalk. "Let's go back to the hotel. You're still shaking and we can't do much more this morning."

They walked in silence for a few blocks then Lara stopped. "I want you to know why I have to find them. They're all I have. Back when I was a child, my mother went to jail for murdering a man. He was a drug addict, her supplier, and she claimed it was self-defence but the court didn't believe her. The court social worker had found a foster home for me before they located Noreen and Henry who claimed me. Turned out that Noreen and my mother were sisters. Even though I was ten, I had never met her, but they've been my family. I lived with them until I left to train with the choir in Atlanta." She sighed.

Jerome cringed at the hurt and fear which flowed across her face. "Does Noreen have any other family in New Orleans? She might be there."

Lara shook her head. "No. Noreen had been on a tour of the city with the Baptist Church from Georgia, where she was born, when she met Henry. He was one of the elders. Her sisters returned home without her. She told me it was hard for her to leave her family, but Henry wouldn't leave his city. She made friends in their neighbourhood and got to love it here."

"What about Henry then? He must have some family here." Jerome exclaimed.

"Henry has a younger brother, Phillip. They were the only ones left in the Devries family. He's a jazz musician who lives in the Garden District in an old mansion he bought or won in a poker game. It's falling apart though. He claims he can't afford to fix it up."

He could tell by the tight tone of her voice, that Phillip wasn't her favorite person. "Would they stay with him?"

"Phillip has always been difficult. But, maybe they would go to his place in an emergency. Where else would they go? I can't remember what the press said about how bad that part of the city is."

Jerome kept his voice calm and slow. "We can try there tomorrow. In the meantime, are there any emergency shelters set up by the city?"

"I don't think so. Most people went to Baton Rouge or even as far away as Atlanta or Texas."

When he bundled her back onto the bus, she sank into the seat and stared out the window until they reached the hotel.

Chapter Two

Bright sunlight streamed through the bus window, when Jerome forced himself to sit up. The tour bus seats folded down into a bed of sorts, but he woke each morning stiff and sore. He'd have to hurry to catch Lara this morning before she left on her search. He pulled on yesterday's rumpled jeans, grabbed a clean white shirt and headed towards the hotel's staff showers.

After the shower, his wet blond curls tangled in the comb which caused him to swear. His blue eyes stared back at him in the mirror, brighter than usual. When he entered the breakfast alcove, Lara was waiting for him while she studied the map given to them by the bell captain.

He slouched into the chair beside her. "We're headed for the Garden District this morning, aren't we?"

She nodded. "From what I've heard so far, most of the drunkenness and looting is in the uptown area. So we should be okay."

He shrugged his shoulders. "The guys told me the city hasn't cleaned up the streets there yet. Do you think it's a good time to go?"

"That's why I've got the map. The bell captain showed me a route around the major damage. Grab some breakfast and let's get going. I've got to find Aunt Noreen and Uncle Henry and that's where his brother lives. It's our best shot."

She waited while he crunched the last of his toast and gulped his coffee. Jerome followed her across the lobby and out into the sunshine. The warm sun felt great on his face after last night's cold wind.

New Orleans still felt new to Jerome. He'd had that one short visit last summer when he tried to get hired on by one of the local jazz bands. Last night was the first time he saw the lush gardens along the riverfront and the old steamboat with its antique organ now silenced. Jerome had decided even then he wanted more than one or two night gigs in small clubs and bars of Jacksonville and this was his best chance for becoming known.

He took Lara's hand as they continued to travel through muddy streets and debris. "You must be shocked by the mess the storm left in your home town."

Lara gave a deep sigh. "As I told you, I'm living in Atlanta now. We had hundreds of evacuees arrive in town, so I knew it was bad."

Jerome was enjoying the feel of her soft moist hand in his with the sun beating down on their heads. They covered block after block. "We've walked a long way. Are you getting tired?"

"No. We need to keep going."

"What made you leave such a vibrant city? Every musician who doesn't live here wants to be here."

"New Orleans always had two sides. I loved the hustle and friendliness of the markets during the day. But, then you'd see the ominous shadows and crime of the Quarter late at night when it was taken over by the drunks and the addicts. That's why I left." Her face showed the strain.

"Yeah. I imagine it's different for a girl. Being in a band, everyone assumes you're into drugs. I just let the guys think that, and they leave me alone." He wiped the sweat from his forehead. "It seems like hours since we started out. How much longer?"

"That's St. Charles Avenue ahead, so probably another twenty minutes. Phillip lives in an old Georgian mansion on Chestnut

Street. If they're with him, that's where I'll find them." Lara picked up the pace, as she scanned both sides of the street and he had to hurry to keep up.

After another couple of blocks, he began to slow down. "How do you think your aunt and uncle will react to us together? I've dated black girls before in Florida and some of the fathers didn't like it one bit."

Lara started to giggle. "We're not dating. I only met you last night, Jerome." She stopped in front of him. "That's important. We're just friends."

Her dark eyes were so very serious. He put his arms around her, as he held her loosely, not wanting to frighten her away. "It feels like a date to me. My gig with the band is only short term. But what do you say? Can we see each other again?"

Sighing, she broke away. "Let's be friends for now. I don't expect to be in the city for long myself. I'm here to check on Noreen and Henry. But, I have a concert in Atlanta that I must be back for at the end of the month."

As they rounded the corner onto Chestnut Street, Lara came to an abrupt stop. She covered her mouth with both hands and gave a high pitched cry. They were facing a large white mansion with Doric columns which surrounded oak double doors. One full section of the grey cedar roof was lying in the back yard against an uprooted cypress tree, which left the upper floor open to heavy rains.

"God save us. What about by aunt and uncle? Phillip's house is at the end of this block." Her breath came in short sharp gasps.

Jerome gazed around as he followed her down the street. "Hold on Lara." He grabbed her hand. "They may still be okay. We'll be there soon."

They passed two more mansions, slightly smaller, but still in the same Greek style with huge landscaped yards, somewhat overgrown with bougainvillea vines. Here, the storm had devastated the grounds, but the houses, although weathered, appeared untouched.

Lara took slow cautious steps forward as they neared the end of the street.

Jerome continued to coax, "Let's keep going. We've got to be close."

Lara stopped in front of an older mansion, white paint peeled in several large strips on each side of the front door. She scanned the yard. "Well, there's a tree leaning against the upper balcony, but the roof is still intact."

"Is this it then?"

She nodded. "It looks like Phillip was lucky. From the amount of debris on the porch, the wind blew through here, but missed the main part of the house."

Jerome grabbed her hand and pulled her towards the stairs. "Let's see if they're here." When they reached the stairs, he held back and dropped her hand.

She reached the bottom of the wooden steps just as a woman jumped up from a rocker on the porch. As the woman screamed in excitement, she hurried down them towards Lara.

"Oh honey. I couldn't believe I was hearin ya voice comin down that street. We didn't know how to reach you," said Noreen. She threw her arms around Lara in a big hug.

Lara hugged her aunt and stepped back. "You're okay? When I saw our house, I was scared for the two of you. But Phillip's was the only place you could be. Thank God, you were spared."

An older man, Jerome assumed must be Henry then ambled down the stairs behind Noreen and clasped Lara to his chest. "So good to see ya girl."

Lara clung to him for a few moments and then turned back to Noreen. "Was it bad?"

"You know we've been in floods before in the years we've lived here, but nothing like this one. The water poured right over the levee. The people in the Lakeview and Warehouse Districts were badly hit. Let's go in and I'll get us some cold lemonade."

Noreen hesitated and pointed towards Jerome. "Who's your young man, Lara?"

"Oh, I almost forgot. Noreen and Henry, this is Jerome, a new friend who's helped me in my search for you. He's a saxophone player at the Royal George."

Henry turned to look at him. "Phillip will enjoy meeting you. What do you play Jerome? Dixie or classical jazz?"

Jerome smiled. "I play whatever they want."

Henry chuckled. "Good answer."

As Noreen led them into the house, she stopped in the entranceway which was littered with old garbage bags and broken garden furniture. "There's been no garbage collection since the storm. Most of it's in the garden shed."

When Jerome's eyes adjusted to the dim light, he could make out a muscular man with curly black hair leaning against the banister. He didn't like the way the guy stared at Lara.

He could see every muscle in Lara's shoulders and chest tense. "Phillip, this is my friend, Jerome."

Jerome continued to stand back since he found this new man somewhat rough and a little sinister. He nodded a greeting but Phillip was interested only in Lara.

Phillip moved forward in slow motion, as he watched Lara's every move, his gaze scanning her body. "It's been some time since you folks visited me consider we live in the same city. Life over in Georgia sure suits you. Youse all grown up."

Noreen's face clouded over as she pushed between them. "Now, Phillip. You behave yourself. Like I told you, Lara is your niece. And this young fellow is a musician like you."

Frowning, Phillip turned towards Jerome. "White men can't play jazz anyways. It's not in they blood." He gave a high-pitched laugh. "I'm just jokin ya. What band ya with?"

Jerome took a deep breath and linked arms with Lara. "It's called The Spirits. We're playing at the bar in the Royal George for the next while, if you want to check us out."

"I've got a permanent gig at the Orleans Hotel in the Quarter, if you want to hear real jazz." Phillip stared at Henry who was frowning and shifting his feet. "Look, Noreen is right. All you are welcome to come into my parlour over there for a drink. It's not much, but we can talk."

As they entered the room, Jerome picked up a smoky pungent smell in the air. Phillip lifted a half-burned joint from a dish and relit it, and inhaled deeply.

Noreen passed glasses of lemonade to Lara and him. She then poured bourbon for Phillip and Henry. "Once the water came up the lower part of the city, it jus kept comin higher and higher," she said helping herself to a large glass of the lemonade. "We had to get out. I really miss our place."

The hair on the back of Jerome's neck prickled as Phillip jerked upright in his chair. "You can leave anytime, Noreen. I got people in the band who'd love to have those rooms."

Henry patted Phillip on the arm. "She didn't mean she doesn't appreciate what ya done for us, Phillip. It's just that we need to be home soon as the power is back."

Phillip relaxed. "Where you two staying at?" He gestured toward Lara and Jerome.

Jerome glanced around at the worn and dusty velvet furniture and brocade draperies. The mahogany coffee table had a broad line of cigarette burns next to the round mirror still covered in white dust. However, the wooden staircase leading upstairs was intact. That was the problem with band members. They spent most of their lives in bars and hotels and their homes tended to reflect their lifestyle.

Lara grimaced and bit her lower lip. "I'm only booked into the Royal George for two more days. I'd planned to return to Atlanta as soon as I knew the two of you were safe. I've got to practice for the next concert."

Noreen blinked back tears. "Not so soon, honey. We just got to see you."

Henry jumped in. "Phillip's got spare rooms here. Your aunt could use you around for a while."

Lara smiled at her aunt and held her hand. "Well, maybe until next week. I can't afford to miss the next concert."

Henry turned to Phillip. "What about letting Lara stay here? You could invite Jerome as well. The two of you could do some jamming here."

Jerome squirmed with embarrassment. "I'm living in the band bus for next the two weeks. It's just fine."

Phillip smirked. "Lara's always welcome here." He turned to face Jerome. "I know about those buses. They's smelly and crowded. Why don't you stay here with Lara?"

Jerome's gaze turned back to Lara who cringed into the furniture. Did Phillip look at all young woman like that? He knew that Henry would protect her, but he was getting old. But, when she gave him a shy smile, he quickly made up his mind to stay.

Lara inquired. "Why don't you stay for a few days at least? You'll love the old Greek mansions and I'll give you a private tour through the district. We can also visit the Lafayette Cemetery."

Convinced, Jerome took her hand. "How could anyone refuse an offer like that one. Until Saturday then. But for now, I've got to get back to the hotel. We play this evening."

Lara followed him out to the front yard. They stood for a few minutes, comfortable under the warmth of the sun. Reluctantly, he turned to go. "I like your aunt and uncle. But, there's something strange about Phillip. I'm not sure what, but there just is."

Chapter Three

Although tremors had flowed through his chest on the trip with Lara to her uncle's house in the Garden District, Jerome had enjoyed the chance to see another part of the city. The New Yorker had an article on New Orleans which he'd read on the bus that confirmed what he'd seen. The old mansions, he'd learned, were originally owned by former southern families who led a genteel lifestyle with many servants back in the 1800s. At that time, the servants were almost always black. Now, most of the houses were the private homes of local doctors, lawyers and real estate developers. However, some of the really old ones had been allowed to decay.

Back in Jacksonville, where Jerome grew up, historic buildings had been demolished to make way for new condos and subdivisions like his. From what he could tell, the people of New Orleans today were a mix of whites, Hispanics and African Americans. Now on his way back to the hotel, he walked alone through the streets of New Orleans. His face broke into a smile when he recalled Lara's expressive brown eyes and her small rounded breasts, thin waist and shapely butt. Her exotic scent reminded him of his former girlfriend he'd left behind in Florida. He'd missed her since their career paths had left them both in agreement to go their separate ways. He hoped to extend his stay in this new city until he could find out what might develop with Lara.

He knew enough to be careful around Phillip. Jerome had been part of a band long enough to know his type. Like many jazz musicians, Phillip was attracted to pot and blow and to get it, he was probably willing to sell it. As usual that led to an unsavory lifestyle where they all hung around together. He'd learned to joke with them but keep his distance after hours.

Beginning to tire, he was relieved to see the red brick wall of the Royal George ahead. The maroon and silver bus would be in the back lot against the chain link fence. He hurried towards it, glad to be back with the boys to prepare for tonight's concert.

While he stood on the front step of the bus and turned his key in the lock, Jerome felt a rough hand on his right shoulder. Since he still carried a sense of unease from this morning, a twinge of fear crawled up his neck as he turned around.

"Hey, Jerome. Where did you leave that sweet black girl we met last night? The desk clerk saw you leave with her early this morning?"

His breath released in a gush, as he recognized the voice. Jerome faced Lewis. "You and the guys scared her. Your approach is too in your face for young women. You got to be more slow and smooth with them." He punched Lewis gently on the arm.

A slow smile crossed Lewis's face. "You eatin with us tonight? We're going to a creole café in the Quarter. Meet us at the front door in half an hour, if that's what you want. I'll see we're back here in lots of time to warm up."

A dinner out with the guys could be fun. "Sure. I'm game. Let me change my things."

Jerome swung the heavy door open and headed towards the back to retrieve his duffle bag. He left Lewis standing by the front door. Although sometimes a little on the rough side, Lewis wouldn't hurt anyone and he was band leader. They'd play together more easily if they got to know each other and he wanted to stay in New Orleans.

He pulled on a clean white shirt, strolled to the small bathroom and splashed water on his face. His long blond hair was still damp causing the waves to turn into tighter curls. His hands still shook from the brief encounter with Lewis and he'd be relieved to move to the house for a few weeks. He packed clothing into his bag for pick up later after the show.

Where would his former band play tonight? They were supposed to go to dinner as a group before he left. But, since it was their last night, his girlfriend had insisted he spend the night with her. He hated to leave her but she'd be moving to her college campus that week. When he'd arrived in New Orleans, he'd called her brother's place and left a message, but so far no call back.

When he reached the front steps of the hotel, all six members of the band had gathered. He stepped back when the piano player slapped Lewis on the back with his enormous hand. "Lewis, this was a neat thing you did getting us guys together to eat. Gets pretty lonely for me waiting to get back to the old woman in New Iberia. I hear the gumbo is the best over at Snug Harbor on Frenchman's Street."

Simon joined them. "How about Broussard's on Conti? They got a patio where we can be loose." Lewis flagged down a cab for the group. "I like the idea of being outside. Let's go."

* * *

Lara leaned both hands on the railing of the weathered porch, as she watched Jerome disappear down the street. Would he come back later this evening or had this been an afternoon adventure for him? She sank into the wicker chair and closed her eyes, as the last rays of the sun kissed her skin.

"Lara, honey." Noreen let the front door swing closed behind her as she ventured onto the porch to stand beside her. "Don't take any notice of Phillip. He'll listen to your Uncle Henry. He always has." She shook her head. "I sometimes can't believe those two are brothers." Noreen gave Lara a hug. "We want you to have a good time on your visit with us. Never you mind the poor state of things."

"I know, Auntie. Phillip would do anything for his older brother." Lara shivered. "It's just the way he looks at women."

Noreen shook her finger at Lara. "Not all women, mind you. Only the young and pretty ones like you, honey. I don't have a worry staying here that he'd even look at me." Her face screwed up in disgust. "But, I don't like the crowd he has drop in."

Lara relaxed and smiled. "Did Henry say when you will be able to get back into your own house? When I saw it, the kitchen floor was in bad shape."

Noreen shook her head. "It will be at least another two weeks for the power. So much is still under water. The evacuation crew's started first to get those poor souls in the Superdome moved. Some of them were put on buses to Baton Rouge and others even as far away as Texas." She patted the old wicker chair next to where she now sat. "But, come and sit beside me here. Tell me about your singing."

Lara relaxed into the old flowered cushions. "Well, you remember my roommate, Emma, who I met in Bible School before I moved to Atlanta?"

Noreen slapped her thigh and gave a belly laugh. "Yeah. The two of you were going to be preachers."

She touched Noreen's arm. "When you and Henry have a phone again, I promise to keep you up to date. After I settled into my apartment, I looked her up. Our Baptist Church along with other churches had competitions for new choir members. She got chosen first. Emma had the most beautiful soprano voice and got most of the solos in her former choir. She persuaded them to give me a try. I think I got chosen mainly so she would stay."

"Don't you put yourself down, girl." Noreen shook her head emphatically. "I remember those nights with the three of us at

Maxwell's Cabaret when you were asked to sing with the band. I just wish you could have found your place here."

"You know we've been through this before." Lara held her breath and let it out. "New Orleans is home to you, but not to me. I could never be a singer on Bourbon Street. I'm still afraid to walk alone down the street at night."

Noreen clasped her hand. "I know sweetie. You had some really bad things happen to you in the past, which started with your mama leaving you before you was even ten. Now you got to learn to leave it in the past. Can you do that?"

Lara stared into her lap. "I'm trying. But, the nightmares still come. It's like I attract violence. Maybe it's because I grew up in Louisville with Ma. Drugs and petty criminals were everywhere in places we lived. She paused. "I feel safe in Atlanta."

Noreen stood and patted Lara on the head. "It's not your fault, honey. You're such a beautiful girl, and in this city, beauty attracts attention. Let's go inside and have a bite to eat."

Lara stretched her arms to loosen up before she followed Noreen into the house. Darkness had spread across the sky and sound of thunder roared in the distance. She joined Noreen in the kitchen and the two of them hummed an old bible song while they cut up sweet potatoes and turnips to add to the chicken in the fryer.

A short while later, Noreen called up to Henry who joined them. The three of them sat around the small pine table for their supper. The closeness reminded Lara of the time when she lived with them.

Three heads turned when the front door slammed open, and soon Phillip and his noisy group stood at the kitchen door. Henry gave Noreen a troubled glance and rose to greet the crowd.

"Phillip, looks like you caught some rain."

"Yeah. We've had more than enough of that already. My friends here are from the bar. We're going to groove here for a while." When Henry went back to the table to sit down, Phillip followed him.

He stood across from Lara, his black eyes piercing into her. Phillip turned to his buddies. "This here is my niece, Lara."

Henry's back stiffened. "Phillip, you're making her nervous. Why don't you guys find a place in the parlour and I'll bring some chicken and beer."

Lara pushed back her chair and leaned against Henry. "I'm finished. I'll go to my room and rest for now." Guilt rushed over her as she glanced toward Noreen. "Auntie, I'll help you clean up later." She was relieved to see her aunt nod. Lara cringed at the three men's long stares running over her body and hurried up the stairs. She didn't look back.

Noreen glared at the group of men still clustered around the table. "What's wrong with you, Phillip? You'll find your own girls down at the Quarter. Lara's a relative to you through your brother. Better treat her respectful, you hear."

Phillip glanced at Henry and snorted, "Come on guys. We're not wanted here in my own kitchen." As she reached the top of the stairs, Lara heard their loud boots on the wood floors as they crossed to the parlour.

Her fists were still clenched when she opened the door to her bedroom and breathed a sigh. She relaxed as she sat on the deep blue bedspread which complemented the oak four post bed. A moment of doubt crept up her spine. Am I any safer here than I would be back at the Royal George? At least back there, the drunks and cursing was out on the streets and not in the room directly below me.

*   *   *

Although Jerome sprinted down the steps of the St. Charles streetcar, and ran down Chestnut Street, the rain still caught him, and soaked him through to the skin. The suddenness of the rains in New Orleans was something he hadn't gotten used to even now. He hoped the clothes in his canvass bag would still be dry when he got back to the house. He wasn't sure if Lara was still up, but, in case, he didn't want her to see him like this. He shivered as he clambered up the wooden steps and let out a sigh of relief when he found the front door ajar. While he stood in the dim hallway he listened, then took a few steps towards the stairs and called out a greeting.

"Hello. Anyone here?"

There was only silence. As he listened again, he heard the murmur of the Cajun jargon in the distance, and headed towards the sound. The muscles in the back of his neck tightened when he entered the parlour. Phillip slouched into the sofa, surrounded by his friends. All of them sipped beer from bottles and a line of cocaine lay out on a broken piece of mirror on the coffee table.

"Hello." Jerome called out as he approached Phillip. "Good of you to offer me a place to stay."

Phillip placed his long legs still in boots, on the coffee table, smoke drifted in clouds over his head.

The beefy man closest to Jerome stood and scowled at him out of cold black eyes. "You aim to crash our party? How we know you're not a nark?" He gave Jerome a hard punch on the arm.

Phillip gave a high-pitched laugh. "Leave him alone, Pierre. He's sweet on my neice and I don't like to deny the young uns. You get my point?" His boots slammed onto the floor when he stood and slunk over to Jerome. As Phillip reached him, the smell of stale booze overwhelmed Jerome.

He winced as Phillip put his arm around his shoulders and squeezed. "This here boy is a musician like us. Right, Jerome?" From down there in Jacksonville." Phillip jerked back and shook drops of water off his hands. "Shit. You soaking wet. Better get upstairs and dry yourself, before you join us."

Jerome let out his breath, and moved towards the stairs. "Yeah. I'm beat from the gig and cold from the rain. I'll see you in the morning." He glanced back while climbing the stairs to see most of the men settle back into their chairs and Phillip drop to the floor by the coffee table to snort a line.

When he reached the top, Jerome admired the carved oak balusters of the once elegant staircase which led to a long hall with dark oak floors. This must have been a great house in the past. In the dim light, he could see two doors to the right which would be over the parlour and two other doors to the left, both of which were closed. What bedroom had Noreen showed him this morning? It was one of those two on the right but Lara would occupy the other. He stopped outside the first door and listened. He was undecided but didn't want to frighten her. He could hear nothing through the heavy door. A picture drifted across his subconscious of her luminous dark skin and shapely legs in tight jeans. His chest throbbed but he hesitated. She already had her suspicions towards men. Men like the crew downstairs were threatening to her. He didn't want her to think about him like that.

He continued down the hall to the second door and remembered the scarred brass handle from this morning. He pulled it open and recognized the purple comforter. His whole body ached from the strain and the cold. He pulled off his wet clothes and dumped them on the wooden floor. The clean towel from the dresser felt good as he rubbed his skin dry. In the mirror over the old Victorian dresser, he admired his flat stomach and continued down his thighs to his long legs which were now streaked with blue veins. Not bad looking. As a musician, his body image was important. He was a little skinny from not eating regular meals on the road. His muscles were still tight and the bulges in his calves showed strong legs. After he dried his curly hair, Jerome eased into bed and pulled the old bed clothes over him for warmth.

Tomorrow, he and Lara would have the whole day together before he had to leave for his show at six. He meant it when he said he'd like to get to know her better. Jerome could imagine himself kissing her long neck and smooth shoulders in the soft sunlight. When he awoke, he'd thrown off all covers. The sun felt good as it streamed through the thin deep green drapes and over his naked body.

Chapter Four

Lara awoke to the sound of heavy boots tramping on the wooden floors of the hall outside her bedroom. She pulled herself up against the headboard. It sounded like her Uncle Henry, but she wasn't sure. He was an early riser, and this would be about the right time. She shivered and drew the comforter closer around her. She didn't want to take the chance the noises were from Phillip, even though his room was at the end of the hall. She started to get out of bed but instead stopped and listened. If it was Henry, her aunt wouldn't be far behind him. She never left him to make his own breakfast. Yes. She heard a second pair of feet shuffle down the corridor. Probably Noreen and she'd be wearing those old flannel slippers.

Lara threw back the covers, wiggled her feet into her new flip flops and grabbed a cotton gown from the chair to pull over her chemise. She'd locked her bedroom door when she came up last night. Her fear about the gang downstairs wouldn't leave her. Lara awoke sometime around midnight to hear someone stop outside the door, but whoever it was soon left.

Henry and Noreen would be on their way downstairs by now, so the bathroom should be free, unless Jerome got there first. In spite of her unease, her body tingled in excitement at the thought of meeting him in the hallway. She smiled. He had a mellow soothing voice which she could only associate with that of Uncle

Henry. To her, it was like a smooth, slow-flowing stream which reassured her.

Her walk to the bathroom was without incident. She took her time in the shower, pulled on her robe and stepped back into the hall. Lara caught her breath when she saw Jerome strolling towards her. His blond hair tangled from sleep, he wore only rumpled blue jeans. She was shocked by the sudden urge to touch his bare chest. He smiled and walked up to her.

"Looks like I'm the slow one today. Did the rowdy crowd from the parlour keep you awake last night?"

Lara blushed and shook her head. "Sorry about Phillip's friends. My uncle says Phillip always hung out with the wrong crowd. He seems to thrive on danger."

Jerome's eyes showed sympathy. "The main reason I'm bunking in here is to see you're okay." He smiled. "I have to admit, I'd like to get to know you better." He detoured around her and closed the bathroom door.

She could soon hear the water run and continued to her own room to dress. On the way downstairs, she stopped halfway to listen for conversation. All was quiet. Jerome seemed so genuine. Since High school, she hadn't risked linking up with any guy. Maybe he would be the one to change her mind.

She joined her uncle at the table and they sat in comfortable silence. Her aunt hummed as she stood at the stove and flipped the eggs. The plate Noreen placed before Lara was piled high. She nibbled at her fried eggs while one hand touched the yellow tablecloth, so like Noreen, with its bright orange flowers. When she noticed the fourth place setting, she cringed. "Is Phillip joining us?" She stared at Henry.

He shook his head. "No. Phillip likes to take his breakfast downtown at the hotel. It gives him a chance to hear the gossip and find out which bars had the biggest fights. That plate's for Jerome."

Noreen gestured at the plate as she filled her own. "I'm thinking your friend could use some fattening up." She turned to Lara. "Eat up, girl. You looking pretty skinny yourself." Noreen started to add more food, but Lara waved her away.

Henry patted Noreen on the arm. "Lara's just right like she is. Being a singer, she'll want to get into those fancy clothes." He gave Noreen a big grin. "Besides, you know I'll clean up any leftovers."

Noreen set the frying pan back on the stove, and joined them at the table. "Where is that boy?"

A few minutes later, Jerome sauntered into the kitchen. "Morning all. That bed sure beats sleeping on the bus with the noise from all the guys snoring." He dropped down next to Henry.

Noreen rose and returned to the stove to put together another plate of food. "Here you are Jerome. My cooking is better than any hotel."

Jerome ate quickly. The series of fast food meals he lived on didn't satisfy. "Hmmm. Noreen, this is great food." He continued to wolf it down.

"This morning, I'll show you more of New Orleans." Lara's eyes engaged his. "We'll see the rest of the Garden District and then I'll take you on a tour of the Lafayette Cemetery. In the daytime, we'll be safe enough. It's only during the night you'll find all sorts of weird characters hanging around. I hear there are regular attempts to rob the vaults."

Jerome's face tensed. "I've heard the ghosts of vampires still float through the cemeteries. How do we skip running into any of those?"

Lara laughed. "Visitors to the cemetery are regaled with different ghost stories to keep them coming back." She and Henry exchanged a glance.

"Ya ever notice how people are scared of danger, but drawn to it as well? Henry asked.

Tension pulled Lara's face tight as she turned toward Noreen. "Was my mama like that? As a kid, I mean. Was she attracted to danger?"

Noreen dropped her head and stared at her hands. "Your mama lost her way with all the drinking. I tried to tell her not to run off with that rock singer, Maynard Jackson. She thought he'd be famous, and her still in her teens, was star struck. It just made her mad at me." She turned to Lara. "I didn't even know she had a child until the social worker called me from Louisville."

Lara sighed and took a peak at Jerome, whose jaw had dropped. She felt embarrassed they'd disclosed sordid family history with breakfast. Oh, well. If the two of them were to become friends, her secrets would be out in the open soon enough.

Lara sat up straight. "Life with Mama was difficult, but I did have some good times. I cried when the woman from social services came to pick me up from our rooms in that old house. When they took me to a foster home, I didn't know if I would ever have a real home again."

Noreen squeezed her arm. "Well, you got us to watch over you now."

Lara stared at her plate. "I still remember the small round table in the front room with the faded wallpaper covered in pink flowers, where I did my homework."

"I remember how shocked I was when she called us and asked if we could take you." Noreen smiled at Lara. "Best decision we ever made, right Henry?"

Henry nodded his eyes misty.

"The Lord saw I found you and Uncle Henry." Lara's face cleared. She smiled at Jerome. "Now we've told you our family secrets. You're still sure you want to get to know me?"

"I'm grateful to know the three of you. It's lonely here sometimes and where else would I find this kind of hospitality?" Jerome raised his coffee cup in a toast. "I'm a city boy from Jacksonville, Florida. Parents lived in a trailer park and marina.

When dad left us, my teacher talked me into joining the school band. I stayed when I discovered I loved music."

Henry's gaze fixed on Jerome. "Sorry about your family troubles, Jerome. We'll see if we can't find some fun for you." He turned to Lara. "He needs to see the real New Orleans, not just the tourist area. Lara, honey, you got to take Jerome to meet a conjure man in the bayou It's the way he'll understand the Creole heritage."

Lara shook a finger at him and laughed. "You're not going to tell him about the voodoo stuff, are you, Uncle?"

Henry replied. "Voodoo is part of our culture. The stories of Marie Laveau, the voodoo queen can still be heard throughout the Lower Ninth."

"That would be great," Jerome chuckled. "A new song about a voodoo queen could be a big hit."

Lara crossed the floor, grabbed his hand and pulled him up. "Come on now. We'll see no sights if you stay here all morning listening to those two. Let's get our things and get going."

*   *   *

The sun shone through the green branches as Lara and Jerome strolled down Chestnut Street. The sounds of men yelling back and forth to each other in the yards around them flowed through the crisp air, as they unloaded trucks of lumber to replace broken porches and railings. Jerome breathed in the fresh smell of the dripping tree branches and green grass after the rain and the pungent odor of newly sawed wood.

"You could do a lot worse than New Orleans when you choose where to settle down, Jerome murmured. "Why are you so determined to leave again?"

Lara's voice caught in her throat as though she thought twice about confiding in this stranger? "Aunt Noreen and Uncle Henry understand why I can't stay." She paused. I'll tell you about it sometime." She grabbed Jerome's hand and pulled him ahead. "Look, we're at the Lafayette Cemetery."

Jerome stared at the grassy square with its rows of above-ground grey stone vaults. Some of these stones were very ornate and others plain granite with a brief inscription of the family name. Lara watched him closely. "I wondered how you would react to the strange sight of these graves."

Jerome walked with his head down as they moved between the crypts. He didn't know what to think?

"This was the first above ground cemetery in the Americas built in the 1700s," she explained.

"It's not very large. Wouldn't they have run out of space years ago?" Jerome pointed to a crypt with three different dates carved into the headstone. "And why does this one show different time periods for the burial?"

"Families had these built above ground due to the water seepage in this lower part of New Orleans, even back then." Lara's face was intent. "We learned about these historic cemeteries in school. When the body deteriorates, what are left are the white calcified bones. The caretaker of the cemetery shovels them into the shallow cavity beneath the crypt and a new body is placed on top." She led him towards one in which the door still stood open.

As they stood in front of it, an older woman, wrapped in a black and purple cape with a red beret, strode up to them, muttering in Creole. She faced them and pointed at the crypt.

"Bonjour. I'm Marie, the local Priestess. Vous ne devriez pas deranger les morts. You shouldn't disturb the dead."

Lara shook her head. "My friend here only wants to know more about our history, especially about voodoo. I was explaining the purpose of the crypts." She pointed towards Jerome who moved back two steps.

Marie faced the crypt, crossed herself and began to chant once more. Finished, she turned from them and proceeded down the path behind where they stood.

"Oh, please. Don't go." Lara pleaded and hurried after her. "We really want to hear about voodoo culture."

Marie stopped to face them, her arms outstretched at shoulder level. "All right then, *mon amies*. If you are genuinely interested, you can come with me to my shop. It's just a block from here." She turned and continued down the pathway, not stopping to check if they followed her.

Jerome stared at Lara for a few moments with an uneasy gaze. "I don't want to be involved in any spells or potions. I know what those little dolls with pins mean."

"Oh, come on, Jerome." Lara smiled. "You don't really believe she'll sacrifice you and eat your flesh and blood, do you?"

Jerome hunched his shoulders and shivered. "The black kids I played with at school in Florida were totally spooked about voodoo."

"Be reasonable. Nothing will hurt you." Lara said.

Jerome sighed. "Okay. Just to the shop and no spells or other weird stuff."

They soon reached the small building and followed Marie through the doorway and across the worn wooden floor. Shelves were lined with jars of crystals, in burnt orange, sage and white. Under the glass counter were rows of necklaces made of bright red, blue and orange beads. In the middle of the room, stood a small table with three wooden chairs. Marie motioned for them to be seated.

"Most Americans are superstitious about voodoo. They don't understand it's one of the oldest religions. I'm a priestess of the Yoruba people and therefore inherited the spirits from my father. The religion started in West Africa and moved to Haiti and the West Indies before coming here."

"So, what do you do in your shop?" Do you have sacrifices here?" Jerome grimaced. He managed to squeeze through the small space between the table and the counter.

Lara shook her head embarrassed. Her voice sounded stern. "Jerome, where do you hear about these things?"

Marie gave a huge chuckle, her stomach convulsed and one foot tapped the floor in rhythm. "Mostly I remove voodoo spells from lost souls who have bought into the accusation they are possessed. I make up the ceremony for each incident, but it does the trick even for those who think they are in death's hands."

Jerome relaxed and smiled broadly at Marie. "Where do they get these rituals? Can we see one of these sacrificial ceremonies which I've read about?"

"Sure. In fact, there is one going on this afternoon not far from here if you want to attend. The group is from the cultural area of Mina who believe a person has two spirits; one which can leave the body during sleep or when that person is possessed as the result of a curse. Follow me."

The exit from the property was through a rear gate which was almost obscured by a wall of tall grass behind the complex of small shops. They followed Marie down a winding laneway into the back of a long low set building between several dilapidated houses. Jerome stood transfixed as he stared at a packed dirt floor with a strange pattern of cornmeal formed into a circle in the middle. His apprehension grew when he realized this was more than the usual cultural display for tourists, he'd experienced before.

A row of black men and women in shorts, cut-offs and bright patterned tee shirts held hands as they danced in a circle, bodies straining against each. The bright colours of their clothing swirled in a rainbow while they chanted in a sing-song fashion, he couldn't make out. Marie walked up to the group and nodded to the leader. He bowed and signalled to the others to drop hands to include her. She clasped the hands on each side while they continued to dance, moving faster and faster as they pulled her along.

The smell of incense here was strong. Fear washed over Jerome as he and Lara clutched each other, trying to keep to the shadows of the room, out of sight. *Oh, God. Please don't let them pull us into the group.* They chanted louder and louder. The dancers perspired and strained against each other as the speed of the dance increased until an older man collapsed and was dragged into the centre of the circle.

Marie joined him in the circle and raised him to his feet. They approached a wooden block a few steps away and stared at something lying on it. Lara grabbed Jerome's hand and inched closer to see what was going on. He made out a live chicken held by two men, in sweat soaked shirts, who struggled to hold on to it. The chicken's wings continued to flap while the men's arms swung wide in an effort to hold it. Horrified, he watched while one of the men lifted a cleaver, and severed the bird's head. He heard the ominous sound of the blade as it hit the wood. One man had to restrain the dead fowl while his partner collected the blood in a metal cup. He offered the cup to the old dancer who lifted it to his lips and appeared to drink. Marie and the other dancers joined the circle as the chicken was plucked and pieces were roasted on a rack over the coals of a fire. The entire group of dancers sat in a circle and gossiped while they drank bourbon and waited for the meat to cook. The smoke from the fire drifted into his hair as he grasped Jerome's hand, bathed in sweat.

While Jerome and Lara quietly stole out the back door into the sunlight, they could still hear Marie's high pitched laughter. They stood stunned for a few minutes but at the crash of a door slamming shut, they grabbed hands and ran down the street at full speed. About two blocks away, Lara stopped to catch her breath and shook her head at Jerome. "So you had to see a real sacrifice. What do you think now?" She laughed out of nervousness.

With the warm sunlight on his face, his fear was beginning to fade. "Well, at least they didn't sacrifice people or stick pins into voodoo dolls." Jerome led Lara to an old wooden bench where they could sit." Every religion has its own rituals."

Lara placed her fingers across his lips. "God doesn't require sacrifices from his followers."

"Oh, I don't know." Jerome tugged her hair in play. "I grew up in the Catholic religion which has its own saints and every church had a statue of Jesus which showed him sacrificed on the cross."

Lara leaned against him. "You know that's not the same thing."

He cupped her face in both his hands and kissed her lightly on the lips. She looked surprised, as he felt her lips move against his and her body begin to lean closer. The strange sensations in his chest and stomach caused him to pull away. She relaxed and continued to sit beside him reaching over to touch his hand next to her. While they sat, he could still hear the chanting swirling inside his head.

Chapter Five

Any recall of the voodoo scene caused Jerome to continue to shake, although he tried to hide it from Lara by his swagger. While they walked, he noticed Lara's laboured breathing and she slowed down as they approached the porch of Phillip's house. Over the railing, he could see Noreen's head, wrapped in a bright pink scarf. Jerome held back as Lara scrambled up the stairs and fell into the chair next to her aunt. When he reached the porch floor, he could hear Noreen humming. Lara had one hand placed on Noreen's arm and had turned to face her.

"What a day we had. We met a priestess in the cemetery and watched a real voodoo dance out in the back alley. I'd forgotten how scary it can be in the Ninth Ward."

"What was her name? I used to know some of the voodoo people, back when your uncle and I first moved there."

Lara shrugged. "She said her name was Marie. We visited a shop on Simon Bolivar which she owned."

Jerome joined them, glad to relax into a firm wicker chair. With his elbow on the chair arm, he rested his head on one hand. "Yeah. The sign said La Marengo or something like that. It was pretty faded."

"I don't believe it. I bet it was Marie Meraux." Noreen jumped up in excitement. "She was part of that group sang Creole music at our old house on Josephine Street. I lost track of them when we moved to Lakeview. It'd be nice to see them folk again."

Jerome sat up. "They told me the Ninth Ward got hit with the waters worse than here. I heard stories about bodies floating in the river and even some lying in the streets." He bit his lower lip when Noreen's jaw sagged and her shoulders slumped.

Lara put her arm around Noreen's waist and directed her towards the door. "Let's get some afternoon tea. We didn't mean to upset you with our stories or give you bad memories."

Shortly after, the three of them gathered around the kitchen table with their herbal tea and sugar cookies. He saw Lara's head jerk up when they heard the front door slam shut. Jerome touched her hand. Noreen hurried to the front door. "Oh, it's you Henry. Join us in the kitchen for tea. We might as well relax while Phillip is out."

Henry frowned. "Phillip's my kin and he's been good to us since the flood." He followed her and found a chair. "Who knows what would have happin to us without his help. He came out to that crowded airport while we slept on the floor waiting for a flight to who knows where."

"Sorry. I'm surely grateful to him." Noreen rolled her eyes at Lara. "Lara was telling me how she and Jerome met Marie Meraux and the crowd from the East Side we used to know." She poured his tea.

Henry warmed his hands on the mug, and shook his head at Jerome. "You two stay away from that group. I'm hearing the police has lost control of the area. Ain't nothin' happenin there but drugs and looting."

Jerome smiled. "Lara wanted me to see the real voodoo and we sure did."

Henry nodded his head. "You don't need to be scared of voodoo. It's been part of New Orleans as long as my family has lived here. People pretend it's supernatural. But it ain't. The real problem right now is drugs."

He turned to Noreen. "I hear our old friends are selling drugs in the Quarter." He shook his finger at Noreen. "Mind what I say about them and stay away."

They heard the door again followed by the heavy tread of boots on the hardwood floors. Phillip stuck his head in the doorway. "Well, doesn't this look cozy? Whole family gathered here when I'm not around." He glanced at Jerome. "I see you've got yourself moved in."

At the tight look on Lara's face, Jerome rose and approached Phillip. "You been wanting to hear me play. How about now?"

Phillip swung around and headed toward the parlour. "Sure. Come on to the other room."

While Jerome retrieved his sax from the case by the door and dropped into the old armchair, Phillip lifted the lid of a silver tureen sitting on the sideboard. "Want some weed to get us started?"

"Thanks. Not my thing when I'm playing. Besides we got a gig tonight and it'll probably run late." He began to tune the sax." As he glanced out the doorway, Jerome was relieved to see Lara climbing the stairs.

He turned back to see Phillip watching him. "You sweet on my niece? I won't get in your way." Jerome was shocked by the dark grimace on his face.

He held his breath, not sure how to respond. Was Phillip jealous or just possessive? "We're friends. Lara's really bright and I like that in a woman." He began to play *Georgia is my Life.*

Phillip picked up his guitar and strummed along with the music, nodding his head with the tune. His manner seemed to soften as he relaxed. The joint in the ashtray continued to burn, giving off grey smoke that drifted above their heads.

*　　*　　*

After breakfast, Jerome had agreed to meet Lara in the front hallway for a trip to find a grocery store that was open. Noreen was running out of food. A quick glance in the mirror reassured him his low-cut jeans looked cool with a tight tee-shirt. He grabbed his denim jacket and hurried down the stairs. Lara waited at the bottom, her shiny red jacket almost covering her white cotton shirt tucked into her jeans. As he closed the door behind them, Jerome braced himself against the wind and took Lara's arm. They soon reached St. Charles Street and Lara grinned at him when they were forced to hold tight to each other to avoid being blown over.

"I'm grateful Noreen suggested we get these groceries for her," Lara said. Phillip seemed touchy about the amount of money he's spending on us, especially with how much the two of them like to eat. I can't understand how he's so thin."

They continued down the street knowing no bus was likely to appear. "We've got the full day to roam since I don't have to get back to the hotel until seven this time," Jerome said. There must be stores open somewhere around here."

She smiled at him. "I'm glad you like my city. But, New Orleans isn't usually like this. Full of wind and rain, that is."

Jerome walked on lost in thought. He needed to find a way of getting to know more about this pretty and smart young woman beside him. He decided to take a chance. "What was your life like before you moved to New Orleans with your aunt and uncle?"

Lara hugged both arms around her body. "I lived with my mother in Louisville. She scared me since she was often drunk and angry. I never knew when she would hit me.

Jerome shook his head. "That must have been awful."

"Yes. But, it was even worse after she went to jail. I was sent to live with foster parents, Mr. and Mrs. Declan who already had four children of their own."

He stopped and turned to face her. "What was it like living with them? I hear some foster parents aren't really interested in the kids. Just the money."

"They weren't too bad. Anyway, I was tired of moving from one rooming house to another when my mother would be kicked out due to loud parties." She sighed. "When she was sober, Mama could be nice to me, take me to Wal-Mart for lunch and stuff like that. She always had to have men around her though. Often we'd have one live with us."

"Did you like having them stay with the two of you?"

"Sometimes. Lucas stayed with us the longest. He was huge, but real gentle with kids. He'd take me to the playground. Problem was we'd usually find Cecily, that's my mama, passed out when we'd return. He'd look after her for a time. Then he got fed up with her, always drunk and her foul mouth, so one day he just left for good."

Jerome frowned. "You must have been scared when she was like that."

"That was my life. Later when the social worker asked if I had any kin, I told her about Lucas. But she said *no way was she leaving a ten year old girl with a black man, not a relation.*"

"What happened to you after that?"

"After a while, Mr. Declan lost his job and food was scarce. A new social worker, a skinny white woman with red hair, showed up. She worried about him being able to continue to provide for me. A week later, she told us about finding an aunt and uncle."

"You must have been thrilled."

"Yeah. When she told me Aunt Noreen and Uncle Henry were living in New Orleans and had agreed to take me in, I was so relieved. But it was a long bus ride. When we pulled into the station, all I remember was a huge crowd."

"Did they meet you?"

"I kept frantically searching the crowd for anyone familiar. Then I spotted a large woman holding up a sign saying *Lara*. She was dressed in a bright red and white blouse and I was so excited, I ran right to her."

"What about your uncle?"

"Oh, yes. Standing beside Noreen was a skinny man with grey hair and a short beard dressed in faded jeans," said Lara.

Jerome laughed. "I bet it was Henry."

"Noreen held out her arms and I rushed into them. She recognized me even without the photo social services sent. *You look just like your mama. My sister, Cecily Jackson who wanted to be a big star.*

"No wonder you were so worried about them after the storm."

Lara's face softened. "Henry just stood there smiling and said something like *we're pleased to have you girl.* So, I had to give him a big hug, too."

Lara gave a deep sigh. "I haven't thought about those events for a long time."

Jerome still wasn't satisfied. "But why did your mama go to jail?"

Lara frowned and stood silent for several minutes. "The social worker told me Mama was accused of stabbing a drug dealer. Apparently, he was her usual supplier, but that time he took her money but didn't deliver. I know she'd get very angry at being cheated."

Jerome pulled back and breathed in. This was much worse than he expected. "Is she still in prison?"

Lara's frown grew deeper. "I'm not sure. About a year later, I asked Noreen if she'd heard anything from Mama. Noreen did receive a letter saying Mama was in a program in jail to get off the drugs. But, she'd been found guilty and wouldn't get out of prison for years. We never heard from her again."

Jerome put his arm around her shoulders. "All of that must have been awful for you."

Lara held her head up. "Not anymore. I'm glad to be here. I was afraid of her at the end. She didn't really feel like my mama anymore." Lara hurried down the street.

Jerome followed. Maybe he'd pushed her too hard. He'd let her take the lead in the conversation for the next while. That is, if he could catch her.

Relieved, he saw Lara slow down to a walk and stop to wait for him to catch up.

When he reached her, she pointed to the abandoned grounds of Tulane University which was across the street from them.

"I remember happier times in this city. When I was in the last year of high school, our group would come here on Friday nights for the football games. We'd all laugh and sing on the bus headed for the Dixie Burgers to celebrate on days we won."

They both stared at the empty fields. The silence reminded him he'd heard most of the students would have been evacuated to either Baton Rouge or Texas. No one seemed to know when the schools would reopen.

They were nearing Carrollton Street where the strip mall Noreen had told them about. Neighbours had told her some stores were still open there. He stopped to stare at a dilapidated bungalow with a hole chopped in the roof. Jerome was startled when Lara grabbed his arm.

"Looks like this 7-Eleven is open." She pulled open the old aluminum door, which squeaked, and walked in.

He hurried towards her, worried what she might find. When he stood inside the entrance, he noticed to his right, some bins of fruit and vegetables, a little withered but edible. Lara had placed some oranges, eggs, milk and flour into her basket and set it on the counter. She pulled her wallet from her jacket pocket and waited for the clerk to finish placing the items in two brown paper bags.

Jerome was walking up to the counter to help her with the bags when the door slammed open and two muscular men with bandanas covering part of their faces came through. The smaller one gestured with a black pistol towards Lara and the store clerk.

"Nobody will get hurt if you just give me your cash." The man's forehead was dripping with sweat. He stretched out his arm and waved the gun at Lara. "You lady. Just give me the bills out of that wallet, you got."

He watched Lara's eyes frozen in fear. She might be remembering the rough crowd back with her mama. Relieved, he saw her take a breath; dump the bills on the counter. Her body blocked Jerome's view of the clerk until the robber shoved her out of the way. Yelling at the clerk to move, the man grabbed the bills as well as a handful of money out of the till.

The taller robber had stood just inside the door to keep watch. He now came forward leaving the first man to guard Jerome and Lara and pointed a gun directly at the clerk. "What's your name, kid?"

The clerk, his hands wet with perspiration shook with fear and replied, "I'm Ron."

"Don't bother with any alarms, Ron. The heat's too busy cleaning up the bodies off the bridge anyway." He gave a harsh laugh. "That is, the cops who stayed. Most of them fled this god forsaken city. Don't try to be a hero."

Jerome stood still since he didn't want to draw the man's attention in their direction. Meanwhile, Ron watched the man stash the bills into his sack and start to leave. Jerome then saw Ron move back towards the cash register and bend as though to reach for something. The movement startled the robber who approached the counter and swung the gun against the side of the youth's head, drawing blood.

"What's with you? Ya lookin' to get killed?"

The closer man signalled to the other one and the two of them plunged out the door. Since he hoped to see where they went, Jerome followed them and reached the front steps in time to see them stick the guns back into waistbands. Both took off at high speed down the nearest back alley and out of his sight. He returned to the store, worried about Lara. He found her still shaking, her face grey. He put his arm around her for reassurance and was glad to see her begin to take deep breaths.

He moved back to the counter to check out the clerk. "How bad is it?"

Ron replied. "A little blood is all. He swiped me with the gun before I got to push the alarm. But, the dude's right. Cops aren't likely to come no how. Even if they got the alarm."

Ron moved back around the counter, wiped the blood off his head with a handkerchief and began to pick up the groceries from the floor placing them back in the bags.

Lara dropped beside him and helped. "He took my money. But I'm Phillip Devries' niece and he shops here all the time. Can I pay you later?"

Ron nodded his head, "I'll let you have the groceries. You can sign his tab." He turned to Jerome. "At least you helped scare them away."

"I didn't do much. Does this happen often? Phillip said petty crime was down since the storm because people can't get out."

Ron sighed. "He's right. At first there wasn't much violence. People were too busy trying to survive. But lately the looting has started up again. This is the third time I've been held up, so now I got this alarm."

Lara shook her head. "This isn't the way the city used to be."

Ron stood and leaned against the counter while he kept the cloth pressed against the side of his head. "People got no jobs and the poor around here got no money. Some of them need their drugs and those are in short supply with all the water and no visitors getting in. Drugs have to come in all the way from Miami now."

As the two of them made the long walk back towards the house, Jerome was proud of how Lara had regained her composure. She shivered some but it seemed to be from the cold.

47

He continued to scan the streets ahead as he watched for any new signs of violence.

They passed house after house which appeared empty, no sounds of any activity. From time to time, they had to cover their noses and mouths as protection from the putrid odours of open waste in the streets. By the time they reached the house on Chestnut Street, the winds had picked up, so hard it pushed them sideways. When the front door shut behind them, Lara leaned against it and gave a deep sigh.

They each carried a bag of groceries into the kitchen. When he saw the puzzled look on Lara's face, Jerome realized she was expecting a comforting hug from her aunt. Noreen would usually be fussing over lunch by now but she was nowhere in sight. After putting the groceries away, Lara headed upstairs probably to check out the bedroom.

Not long after, he was startled to see her hurry down the stairs towards him.

"She's not there. Her housecoat and pajamas were folded neatly on the wicker chair as usual. I couldn't even smell her jasmine perfume."

"She might have gone out with Henry."

Lara stared at him. "No. Henry goes out most afternoons for coffee and gossip with the guys, but not Noreen. She's a home body, especially now." She clenched and unclenched her hands.

"Where could she be? She talked about making some jambalaya for lunch. It's not like her to go out without telling me." He saw her bite her lower lip.

After all they'd been through today, Jerome wanted to calm her but he didn't know Noreen well. "She's probably over at a neighbour's house. You know she told us she wanted to get to know people around here. You told me she's worried about where their former neighbours might be, as well." He shrugged.

Lara still seemed doubtful. "Most of the phones still don't work. I guess she couldn't call anyone. I wish Henry would get home. He might know something."

Jerome grabbed her arm and led her into the parlour. "You need a rest." Fatigue washed over both of them as they sank into the old sofa. He was surprised and pleased when she leaned her head against his chest. He pulled her closer and kissed the top of her head. Exhausted from the morning, they both soon dozed off.

When he next opened his eyes, he was startled to see Henry bent over them. His breath smelled of Lucky Strike. Jerome jumped to his feet and glanced over at Lara still asleep.

"What's wrong, Henry. Isn't Noreen home yet? Lara's been so worried."

Henry frowned. "I just go in. That's what I been trying to ask the two of you. Where is Noreen? She would usually be starting dinner by now."

Lara sat up and rubbed her eyes. "What time is it?"

"It's nearly six. Lara, I got to tell you, I'm worried for Noreen if she went out alone. There's guns all around town these days. One of the guys from the coffee shop got robbed and pistol whipped on the street yesterday. Maybe she went for grub?"

Jerome ran his hands through his hair. "No. We went for food. But you're right. The 7-Eleven got robbed and Lara's money was snatched while we were in the store. "

Henry pulled Lara into a hug. "You all right, honey?" He shook his head. "That's not like the New Orleans, we knew. Always been some drug crimes in Lower Ninth Ward, but not like it is now."

Lara stood in his arms for several minutes, and then pulled back. "I feel safe with you two around."

Jerome fidgeted. "Did you say it's six?" He turned to Lara with a frown. "I hate to leave you like this, but I got to be on stage for practice at seven and it's a long walk. Will you be okay?"

Henry gave his attention to Lara. "Honey, can you stay by yourself for a while? I've got to go look for Noreen. I'll make the rounds of those who know her. She visits with the woman next door, name of Michelle. Lara, I promise to be right back. I want someone to stay here, just in case she comes back."

Lara smiled at the two of them. "Be off the two of you. I'll be okay." Jerome watched her walk back into the kitchen before him and Henry both left, closing the door with a solid pull.

Chapter Six

Lara boiled the kettle and poured the steaming water into the old blue teapot. She stood staring at it until the normal four minutes she allowed for tea to steep had passed. Her mug full of warm tea gave her some comfort as she sat at the table and waited for her family to return. She finished the tea and stared at the faded green wallpaper. Then with the noise of the front door opening, she hurried to the front hall. It was Henry and his face was ashen.

"Not good news, honey. Michelle says Noreen went to the Lower Ninth Ward. Wanting to look up Marie and some other old friends. She's been worrying about them." Weariness seemed to overwhelm him so Lara led him back into the kitchen. He dropped onto a chair and she poured him some tea.

"I been telling her that's a bad group to hang with." He pounded one fist on the table. "I'm going to the cops. But I can't hope for much. I hear they're so overloaded. When I'm finished with them, you can bet I'm going to find Marie." His eyes pleaded with Lara. "I'm hoping ya can stay here by yourself a little longer? In case she returns, she'll need to know where we're at."

Lara's shoulders tensed. How she hated being in this old house alone. Then she saw Henry's worried expression. "Of course, uncle. You know I'd do anything to help you and Noreen. But make sure to close the front door tightly when you leave? You know musicians like Phillip and Jerome will be back late. Probably midnight." She followed Henry to the front hall and watched him close the door which she locked. As she returned to the kitchen, feelings of loneliness and despair which she had held back, flooded through her. The lost and abandoned little girl returned to haunt her and she let a few tears escape while she remembered.

*   *   *

Mama had promised they would celebrate Lara's eighth birthday with an ice cream at Woolworth's, as soon as she got back from her errand. With her hands on the cracked window sill, she stared down the street. What was taking her so long? Disappointed, she dragged her feet back across the wood floor and jumped onto the old flowered sofa. Ouch. Tears gathered as a sharp pang ran through her bare foot from one of the broken springs.

For lunch, Lara had cooked the last of the macaroni and sprinkled it with dried cheese. She gulped down the food without even setting down the spoon. Her mother, as usual, hadn't eaten anything. Cecily just pushed the food around on the plate and then gave the meal back to Lara barely touched.

"I gotta go out now," Cecily growled. Her mother's black braid had unravelled in several places. Her hands trembled which wasn't a good sign.

"I got people to visit down at Joe's, baby. Ya know I need my medicines."

Lara had stared up at her. "Mom, that medicine makes you sick. Lucas has been telling you to stop taking it."

"What does he know? Big lazy bastard. He's long gone now." Cecily then got up from the table and grabbed Lara by both shoulders, squeezing hard. She'd later find two red marks. "You listen to your mama, and not to any man, ya hear."

Cecily pulled on a dirty windbreaker with holes in the elbows and dropped a small bag of money in the pocket. "You remember to be right here when I get back, if you want that ice cream." She wagged her finger in Lara's face, her hands shaking so hard mama could barely open the door.

The next time Lara made the trip across the floor to stare out the window, the sun was beginning to set. While she stood there, both arms around her thin body, Lara caught a glance of Cecily staggering down the street towards the house. But worse than that was the two men following her. Were they coming to her house? She hated it when mama brought friends home. She walked over to the door and stared at it with apprehension.

Slowly, it inched open and mama came through it alone. She smiled although her eyes were glazed. "How's my good girl? Waiting for mama like I told you?" Cecily gave her a quick hug and headed straight for the bedroom.

While Lara stood there, the door opened again and the two men she'd seen earlier, noisily filled the living room. When a tall man with curly white hair leaned over her, the smell of booze was overpowering. His dirty brown raincoat brushed across her face when he stood up again. "You must be Lara? Your mother said you were cute and I'd have to agree with her." She squirmed when he ran his hand over her hair.

"Leave her alone, Morris. We're not here to scare the kid."

Lara turned her head and saw a short man with brown skin and a thin black mustache who came to stand beside Morris. He wore a shiny black and orange baseball jacket.

Lara felt her lower lip tremble while she waited for her mother to return. Cecily came into the room dressed in tight black pants and an iridescent blue top. She went to the small kitchenette and pulled out mix and other bottles from the cupboard.

"Rye or vodka, Manuel?"

"Rye for me. Morris is the vodka man."

Lara shifted from one foot to the other as she watched them. All three were now crowded into the kitchenette, with drinks in hand and loud talk.

"Mama, aren't we going out? You promised."

Cecily froze with the drink still raised to her lips. "Can't you see I have company, girl? Do you want me to be alone all the time?" She grabbed Lara's shoulder. "Get out of my sight or you'll be going to bed instead of out."

Morris stood next to her mama, leering at Lara. "Yeah, kid. Better listen to your ma." He gave an eerie laugh. "She's the boss."

As tears streamed down her face, Lara ran into the bedroom and slammed the door shut. She could still hear the drunken laughter and the high-pitched voice mama had when she drank that stuff. After a while, she could hear the three of them in her mother's bedroom next door making those strange noises. Please don't let them come into my room. She had kept her hands over both ears. There'd be no birthday celebration for her.

*　　*　　*

Lara straightened her shoulders. Time to forget her old life. She would find the strength to help her aunt. Her stomach rumbled with hunger while she heated up a pot of soup for dinner. Maybe Henry would have some news when he returned next time. The bowl was almost empty when she heard the key turn in the front door. Would Henry be back so quickly? She froze at the table listening to the sound of heavy boots on the wooden floors.

"Where's Henry?" Phillip sauntered into the room. She could tell by his blood shot eyes, he was high. He came closer. "Is it just you and me, girl?" He gave one of his throaty laughs.

Lara breathed deeply to remain calm. She recalled what she'd learned from the health teacher at school. *Never let a bully know you are scared.* "Uncle Henry should be back any time now. He went to find Noreen." She clenched both hands but they still shook.

His face turned serious. "Where is Noreen? She never goes out much. These streets aren't safe at night."

Lara sighed. "Henry thinks she might have gone to the Lower Ninth Ward to seek after friends."

Phillip straightened up and lit a cigarette. "Why would she do that? There are lots of drugs down in that area, but it's not her thing. She could get real hurt. I don't much like Henry being down there either."

Shocked at the concern in his voice, Lara responded. "We don't know. That's what Henry went to find out."

"I got some people I can talk to knows that place. I need to see Henry gets into no trouble down there." Phillip turned into the hallway headed to the parlour in back.

Lara was surprised to see how worried he was. She finished her still warm soup while she contemplated what to do next. She couldn't join Phillip to see what he knew because he might get too friendly. But if she went upstairs, what would prevent him from following her? She placed the dirty bowl in the sink. She decided to take the chance and headed towards the stairs. Her own room would feel safer. Just as she reached the bottom step, she felt a hand on her shoulder and turned to face Phillip.

He placed one hand on the stair banister right beside her while she cringed. "Hold on Lara. No need to be afraid of me. After all I'm your uncle. I only want to make sure you're looked after until Henry gets back." He stepped even closer.

Lara knew she'd need to show some strength with him. "Phillip, stop it right now. You know Henry will hate you, if you mess with me."

Phillip dropped his arm. "Okay, then." He gave a sneaky grin. "Maybe another time, we can get together. I know Jerome isn't back until late." He started back towards the parlour.

When she heard the sound of a key turn, Lara stared at the door. It swung open, and Henry stumbled through. He breathed deeply and walked towards her, but stopped when he saw the anxiety written on her face. He turned his head further and stared at Phillip who stood across from her, still in the hall. "What you been doing to scare my niece? Why can't I trust you with my family? If you want us all to leave, just say so."

"Calm down, Henry. I didn't touch her, did I Lara?" He gave her a hard look.

Lara glanced at her uncle's face, noting the stress and fatigue. "No. I'm okay now. Did you hear anything about where Noreen might be?"

She was shocked by the strangled sound he made. Almost like he was crying. It wasn't like Henry to be so emotional. "I didn't find her, but she was with Marie and the gang at the shop. I heard from an old friend who's heard the gangs down there are pretty desperate." If they have her, he said they need cash badly. He thinks they'll contact me asking for something soon." He jerked his head towards Phillip. "Any ideas what they'll want?"

"Yeah. It's money they're after. I also heard about the local drug supply drying up. We need to get her out of there right now. I've dealt with them before and they're not particular about who they hurt."

Henry shrugged his shoulders. "I talked to the cops this morning, but they've got no ideas. The downtown petty crime and looting has given them all they can handle. They're still avoiding the flooded areas waiting for the National Guard."

Phillip patted his shoulder. "I got my own contacts. I'll see what I can find out tomorrow at the hotel. For tonight, we'll just have to sit it out."

Henry grabbed Phillip's shoulders with both hands. "Don't you see, I can't leave Noreen out there alone again all night? She's never been away from me for long since we married. She'll be so scared."

Phillip pulled free and gave Henry an angry glare. "Look, it's the best I can offer. We can't do any more tonight and you know it."

Henry dropped onto the bottom step holding his head in his hands. "I hear Marie has used her shop and the voodoo business as a front. They are bringing in drugs by boat now and selling them to some of their normal users. But, there are still a whole lot of strung out addicts down there and they got no way to get in enough supply for them all." He raised his head and stared at Phillip. "But, you know about the drug trade better than me."

Phillip nodded. "You're right. Musicians often use some dope. Helps them to get down with their music. Before the flood, there was plenty on Bourbon Street. But, I wouldn't be surprised if some of it came from the lower districts."

Henry stood up and moved closer to Phillip. "You selling the stuff?"

"Yeah, You know I'm using. Who's using is into selling. But, our group have never been into it in a big way. Just sell enough to supply our own musicians." Phillip crushed his cigarette out in the ashtray which stood in the hall. "Like I said. I got people I can talk to who might know something. Tomorrow that's what I'll be doing."

Lara touched Henry's arm. "Come on uncle. He's right about us not being able to do anything tonight. Especially when no cabs will go down there. We'll start again tomorrow."

Henry turned to the stairway and dragged himself up, his shoulders sagging like an old tree blowing in the wind. "Okay honey. I hear you. Until tomorrow then." She followed him up the stairs.

She heard Phillip stomp back into the parlour. She could imagine him opening the silver urn on the table to take out a joint like he did most nights.

Chapter Seven

Noreen enjoyed the stroll down the dusty laneway which led away from the cemetery, old memories tugging at her. When she and Henry had lived down here, Saturday was shopping day on the stretch of one storey shops on Louisiana Avenue ahead. Noreen stopped when she reached one of the small shops, a well-known landmark in that area. The bell jingled when she forced open the old wood door, swollen from years of water. She was relieved to see a familiar face move towards her.

Marie, the shop owner, smiled in recognition. "Noreen. I haven't seen you in years. What ya doing in my part of town?"

"Since the flood, we're living over in the Garden District with Henry's brother until our place is livable." Noreen sighed. "I got lonely and then I remembered that the group used to hang out at your shop. So here I am."

Marie took Noreen's hand in both of hers and touched it to her lips. "Wonderful to see you. Let me make us some tea and we can catch up."

Noreen breathed in the aroma of chamomile tea brewing as she seated herself on one of the sturdy pine chairs. After taking the cup from Marie, she held it up to her nose to savour the smell. When the front door burst open with a bang, moments later, her back jerked against the chair, almost spilling the tea. Shock hit her as she stared at the two large muscular men, with menacing faces, blocking the doorway. Her cup crashed to the wooden floor. Marie jumped to her feet and moved towards them.

"What you wanting here, Jackson? I told you before that I don't need your type of drug. Herbal drugs is my type. Much betta for our people."

Marie turned back to Noreen. Before she could reach her, one of the men, who appeared to be Creole, pulled Noreen off the chair and jerked both arms behind her back. His muscled arms bulged against his tight black cotton shirt.

He roughly tied both hands with a rope making sure she couldn't move them. While she wailed in fear, he tied a bandana over her eyes. Everything went dark. Her heart pounded when she felt him drag her towards the back door. She could hear Marie follow behind them.

"You leave her alone. She don't even live here. Just havin a visit with me for old time's sake."

He grunted. "Get out of my way and you won't get hurt. This ain't no affair of yours. Don't even think about calling the cops."

Noreen attempted to brace one foot against the doorframe while he continued to drag her out the door and into some sort of back lane. She heard the second man slam the door shut before he joined them. Pain shot up both arms as she felt herself lifted into the back seat of a vehicle. She heard the driver crank the motor until it started. Then they drove off down the street. The man beside her held a cloth with a pungent odor under her nose. She felt her mind closing down while her tongue grew thick in her throat.

*   *   *

When Noreen came to, sweat was dripping off her forehead. Startled, she felt the bandana ripped off her eyes. What was going on? She blinked in the low light and attempted to focus. Someone was standing over her. When her vision cleared, she could see a skinny white woman with straight straw-coloured hair. Noreen found herself sitting in an old wooden chair. She looked around at the stained wallpaper with small blue and yellow flowers and the painted floor.

"Where am I? What's happened to Marie?"

The woman waved a shiny knife towards her face. "Forget about her. She's not part of this job. The shop was just a good place to grab you when we saw where you was headed. It's that brother-in-law of yours, we got business with."

Noreen shrugged. "You must mean Phillip. But, I got no control over what Phillip does. You'll have to talk to him. What's your name, girl?"

"Keep quiet. We know your old man can get to Phillip." She dropped the hand which clutched the knife to her side. "You can call me Lucy."

Lucy continued. "Back in the quarter, the gossip is those two been looking after each other since they were kids with both parents gone. And Phillip owes us plenty." Lucy's pale blue eyes stayed fixed on Noreen as she waited for a response.

Noreen squirmed in her chair. What had Phillip done to get her and Henry into this trouble? As she continued to move, she could feel the ropes around her hands begin to loosen. If she could distract Lucy for a while, she might be able to free herself. Noreen whimpered. "I need to go to the toilet. Can you bring me somewhere?"

"Shut up your crying. You'll have to stay here as I got to wait for Jackson." Loud noises in the hall outside the door caused Lucy to turn her head in that direction. When she turned back, she waved the knife at Noreen. "I've got to go see what's happenin across the hall. Now, don't you get any ideas cause we'll be over there in the next room. We don't really need you in case you get to be too much trouble for us. I hope you get what I mean."

Noreen settled against the hard back of the chair and breathed out. "I'm not going anywhere, Lucy."

As soon as the door slammed behind her guard, Noreen slumped forward in the chair, her head almost on her knees and wiggled back and forth until the ropes were looser. She felt one hand work free and struggled to pull the other one out. With a sigh, she brought both hands up to her face and felt the wetness of her tears.

* * *

The morning after Noreen disappeared, Lara packed large slices of ham wrapped in cornbread and covered with wax paper into a bag. She placed them together with a small thermos of black coffee into a knapsack for Henry. When she finished with the lunch, Phillip joined them in the kitchen.

"Where you off to now, Henry?"

"I'm gonna check the Lafayette cemetery district. Just in case Noreen wanted to find Marie."

Phillip shook his head back and forth. "Don't you do that. I talked to the guys at the hotel this morning after breakfast. They tell me the shop is where the dealers hang out. The gang is pretty mad over losing their payoff money since they're all short of cash. Most of the banks are still closed and money lenders aren't lending since they don't know when they can get more."

Henry glowered at his brother. "Look here, Phillip. You seem to have all the drugs you want and the band isn't looking strung out. Where's your supply coming from?"

Phillip grabbed Henry's arm and pulled him forward. "You're not going out there, ya hear. I won't let you get yourself in trouble with the gang."

Henry glared back at Phillip and then yanked his arm free. He grabbed his bag and headed for the door. "I'm not waitin any longer. From what you tell me, it's worse than I thought and Noreen's in danger. She's done nothing wrong."

Phillip followed Henry into the hallway. "I've told Dominic I'm ready to meet."

Henry stopped. "Where at?"

"At one of our old haunts. I'll be there around eleven. Can you wait until then?"

As he shook his head, Henry opened the door and left.

*   *   *

Jerome's eyes sparkled and his smile stretched across his face as they wound up the session that night. It had gone so well. The crowd had clapped with enthusiasm when Lewis wowed them with his clarinet solo. Lewis was now a good friend. Although he had a tough side, he was very loyal to those whom he befriended. Jerome continued to worry about leaving Lara alone at the house. But he also knew the information he needed to find Noreen would be found right here in the Quarter. Lewis must know something.

Jerome gestured to the bar. "Lewis, join me for one drink to celebrate. I know it's midnight, but let's have a quick rum before I have to go back to the house."

Relaxed on the cracked leather bar stools, they sipped their drinks. "Now this is what I call a good drug," said Lewis. "Warmth calms your mood. Not like the hard stuff your friend uses."

"You mean Phillip? He's so unlike Henry." Jerome set down his glass. "Henry's the straight one."

"Yeah. That's him, Phillip. The one who hangs out at the New Orleans Hotel."

"It's mostly pot with him." Jerome stated. "At least at the house."

"That's what you think. He and his boys are into blow in the backroom almost every day. I don't know where they're getting it right now, but I hear he owes big money for his last supply."

Jerome finished his rum in one swallow and stood ready to go. "Does Phillip have anything to do with Noreen being kidnapped? Henry's worried it's a gang of drug dealers which has her."

"Yeah. I hear she was grabbed by the Marrero gang to put some pressure on Phillip to pay a debt. They'll hold her hostage until they get paid. I'd worry about what they might do after the pay off."

Jerome pulled on his jacket. "Does Phillip know about this?"

Lewis nodded. "He knows. Probably afraid to tell his brother. Phillip doesn't have any real friends besides Henry." He finished his drink and followed Jerome to the door.

"I got to get back to see if I can help. Lara would be devastated if something happened to her aunt."

"Why don't I come with you? I know the area and the normal hideouts for the gang. Give me a few minutes to stash my clarinet in my room."

"Okay. I'd appreciate your help. But I have to pick Lara up back at the house. She'll want to join in the search for her aunt," said Jerome.

"All right by me. We'll head straight to Chestnut Street." Lewis hailed down a cab.

*   *   *

Henry felt defeated as he left Marie's empty shop and pulled the door shut behind him. He stood in the dusty street gazing from North to South. Where would they go from here? Marie was his only link to the gang and she wasn't here. Funny that she left the door unlocked. He stood at rigid attention as he watched a tall man in black leather vest and tight jeans walk towards him.

"If it's the good stuff you're seeking, the New Orleans Hotel is the place right now. It's not down here anymore." He pointed north.

Henry decided if the man thought he was a user, he might find out something. "I'm new to town. Who do I ask for?"

"You ask for Phillip. He'll know where it's at." The man nodded his head and wandered on down the street.

Henry was in shock at the news. Phillip wasn't getting away with this again. With no cabs in sight, he'd have to walk back uptown but it'd be worth the effort. An hour later, hot and sweating, Henry entered the familiar long bar at the New Orleans Hotel. He slipped into a seat at a table of men who were quietly sipping their bourbon and gestured to one of them. "You know where Phillip is at?"

The man had thin arms and a sunken chest which suggested to Henry he might be an addict. "Ain't you his brother?"

"That I am. And I need to see him right away. I got business with him." Henry kept his eyes on the man's face to see how he would react.

"You needing a strong fix?" The man gestured towards his nostrils.

"No. Not that. I got other urgent matters with him."

The man snickered. "From what I hear, Phillip got some urgent matters of his own. He owes the Marrero gang big and that's not good. They're not too tolerant of uncollected debt, so I hear." His two companions smiled.

The stocky one with dark curly hair turned to him. "I hear they took a relation of his hostage to hurry him along. A woman."

Henry felt prickles along his skin. "What did you say? Who was it?"

The guy shrugged. "Don't know. Just heard she was black and not originally from this city."

Henry got to his feet, a snarl on his lips. "I need to find Phillip and right this minute."

"Can't help you. I hear he left the hotel this morning after breakfast and hasn't returned." The thin man's eyes brightened.

"You let us know if you find him. There's lots of people looking for him right now."

As he hurried out, Henry hit the door hard with his shoulder. Bursting into the street, he tried to find a cab. *Wait until Phillip returns to the house. He'll find me waiting for him and he better talk fast.*

Chapter Eight

Back at the house and impatient to get the search started, Jerome rushed up the stairs, pushed open the heavy front door and called out. "Lara, where you at hon? The cab's waiting so we need to move fast." Lewis, who had followed him and stood at the bottom of the steps, kept an eye on the taxi.

From the hallway, he heard Lara's rapid footsteps on the stairs before he saw her. Her face was pulled into a frown with her hair pulled severely back from her face in some kind of a bun.

"We still have no word on Noreen as yet." Lara sighed. "Henry's gone out again, but he asked me to stay here."

Jerome pulled her into a quick hug. "Lewis and I are on our way out to Lafayette, but I knew you'd want to come with us." When she hesitated, he continued. "That's if you want to join us. You can stay here until we get back, if you'd prefer."

He watched her take a deep breath. "Of course, I want to find my aunt. Forget what Henry said. I have to go with you. It wouldn't be right not to try." She grabbed a navy-hooded jacket from the closet by the front door and they followed Lewis out to the street.

Lewis gave her a big smile. "So you're the reason Jerome has been staying way out here." Lara blushed. She grabbed Jerome's arm and the two of them jumped into the back seat of the cab. Lewis joined the driver in front and gave him directions.

"As long as you're helping Jerome to find my aunt, you're a friend of mine, too."

Jerome smiled. "Lewis has been a big help. He insisted on coming with me out to the shop." He put his arms around Lara and kissed her on the cheek.

He felt the light weight of her head on his shoulder as he watched a stream of broken houses along the water-logged streets. They'd just passed a yellow vinyl bungalow with all the windows smashed and the front section of the roof ripped right off. Wind and rain had turned the wallboard in some of the rooms into mush. "You been out this way before, Lewis?" Jerome asked. "Since the storm, I mean."

"No. the band members stay out of this part of town. Who lives here is mostly poor brothers who can't get any work since the storm. They were your porters, busboys, shoe shiners and hotel cleaning staff. Folks like that. With this mess, tourism is still down from what it was before the hurricane.

Jerome gestured to the street. "What they livin on now?"

Lewis frowned. "Turnin to petty crime, I imagine. Break ins are all up, from what I hear. Some turn to selling dope. That's why I stay downtown."

Shortly after, the taxi pulled up to the same old store where Jerome and Lara had met with Marie only a few days ago. After he asked the driver to wait, they got out and walked to the front door. Jerome recognized the sound of the bell as it opened. Marie dropped the bag of incense she'd been wrapping, and her mouth fell open. She seemed reassured when she recognized them. "What you two doing back here? Didn't we scare you off last time with our voodoo dance?" She chuckled. Her manner changed when she noticed Lewis. "And who's this friend of yours? I told you not to bring anyone here."

"Where's my aunt at? Lara demanded. "She was last seen right here in this shop. You'd better tell us where she is." Lara stood face to face with Marie across the counter, glaring right into her eyes.

Marie stared back. "I don't know nothing. You're right. Noreen was here. But, she joined up with some locals and they all left together. Didn't tell me where they's going."

Jerome was proud of Lara's initiative in challenging Marie. He decided to push the issue a little farther. "We're not leaving until you tell us where she is. I can tell by your responses you do know more than you're telling us."

From behind him, he could feel Lewis move forward. "Come on now, Marie. We know the gangs are out of control down here. You part of the group now?"

Marie's eyes turned fierce. "You know me, Lewis. I make an honest living in this shop. The old crowd is into lots of stuff, but I keep to myself." She came out from behind the counter, smoothed the front of her multi-coloured skirt and sat in the chair. "They try but no way I'm joining them."

Jerome smacked the back of the wooden chair beside her with his clenched fist. "Marie, you've got to tell us. Think about what could happen to Noreen. Isn't she your friend?" In frustration, he grabbed her arm and squeezed it. "Who took her? You better tell us."

Lewis stood on her other side, his face inches from hers. "You'll tell us what you know. And now."

Marie's shoulders slumped. Jerome watched guilt and fear drift over her features. "What about me? They promised to kill me if I talked to anyone. They're desperate and will do it. I can't tell you." She stopped to catch her breath. Shrugged and continued. "Besides, I don't know where they took her.

Lara took the chair next to Marie and put a hand on her shoulder. "Back off for a minute, guys. Marie, we'll not let them hurt you. But, we have to hear what you know. If they threaten you, let Henry or I know and we'll send someone to help. We're over at Phillip's.

Marie seemed to calm down. "It's the Marrero's who's got her. Took her right out of my shop and dragged her away." Marie put her face in her hands and rocked back and forth. "If Phillip doesn't pay them what's owed, you won't see her again."

The three of them stood waiting for her to continue. In the silence, Jerome asked, "What has Phillip got to do with this? Why would he hang out down here?"

"They're his main supplier for uptown now that offshore smuggling has stopped due to the high water. I hear he's got a big debt with them."

"But why take Noreen? She had little to do with Phillip before now." Jerome began to pace.

"They wanted to get to Henry, but he's too smart for them. They figured grab Noreen and Henry would put the pressure on Phillip for them." Marie gave a deep sigh. "That's all I know. I want to help Noreen, but it's too much danger for me. You go now. Phillip is your answer."

Lewis turned to Jerome. "So we're back on our way to the New Orleans Hotel. We could search every shack down here and never find her."

The three of them left and headed to the waiting taxi. Once in the back seat and headed back uptown, Lara clasped Jerome's arm. "I knew Phillip couldn't be trusted. It's too bad he's Uncle Henry's brother. This'll go hard with Uncle."

Chapter Nine

Spurred on by his deep anger, Henry strode across the familiar veranda of the hotel and headed straight for the back entrance. He knew this late in the afternoon, the guys would be in the back bar, probably already high, and he would be able to surprise them. With a solid push to the old grey door, he entered directly into a small room with a dozen men huddled around two dilapidated tables. Based on his hunch, Phillip was likely somewhere in this group.

Henry approached the first table through the smoke. In his loudest voice, he demanded, "Phillip, you in here? I need to have a talk with you about Noreen gone missing." He held his ground while met with silence. A moment later, Phillip withdrew from a crowd at the bar and approached. "Hold on now brother. What have the guys been telling you?" As he stood head to head with Henry, he continued. "I didn't do nothing with Noreen. I don't know where she's at."

"Maybe not. But I know you're the problem. What you been up to with the Marrero's? Sounds to me like they're the ones who took her." Henry refused to back down or drop his gaze from Phillip. "I hear you owe money to them. The gang down in the lower east side. You pay up and Noreen goes free."

Phillip shook his head and turned back to the bar. "I can't help you right now. You go home and calm down. When I get back later tonight, we'll talk about a real plan to find Noreen." He picked up his drink, walked back to his buddies.

Henry felt the heat on his face. He walked over to the bar, grabbed Phillip by the arm and spun him around. His punch hit Phillip in the chest and caused him to stumble. "Right. Your friends are your own business until it affects me and my family. Noreen and Lara are my only family since I no longer have a brother. Noreen's my number one priority and I'm going to get her back myself."

Built up anger propelled Henry towards the door which he kicked open, marched back across the veranda and into the street. He stopped. What would he do now? If Phillip wouldn't help him, who would? Henry knew Ray Marrero from back when they both lived on East Jefferson Street and worked in the dry wall business renovating homes in the Garden District. Ray was a little crooked, but never anything like kidnapping.

Maybe he could approach Ray and offer to pay him off for Phillip. He had some money put aside for him and Noreen to retire, but it wouldn't be enough. And could he find Ray? Henry flagged down a yellow cab and fell into the ragged back seat.

"Take me to the Paddock Bar." He knew Ray used to hang out at the bar back when the boys bet on racing for entertainment. It was worth a try.

The young driver shook his dreadlocks and turned to stare at Henry. "Why you want to go there, man? Not safe anymore since the storm."

Henry nodded. That information confirmed for Henry drugs would be available at the bar. "All the better for me."

The driver shrugged. "Okay, man. It's your skin. But I don't wait for no fares down there."

How much did Phillip owe those guys? Who could he borrow from if he didn't have enough?" Henry sunk back against the seat, with his energy fast drained away. Before Katrina, he could go almost anywhere in lower New Orleans and be welcomed. Many of the locals had gone to school with him. They were now owners of small shops or worked in the tourist district. Now, everyone was out of work and he knew some of them would be pretty desperate. The cab pulled to an abrupt stop which jerked his head into the back of the seat.

"We're here." The driver turned and held out his hand for the fare. "I got to be moving. No work for cabs around here right now."

Henry paid him. "Couldn't you give me five minutes?" After he waited for a response and stared at the driver's back, he pushed open the door. He heard the car engine rev up as his feet hit the pavement.

"Okay. Take it easy. Don't run me over, I'm going." He found himself standing on the muddy William Boulevard as he watched the taxi leave. He could make out Jefferson Downs across the way, deserted at this time of year with the grass peeking through the layer of silt. As he approached, he remembered the weather-beaten walls of the Paddock. It now had more peeled paint and the wooden walkway had several broken planks.

Henry pushed open the door and entered yet another smoke filled room. Through the haze, he could just make out several groups of men gathered around the dark pine tables. Some sat in the green vinyl chairs while others clustered around them. No race forms were in sight. Through the expanse of window, he could see the race track was deserted.

Henry walked up to the table closest to the door, dropped into a seat and signaled the waiter to bring a beer. He was aware of six pairs of eyes focused on his face.

"Any of you seen Ray Marrero?"

"Why? You lookin for blow?" He turned to face an older white man with a long grey ponytail and denim vest who sat next to him. "Does he have some good stuff?"

Henry didn't respond. He continued to check out the other men at the table seeking a friendly face. "I'm an old friend of his. Just trying to reconnect. See how his family is. With the flood and all."

The guy with the ponytail extended his hand. "I'm Joel. I'd like to help you man, but I don't know the dude personally."

The heavy set brother who sat on Henry's other side blew out a puff of smoke. "You'd want to talk to Dwayne, other there." He gestured with his cigarette toward the table next to the bar. "He's part of that gang."

Henry stood and offered his hand. "Thanks. Appreciate it." He crossed the wooden floor toward the bar. As he neared the table, an electric sensation crawled up the back of his neck.

Dwayne was a brown-skinned, muscular man with black wavy hair. Probably one of those Creoles who claimed to be the original people of New Orleans. "You know where Ray is at?"

Dwayne stood to face him. "Who wants to know? What's your business with Ray?"

Henry held his position. "You tell him Henry has got word for him from his brother, Philip. He'll know what I mean." Henry pointed. "I'll wait over in the corner there until I hear from him." Without waiting for a response, Henry headed to one of the old leather booths, slid in and placed his beer on the table.

Dwayne followed him and stood by the table. "Okay, I can get to him, but you got a half hour wait. And it better be good news." He banged his fist on the table. "Right now, Ray's out of patience with your brother." Dwayne gave him a final glare before he strode out the door.

Henry settled back. He could do nothing further except wait, and pray Noreen was still safe. Never before had he felt like a stranger in his own town.

Chapter Ten

As she trembled in fear, Noreen eased the wooden door open by a small crack and peered into the dingy hallway. Although the door directly across from her was closed, she could hear the low hum of voices and an occasional high pitched laugh. She was sure it was Lucy. Would she be able to sneak passed them, down the hall and out the door which led into the street? Her heart raced as she stepped into the hall. What choice did she have? If she stayed in this room, she would remain at their mercy. She had to take the chance. Noreen removed her red slip-on shoes and stuck one in each of the oversized pockets in her bulky cardigan.

Easing the door wider, she held her breath as she tiptoed into the hallway. Her body felt heavy as she gingerly moved her feet forward, a few steps at a time. With the end of the hall clearly in view, Noreen clasped both hands over her heart, mumbled a silent prayer. A sudden noise caused her to glance over her shoulder in time to see Lucy running towards her, knife in hand.

"You, stop right now. Jackson stay close to me in case she puts up a fight," yelled Lucy at the man behind her.

"We wouldn't be facing this right now, if you had stayed with her like I asked you," he shouted back at her.

Noreen, with her heart continuing to pound, charged towards the outside door with a spurt of energy. Her entire body shook with the effort and a high pitched sound escaped when Lucy grabbed her around the neck from behind and held the knife to her throat.

Lucy's voice grated with fury in her ear and she tightened her grip. "Where do you think you're going? Didn't I tell you to stay in that chair?"

Noreen felt her body collapse, her face wet with tears. "I can't get you your money. Please just let me go home."

Lucy loosened her grip and turned Noreen around to face her. Her manner was more subdued. "I told you, it's Phillip we're after. Just get back to your room like a good girl and we won't hurt you."

Jackson moved in front of them, blocking their path. "Why don't we do away with her now? She's seen both of us. We can't let her go."

Lucy glared at him. "We wait like I told you. Phillip knows we have her so she'll bring him to us. He'll want to know she's still alive." Her face hardened. "There's no way he's getting away with robbery like he did to us."

Jackson stepped aside and stood, arms crossed, with his back against the wall. "From what I saw in the bar, Henry's put pressure on Phillip, but he's not making any moves to settle."

When they reached the door, Lucy turned the handle and kicked it open with one foot. She shoved Noreen into the room. "Back to your chair, woman. This time I'll use a rope."

Noreen fell onto the chair and buried her face on her crossed arms. "Lord, why don't you help me?"

Jackson, who had followed behind Lucy, handed her the rope which she wrapped around Noreen's waist and secured to the chair. "In case you haven't noticed, the Lord left New Orleans right before that big storm. We all got to look after ourselves now."

Lucy pulled Noreen's head against the chair back and stared into her eyes. "We'll take no more of this nonsense from you." Noreen felt the sting when she slapped her right cheek hard. "From now on, one of us will be on watch with you at all times." She slumped into the old stuffed arm chair in the corner, her eyes trained on Noreen. "I'll take the first shift. Jackson. Try again to make contact with Phillip."

*　　*　　*

The taxi was slowed to a crawl by the traffic on Bourbon Street as Jerome and Lara neared the hotel with Lewis still in the front seat. Jerome watched people huddled in groups of three or four, laughing loudly as they ambled in slow motion down the sidewalk. He remained fascinated by the street, the Georgian brick buildings with their French balconies which flew flags from every country. The neon signs advertising live jazz and blues on every block. The forced gaiety of the crowds fueled with alcohol and music that spilled from the doorway of every bar.

When their cab stopped to wait for the vehicle ahead to discharge its passengers, Lewis gave an impatient jerk of his head, opened the door and jumped out into the street.

"Jerome, I got to rehearse the guys before our next set. I'll get there faster on foot. I'll look for you as soon as you can get back."

Finally, they stopped in front of the hotel and got out. Jerome could see the balcony was already full of men with glasses in hand, eyes on the street, ready for action. He felt Lara by his side flinch as she stared at them.

"Jerome, maybe we should come back in the daytime." She grabbed his hand and squeezed it. "I don't like the way they're looking at us."

"I'll have to join Lewis and the rest of the band soon anyway. Let's just go into the bar to see if Phillip is there." He squeezed her hand back and led her up the weather-beaten stairway.

The two of them stood in the doorway of the bar, and peered through the crowd, trying to spot Phillip. Jerome saw him first with his body pressed against the bar by the surge of people. His black curly hair complimented the bright blue of his shiny shirt, making him stand out in the group of men. Jerome motioned to Lara and they approached him. Jerome called out, "Phillip, we've been looking for you."

Phillip shifted to face them. "What are you two young people doing down here?" He stared right at Lara's open-necked blouse. "Not that I'm not glad to see you."

Jerome felt the surge of heat on his face as Lara took a step back. "Phillip, leave her alone. We're here about your debt problem which has now become our problem due to Noreen. Can we go somewhere to talk in private?"

Phillip shrugged. "This is as good a place as any." He led the way to a booth at the back." When Lara slid into the booth and moved over against the wall, he pushed his way in beside her. "I like to keep an eye on my niece here."

Jerome stiffened and clenched his fists, but he slid into the other side across from Lara. "Don't touch her or you'll have me to deal with as well as Henry."

Phillip shifted closer to the aisle and Jerome could see Lara breath more freely. He watched as her eyes narrowed and her mouth settled into a grim line. Lara turned towards Phillip. "You should be ashamed of the damage you're causing our family. Your brother has always been good to you and this is how you treat him."

Glad she was taking a firm stand with Phillip, Jerome relaxed.

Phillip shook a cigarette from his pack, lit it and took a slow drag. "Just what is it you kids are trying to get out of me? Monies that I owe are my problem and maybe Henry's now the gang has Noreen. Where's Henry?" He paused. "You better stay out of this or the gang will be after the two of you as well."

Lara's voice deepened. "Tell us about Noreen? Is she in danger because of you?"

Phillip grabbed her arm and pulled her closer. "You better remember this. I had nothing to do with the guys taking Noreen."

Jerome lunged across the booth at Phillip and grabbed his arm. Startled Phillip let Lara go. "I told you not to touch her."

Jerome watched relief flood across Lara's face as Phillip turned his attention back to him. The three of them were frozen in silence when they noticed the bouncer approach from the bar. The man had the body build of a former wrestler, a shaved head and a bull neck.

"You're wanted out back. Both of you guys." He gestured toward the two men. "I been told Ray's looking to talk to you."

Phillip stood, ground out his cigarette out with his foot and headed toward the rear door. Jerome started to follow.

Lara's voice broke. "Jerome, don't leave me here alone." She gestured at the bar.

Jerome kept his voice low and soothing. "Don't worry, hon. You'll be safe here until I get back. It's our best chance to get information about where Noreen is kept. Just stay right here, I won't be long." He hurried to catch up to Phillip who had already slammed the door.

Lara remained in the booth where she was pressed against the wall. The bouncer disappeared into the crowd in front of the TV. She began to feel a creeping sensation grow in her stomach, almost an intuition that something wasn't right even before the stranger approached. He was skinny with black matted hair, dressed in torn jeans and a dirty grey t-shirt.

Before she realized it, he was standing beside the booth, staring at her. "Why you sitting back here all you yourself, babe?"

Lara remembered her aunt's advice. When accosted, try to stay calm and sound assertive. "I'm just waiting for my boyfriend. He went to the john but he'll be right back. He won't like you being here."

The man threw back his head. "You can't fool me. I know the two guys was with you are out back now with the brothers from Ray's gang." He slid into the booth and tried to pull her towards him. "You and me can have some fun while you wait." His hands pawed at her chest.

She'd pushed back in desperation. "Leave me alone or I'll scream."

"Scream all you want baby. I love it when my girls are noisy. With the rest of the Marrero gang all over at the bar, ain't nobody gonna do nothin' for you. Besides, I'm friends with that crowd out back."

She pushed and strained to shove him away. His breath so close to her face made her nauseous. Shock hit her at the sound of her blouse tearing as he grabbed at her breasts. Repulsed by his odour, and overwhelmed by fear, she struggled even harder. All of a sudden, the man's grip loosened. All she could see past his dirty hair was Lewis's angry face. He had his hands around the attacker's neck.

"Okay, now weasel. You'll lead our way outside but I'll be right behind you. Don't try anything."

When they reached the door, Lewis turned to her. "You going be alright, Lara? I'm going to have to dump this piece of trash out back."

Lara had stuttered. "Yes. I'm okay. She sat up and pulled her blouse together tying it as best she could. "But, it sounds like the creep might know something about the missing money."

Lewis had loosened his grip allowing the man to begin to pull the door open.

"Phillip ain't going to like this one bit," the guy snarled.

Lewis pushed him through the door and followed continuing to jab the guy ahead. Lara trailed them at a safe distance. At first the street was so dark in the dim light from the one working street lamp that she couldn't make out what had happened. The alley was still damp from the storm with the smell of rotting garbage and sewer gas.

The three of them moved ahead, a few steps at a time until they could hear loud voices from the backyard of what appeared to be an abandoned building next door. Lara could make out the shape of four men standing in a circle with a lone figure crumpled on the ground. One of the men in the group was Phillip whom she recognized from his tall wiry body and curly hair.

Lara ran toward the group. "Phillip. Where's Jerome?" As she reached them, she heard a low moan from the body on the ground and watched the man try to roll over.

"Wait, Lara. Let me do this." Yelled Lewis, as he pushed her behind him. He kept his grip on the man from the bar whose eyes had widened.

She could hear the tremor in the skinny man's voice and saw his hands were shaking. "Look guys." He turned to face the gang. "I don't want any trouble from you. I'm just trying to clear up a misunderstanding for my friends here."

"Ratface. How did you get yourself involved in this?" Another member of the group gestured toward the man with his pistol. "I thought it was women who were your vice."

Phillip turned toward Lewis with a surprised look on his face. "What you doing here? It's none of your business." He sneered at Lara. "Your boyfriend doesn't handle himself well in a fight."

*   *   *

Jerome remembered hearing Lara scream in horror when she realized who was lying on the ground. She ran to him, dropped to her knee and cradled his head in her lap. "Phillip, you're a monster. You had no reason to beat on Jerome?"

"It wasn't me. Jerome tried to take on Ray over there and got the worst of it."

Lewis advanced to stand face to face with Ray, his knife in hand. "I'm here to take back one of my band members and now I find he's injured. You owe me for that."

"What about the drug money? That's what Ray's here for." The skinny man sidled over to stand by the two Marrero brothers. "That right, Ray?"

"You're out of your league, Alvin. Stick with the street girls. It's what you know." He turned his attention back to Lewis. "All I know is that I'm owed. I delivered the goods, but someone neglected to pay." He jerked his head in the direction of Phillip who shook his head, lit a cigarette and inhaled deeply.

"What I already told your men, Ray, is that I got held up myself down in the district. The place is crawling with imports from off shore trying to take over our territories."

Ray nodded. "And I told you, Phillip, that it's not my problem. I still expect to be paid, is all."

"You'll get your money once I collect on a few more debts owed to me. Phillip narrowed his eyes. "How about you let Noreen go while you wait for it?"

"Not likely. I hear your brother has money hidden away and he wants his honey back pretty bad. He'll pay." Ray nodded to his two companions and the three of them headed back towards the door to the bar.

Jerome watched Lewis as he patted Lara on the shoulder. "Let go of Jerome now, so Phillip and I can carry him to the street. You can go ahead and wave down a cab. They'll stop for a young woman, even in this area at night." He turned to Phillip, "Grab him under the left arm and I'll take the right. "Jerome, can you stand?"

He sucked in his breath which was agony and tried to raise himself. "No, I don't think so." He was surprised his voice was barely audible.

The two men lifted him and headed for the street, dragging his feet behind.

With the gang out of sight, Phillip's tone sounded almost gentle. "We better get him to the hospital. Ray beat him badly. He has balls, though. He stood his ground for the first few rounds."

Lewis glared at Phillip. "What will you do about your brother's wife? The gang won't hesitate to hurt her if nothing is paid."

"Henry's my brother and I don't want him to hate me like this. Who do I have without Henry? I'll get the money. It's just a matter of time."

"If I was you, I'd talk to Henry yourself. He's feeling pretty desperate. Maybe the two of you can work something out."

Lewis and Phillip carried Jerome to the waiting cab. He winced when they lifted him into the back seat. Lewis gave the cab directions to the nearest hospital. "Lara, you get in here with Jerome and me. He'll want to see you're okay when he gets there. Besides, I can't stay with him long, since my band is now short two players." He waved Phillip away. "You know what you got to do."

Chapter Eleven

A grey sheet of mist clouded his eyes as Jerome became aware of movement close beside him, but he felt unable to lift either arm. Where was he? The scene had begun to come back where Ray's fist slammed into his right cheek bone and he could feel himself drop to the muddy ground. But, that all seemed so long ago. Then he became aware of the narrow bed and white sheets unlike either the tour bus or his bedroom at Phillip's. He felt a soft hand touch his arm.

"Now, honey, you take it easy. You got beat up pretty bad. Thank goodness for Lewis. He was the only one who had the courage to intervene."

As his vision cleared, Jerome could make out Lara, where she stood right beside his bed. He could see her attempt a smile but frown lines ran across her forehead.

Jerome was able to raise one hand to lay it on top of hers. The pain in his head made him wince. "Thanks for staying with me." Guilt washed over his face as he remembered what had happened. "I should never have left you in the bar alone, prey to that bastard. If Lewis hadn't arrived, I don't want to think about what the creep would have done."

Lara nodded. "You're right. Alvin is a local slime bag who saw his chance to corner a woman alone. But Lewis taught him a lesson."

Jerome made an attempt to sit up but fell back against the pillow. "I realize now what a mistake I made when I followed Phillip into the back alley. It didn't resolve anything toward finding Noreen."

Lara stepped back when the doctor entered. He went directly to Jerome, took his pulse and checked his chart. "I'm glad to say you're looking much better. You've had a nasty concussion and will require bed rest for a while." The doctor turned to Lara. "Young lady, I'll have to ask you to leave for now. We need to do some further tests."

"Okay." She turned to Jerome. "I've got to find Henry anyway. I had to see if you were awake yet." She gave him a light kiss on the cheek. "I'll be back later to check on you."

The doctor followed her into the hallway right outside the door. "Are you family?" When Lara shook her head, he continued. "Do you know if he has family here? I like to notify the family when there's been a head injury. In case it gets worse."

"No. His family are in Jacksonville, Florida. I don't have any contact numbers. But, I'm a friend. You can contact me at this number if there's a problem. It's a relative's house. She scribbled her contact information on a slip of paper and gave it to him."

Jerome, who heard them from his bed, relaxed his tight shoulders. It was great to have someone like Lara ready to take care of him.

"Okay. That'll have to do." The doctor started back into the room and turned. "I bet you'll be in later anyway."

When he returned to Jerome, the physician looked into each of his eyes with a light and felt around his skull. Although he could feel the pain, Jerome tried to remain still.

"You're going to be a good patient." He smiled. "The nurse will be in shortly to take more blood tests and check your blood pressure. I'll see you tomorrow."

*   *   *

Lara carefully made her way down the slippery front steps of the hospital. Silt was still piled up in spots which made them treacherous. She needed to find Henry and could only hope he'd have returned to the house by now. Worry made her throat dry and her hands clench as the cab inched its way down Chestnut Street. From the window on her left, she could see two yellow landscaper trucks filled with broken oak branches parked in the front yard of the old Georgian mansion next door. She could also make out three men in overalls rebuilding the roof over the front entrance to the house.

As they pulled up to Phillip's house, she could see Henry on the front porch. There was another man with him and they seemed engrossed at something on the table. Lara got out of the car and ran up the stairs to join them. With deep brown skin and black eyes, the stranger looked Mexican. No accent like you'd expect with a Cajun.

"Uncle, we did find Phillip. But, he refused to help us."

Henry's eyes narrowed as he gave her a look of warning. "Lara, this is Dwayne. He's a friend of Phillip's. He says he can find out who has Noreen for me." He turned back towards the man. "I already told you. I got money to pay Ray if he's willing to meet. But, I need to talk to Noreen before he gets it."

"How much you got?" Dwayne crossed his browned arms and glared at Henry.

Henry put both hands on the table and stared back. "I got the twenty grand he's asked for. But, it'll be an exchange. He gets the money when I get Noreen and no other way."

"Okay, I'll arrange the meet up." Dwayne stood and began to leave. "You be right here when I get back. Any contacts outside of us will go hard on Noreen."

Lara and Henry stood on the porch until Dwayne disappeared down the street. Lara clutched Henry's arm. "I need to tell you

85

what happened. Jerome and I ran into Phillip in a bar over on Bourbon Street. Jerome followed Phillip into the back alley where he was to meet up with Ray. There was an argument and Ray beat up Jerome so bad he's still in hospital."

"Ray can be a bastard. Didn't Phillip help?" Henry stared at the floor. "No. I guess he wouldn't. Nothing in it for him."

"Then Lewis arrived and stopped the fight just in time." Lara breathed out. "Phillip told Ray he'd find the money to free Noreen. He's looking for you to let you know to stop your search. He'll pay as soon as he gets the cash."

While they stood there, a cab pulled up and a man dressed in a dirty navy blue shirt paid the driver. Lara recognized Phillip's swagger as he came closer.

"Glad I caught you here, Henry. Come on." He gestured toward the front door. "We got work to do. " Phillip brushed passed them and entered. "I've been able to collect nine grand from friends who owe me, so if you can borrow the balance, we've got a deal for Ray."

She and Henry followed into the parlour. Henry paced. "I've no reason to trust you, Phillip. You and that crowd of yours got us into this mess."

Phillip stood his ground. "We don't have time for your tantrums, Henry. Can you get the cash of not?"

Henry nodded. "Yeah. With the storm coming, I withdrew most of my cash from the bank and hid it. I have ten grand. That's close enough."

Phillip lit a cigarette. "So, what's our next move?"

"We wait. Dwayne's to come back with word from Ray." Henry motioned for Lara to go upstairs.

Phillip shook his head. "No. She stays here. We can use an extra pair of eyes with this group."

Lara dropped into an armchair. "Uncle, Phillip's right this time. Besides, I want to help. I can watch what's going on and pass messages, if needed. I need to do something to free Auntie."

Chapter Twelve

Silence hung over the small group on the porch. Lara's heart raced when she heard the tone from Phillip's cell phone. He grabbed it from his jeans pocket, leaned against the railing and flicked it open.

"Yeah, Ray. I know Dwayne's talked to Henry. He's right here with me."

Henry mumbled. "Tell him we've had more than enough of his shit?" Phillip frowned and shook his head at Henry.

"Yes, Henry knows what this call is about." Phillip grimaced. "I don't care about him knowing our business. He's my brother and he'll keep it quiet." Phillip motioned with his phone to silence Henry and then put it back to his ear.

"We can have the money for tomorrow. Where's the meet up?" When Henry started to protest again, Phillip put his finger across his lips.

Henry blurted out. "You understand, Noreen better be there or no money changes hands."

Phillip scowled, cupped the phone with his hand and continued. "We'll be at Marie's at ten tomorrow morning then. I hear you. Lewis won't be with us. Just Henry and me." He snapped the phone shut and Lara followed the two men back into the house.

Henry paced back and forth across the parlour. "Do you think he means it about Noreen? Can we trust him?"

Phillip put his hand on Henry's shoulder. "It's our best chance to get her back. Can you have the money ready by the end of the day?"

Henry shook off the hand. "If they harm her, Phillip, this is on you." He took a step back sucked in his breath and continued. "Of course, I told you, I've got the money stashed."

Phillip moved to face his brother. "Look, Henry. Don't think I don't know it's my fault. But I never intended this. Things have changed so much since Katrina hit. People I've known all my life are different. Much harder. I've got one more collection to make." He strode down the front steps, and disappeared down the street.

With Phillip gone, Lara relaxed. "Can't I come with you, Uncle? I want so badly to see that Auntie's okay. I'd really like to come."

Henry led the way back into the house and over to the sofa. They sat close together. "No, I can't do that. She'd want you to be safe. Besides, you heard what Dwayne said; only Phillip and me. If things go badly, I'd rather you not be in danger." Henry got up and headed towards the door. "I hate to leave you here by yourself, but I got to get the money."

"Thanks for listening to me, Uncle. Give me a minute to get a jacket and I'll come with you downtown and stop at the hospital to see how Jerome is."

"Sure, honey. But hurry. We need to go right now." Henry pulled on his faded denim jacket from the coat rack by the door and left together to hail a cab.

*   *   *

Jerome flicked the remote from channel to channel but couldn't concentrate. His headache had dulled but he felt drained. He managed a smile when he realized it was Lara who stood in the doorway, tentatively looking at him.

"Come in. It's great to see a friend with all these strangers about."

She sat on the side of his bed and took his hand in hers. "How's your head feel today?"

"Better than yesterday. I must have slept last night. What time is it anyway?"

"It's already eleven-thirty and they'll probably want me to leave soon while you have lunch"

"Did Henry find Noreen yet?"

"No. But, he and Phillip are working on it together." She squeezed his hand. "I just had to stop by to see if you were okay. You looked half dead when we brought you in here."

Jerome swung his legs over the side of the bed and as he grabbed hold of the bed rail, he managed to stand. "They want me to try to walk as much as I can. Let's go as far as the patients' lounge. It's usually empty and we can talk."

Lara put her arm under one shoulder to steady him. "Are you sure you'll be okay?

Jerome grimaced but nodded.

"Great. I'd love for us to be able to talk in private."

After a difficult walk, they reached the room and settled on the faded brown vinyl sofa. "My doctor said I can leave tomorrow afternoon. That's if the headache stays stable." He put his arm around her. "But I'll need to have someone with me at all times to check on me."

Lara's face broke into a smile. "Don't you worry. I'll be happy to watch over you. You can't go back to the bus with the guys right now."

Jerome frowned. "There's just one problem. I'm not sure I want the two of us to continue to live with Phillip. He didn't hit me, but he just stood there and watched me get beat up."

Lara sighed. "I don't like being there either. But let's be honest. We've got nowhere else to go right now. As long as

Henry's at the house, we're safe and I'll need to help Auntie when she gets home."

He leaned against Lara for support. "Have you thought more about a move back to New Orleans after everything returns to normal?" He watched her face in hope. "I don't understand why you want to go back to Atlanta when I see how close the three of you are."

Her body stiffened. "You don't know the whole story about why I left. Noreen understands.

Jerome squeezed her shoulder. "Can't you tell me? I want to know everything about you."

When they reached the bed and he got in, she moved a few feet away. The strain on her face was deep, her eyes dull. "Downtown New Orleans still scares me with all the drunks at night. Back when I was sixteen, I was walking alone from Galatorie's on Bourbon Street after a late night jazz session with my friends." She stopped.

Jerome coaxed. "What happened? You can tell me."

"I was attacked. I remember the footsteps behind me, and the fear when an arm grabbed me around the throat. I did my best to resist, but I could feel myself being dragged down the alley."

He could see the fear and anxiety on her face. "Did he hurt you?"

"In my nightmares, I still see his icy black eyes, his black face stretched into an evil grin. I hit him with my fist. All I remember after that was him standing over me with an iron bar. Then I felt it hit me. I must have blacked out."

"That must have been awful for you. How did you get away?"

"What they told me later at the hospital was some tourists scared him off and told one of the street cops what happened."

Jerome could feel the tears in his eyes and he grabbed her hand again. "No wonder you don't like to be left alone. I can understand the bad memories. I wish I could have been there for you."

She shook herself as if to throw off a bad experience. "I'm telling you because what happened yesterday in the Quarter when you were attacked, it reminded me there was always crime in this city. The hurricane didn't just bring it on. It's why I'm so worried about my aunt."

Weakness had begun to creep over Jerome. He struggled to keep his eyes open. "Do you think Henry will find her okay?'

He watched Lara compose herself. "Yes. Don't worry. He and Phillip will be meeting with the gang tomorrow for the exchange."

"You're pale and tired looking again, sweetie. I'll leave you to get some sleep before lunch. We want you to be well enough to come home tomorrow." Back outside, her mind flashed back to the awful event which ended up with Jerome in hospital.

*　　*　　*

The house was in darkness when Lara opened the front door. She crossed the hall and headed up the stairs. As she reached the top, she could make out a faint light from Phillip's room on the left. She turned right towards her own. Just to be safe, she continued down the hall to the room at the end and peeked through the partially open door. Henry was in the faded blue pajamas, sprawled across the bed, his head on Noreen's pillow. He snored softly. Lara smiled and felt reassured. She felt safe enough to go to bed now, but still hesitated.

She felt unclean after the encounter with the creep, Alvin. Maybe a shower would help. The warm water tingled across her shoulders, loosened the muscles in her back and trailed down her legs to pool at her toes. The images of Alvin's evil snarl began to recede with the water. She scrubbed her breasts with a bar of camomile soap until they were red. She choked back a sob praying Henry wouldn't hear her. Why did she attract these predators like Alvin and the guy in the alley before him? Was she turning out like her mother after all?

Chapter Thirteen

The next morning, Henry and Phillip sat at the table in silence while Lara spooned scrambled eggs and fried ham onto their plates. Henry breathed in the aroma when she poured freshly brewed coffee into the three mugs.

"Toast will be done in a few minutes."

Henry forced a smile. "That's great, honey. I'd like you to stay here until I call, in case I need you to contact someone."

"Of course, I'll be right here until I see Noreen come through the door."

Phillip wrapped both hands around his mug and then lifted it to his mouth for a swallow. "You're both damn sure you'll succeed in this little mission, aren't you? What's your back up plan in case things go south?"

Lara gave a pained look at Henry as she dropped the toast onto the table. "Sorry. I couldn't live with any other result. Could you?"

"No, girl. I sure could not. We'll bring her home safe." Henry took another mouthful of ham and chewed it carefully. "I won't be coming home this time without her?

Lara watched while the two men climbed into the back seat of a cab to head out to Josephine Street. They sat stiffly and didn't look at one another.

*　　*　　*

Noreen's body tensed when she heard the door slam open and Lucy strode towards her. What did this mean? She knew it wasn't time for a washroom break. Lucy grabbed her wrists and pulled at the knots in the rope which caused a jab of pain. At her gesture to stand, Noreen tried to respond but fear caused her to whimper.

"On your feet woman. We're moving you this morning," Lucy growled. She shoved Noreen towards the door.

Noreen couldn't keep her voice steady. "Where are you taking me? I thought you say we is waiting for Phillip to arrive with the money?"

She felt Lucy jab her in the neck with the blade of the knife but couldn't feel any blood. "Just shut up and keep moving like I told you."

"What about the blindfold? Why aren't you putting it on again?" Fear flooded through her. She could see her chances of getting out of this situation were about to slip away.

While her annoyance showed, Lucy just nodded. "That will come later. Can't you see, I'm the only one here right now?" The two of them moved into the empty hall and Noreen was prodded toward the door at the end. Before they reached it, the entry swung open with Jackson, the heavyset man with the goatee framed in it.

With the fine hair on the back of her neck zinging, Noreen heard him come up behind her and secure the bandana over her eyes.

"Okay. Let's go." Jackson gave her a push.

Noreen stumbled down the stairs and into the rear alley. The warm sun felt good on her bare arms. She heard the purr of a motor followed by the slide of a van door before she was pushed head first onto the floor. The sound of two new voices caused her to stiffen, before she felt the motion of the vehicle below her as it accelerated. In what seemed like minutes, the van screeched to a stop. She tried to get up but was dragged back out by her collar and fell. As she sat up, her dirty hand wiped blood off her scratched cheek.

Both arms trembled as she was pushed and prodded down another dirt road until she heard a wooden door creak open. Manoeuvred into a wooden chair, she was relieved at the smell of familiar herbs.

A loud gasp came from her left. "Noreen. What have they done to you? Your face is bleeding."

It sounded like Marie's voice. But, why had they come back to Marie's shop?" The room where they held her must have been close by. She turned her head toward the sound. "Don't worry. It's just a scratch." She didn't want Marie to get on the wrong side of this crew. Her head was jerked forward and she felt the bandana loosen. She gave a cry when the blindfold was roughly pulled over her head.

Lucy waved the knife at Marie who scurried back behind the counter. "I told you to watch for the guys. They should be here any time."

Marie's response was sharp. "Watch for whom? Who am I expecting?"

"Phillip. Who else would be paying the money?" She started toward Marie, but Jackson shook his head. "It's okay. She hasn't heard a thing I been telling her."

"Remember ladies. We're here for one thing and that's to get back what's owed us," Jackson grumbled.

"Do you mean we'll let her go?" Lucy demanded. "She's seen the two of us."

"If that's what Ray wants, then we let her go." He glared at Lucy. "She's too scared to tell anyone and Henry knows to keep his mouth shut."

At the mention of Henry, Noreen couldn't stop her sobs. Would she ever see her husband again? "Is Henry coming here?"

"You get the picture. They're both on their way and if you behave yourself, the three of you can leave together." Jackson started to move toward the front door. "If we get our money, that is."

Noreen's eyes remained fixed on the front door. Shortly after, it swung open and the sound of his boots reached her before she looked up into Henry's worried eyes. He wrapped her in his strong arms.

"Honey, I'm so sorry for what Phillip done. But we're here now to take you home."

Henry stiffened when Lucy poked him in the back with her knife. "Wait just a minute. We're waiting for payment before you go anywhere."

Henry pushed her arm aside. "Phillip's taking care of business with your partner right now. Don't you try anything with that knife again or I'll be forced to pound you for what you did to Noreen."

Noreen watched Lucy's face for some sign of fear. She dropped her arm, but continued to keep the knife ready in her hand. "Jackson, you got the twenty grand yet?'

She watched Jackson rifle through the bundle of bills until he grunted. "Looks like it's here. If you're short, we'll send Dwayne after you. We'll be keeping an eye on you, Phillip."

Phillip sneered. "Yeah. Whatever you say, Jackson. After all, this is a small town. We're bound to run into each other."

Henry had his arm tightly around Noreen as the three of them exited into the dusty street. The street was empty except for two young men with bare chests and dirty jeans. Their hands were full of loot which they had grabbed through the broken windows of a few storefronts.

Henry had urged Noreen to walk with him toward the intersection with Clairborne Avenue where he knew he'd likely find a cab, but her feet dragged in exhaustion. He gave her an anxious glance. "It's not much farther now. Can you make it?" He put his arm around her waist to steady her.

Her voice quivered. "Thank God you were able to come for me, Henry." Phillip strode along beside them in silence. She gestured toward him. "The two of you, that is. It's hard to believe the Big Easy has come to this."

While Henry held the back door open, she clambered into the old black Ford. Her nose twitched at the smell of mould which had seeped into the seat cushions. She leaned against the open window for fresh air. Henry climbed in beside her and squeezed her hand while Phillip got into the front with the driver to give directions.

"You'll be home soon now, honey." He patted her hand. "Lara will make us some nice hot soup."

She clenched her hands and rubbed the tears from her eyes. "Lara is such a good girl. I'm glad she's here with us right now."

Henry pulled her closer. "She'll stay with you if you want her to. You know that."

Noreen leaned her head against Henry's shoulder and snuggled into the warmth. "It wouldn't be me wanting to spoil her career. She's got her own life. Besides, there's nothing left for her in this city."

Noreen jerked upright when the cab stopped. Through the grey streaked window, she could make out their porch where she sat most afternoons. She smiled at Lara's squeal of delight when she reached the cab.

Henry helped her out the door and stood back to watch her enfolded in Lara's arms.

"I'm so grateful, you're safe, Auntie." Lara held her back for a minute and searched her face. The grey lines of fatigue and dull eyes told its own story.

Noreen walked slowly towards the house. "Shocking. To think my people could do this to me. I don't understand it."

At the entrance way, Phillip lit a joint and headed towards the parlour seeming lost in his own thoughts.

"Auntie, let me help you up the stairs. You're looking very tired. I've made some soup for lunch. She took one arm and Henry the other while they guided her up the stairs. When they stood on the porch, Noreen hesitated to go in.

She pointed to her favorite wicker arm chair. "I want to sit here a bit. Can you bring the soup out here?"

Lara pointed for Henry to sit with her while she headed back through the front door. "Of course. Whatever would make you feel better." She glanced at the strained and glazed look on her aunt's face and shook her head at Henry.

Shortly after, she returned with a tray of hot shrimp and rice soup in a blue ceramic bowl and set it in front of Noreen. "Can I put a bandage on the scratch on your neck?" When Noreen set the spoon down, she lifted Noreen's hair off her shoulder and taped a clean piece of gauze over the wound. Henry followed with mugs for them.

Lara sat beside her and watched Noreen slurp the soup. "I can tell you're enjoying your hot lunch." She and Henry exchanged worried looks.

"Hon, what did they feed you in that place?" Henry asked.

"Mostly pizza or a burger, usually cold. Lucy brought it from a takeout." She continued to gobble the soup until the bowl was empty. Then she leaned back in the chair and closed her eyes.

"You'd be more comfortable inside. Let me help you up to our bed." Henry put his arm under hers, but she pushed him away.

"No. I was shut up for too long. I need to feel the sun. They never let me out." She shivered while she settled back into the chair.

Henry waved Lara away. "I'll sit with her while you finish the cleanup. Didn't you say Jerome was expected back later this afternoon?"

"You're right. Lewis will bring him. He didn't want Jerome to travel alone." Lara bit her lip as she headed back into the kitchen. How could those people have treated her kind and gentle aunt that way? Noreen had lived in this city for twenty-five years since she married Henry and she knew the locals.

What about how they had treated Jerome? She had better hurry to change before he arrived. Lara dried the last dish, hung up the towel and started up the stairs. Half way up, she heard a creak on the bottom stair and turned to stare at Phillip who was following her.

"Calm down, girl. I don't intend you no harm." He stopped where he was. "Our family has been through enough in the past few hours."

Lara held her breath and let it out. "Thanks for helping Auntie. Henry couldn't have done it alone." She continued to climb to the top of the stairs, and turned right towards her bedroom. As she closed the door, she listened for his footsteps, but all was silent. Her white t-shirt and denim shorts were already sweaty when she peeled them off.

After a quick rub with the towel, she began to relax as she pulled on clean shorts and a bright pick Lycra top. She ran damp hands over her hair and put on a touch of bronze lipstick before returning to the front room to wait for Jerome.

Besides, she wanted Henry and Noreen to have some time alone. With the drapes pulled back, she could see the street through the large window. When a cab stopped in front, she rushed to open the door. Lewis got out of the cab and reached back to take Jerome's arm. Although unsteady on his feet at first, Jerome took slow steps towards the front porch and met her at the bottom of the stairs. She supported him as he climbed the few steps.

On the veranda, she could see Henry still held Noreen's hand, although they were both asleep. She and Jerome used cautious steps to continue passed them and turned at the doorway.

"You take good care of him, now, Lara," Lewis smiled. "We're badly in need of his sax back in the band. The replacement the union sent is too low key. No life in him."

Jerome tried to return the smile. "I'll be back before you know it." He moved into the parlour and fell into a large armchair, dropping his head into both hands.

"Does your head hurt, Jerome?" Lara rubbed his shoulders. "The doctor said to watch for that."

He sighed. "It comes and goes. I just feel very weak, is all."

Lewis had followed them inside. He picked Jerome up in his muscular arms and headed for the stairs. "I promised the doctor I'd be putting you to bed." He glanced at Lara. "Which way is it?"

"Turn right at the top of the stairs. His room is next to Henry and Noreen's at the end of the hall. I'll be right behind you." She trailed the two of them up the stairs. Lewis had Jerome in his arms like he was a child. After he deposited him on the double bed, she carefully removed his shoes and socks and covered him with a blanket. With his blond curls spread out across the pillow and his blue eyes half closed, he looked like an angel.

She gestured at Lewis. "You can go now." She smoothed the covers. "I'll take good care of him."

"Okay, mam." Lewis turned in the doorway and chuckled. "Just remember he needs rest and nothing strenuous, if you get my meaning."

Lara and Jerome looked at each other in embarrassment. He touched her hand. "There's lots of time for that later when I'm well." His eyes smoldered for a second before he winced with a spasm of pain.

Lara smiled while she tucked the blanket around his chin. "You're being punished for your thoughts." She kissed him on the forehead. "You get some sleep while I check on the other two downstairs on the porch. I guess I'll be playing nurse in this household for the next few days."

Chapter Fourteen

Each morning, Jerome could feel his strength return with the sun which shone in through his bedroom window. Still, he lay in bed for a while and listened to the noise from the construction work outside his window before he got ready for the day.

After his shower, he made an attempt to pull the comb through the matted waves in his blond hair. One look in the mirror, told him it was far too long. Maybe by the weekend he'd make the trip to his barber.

The kitchen was far too quiet when he entered. Lara and Henry sat across from each other finishing their mugs of coffee in silence. He missed Noreen's constant chatter and the clanging of the metal flipper against the cast iron fry pan while she turned the eggs. Yesterday, he could tell Lara was still worried about her aunt.by the tightness around her eyes while she poured the coffee. He expected it would be some time before Noreen returned to the kitchen. Lara waved him to a chair and went to the stove to fill a plate for him.

"Was Noreen awake when you came down, Henry?"

He nodded. "Her eyes were open but the sparkle is gone. I'm worried. She went through a bad time when we had to leave our home after the storm and had just started to get over it. Now this." He slammed the empty mug on the table and pushed back his chair. "It's all Phillip's fault. I can't forgive him for his betraying us."

Henry pulled on his jacket and his battered navy beret. "How you coming along, Jerome?"

Jerome made an attempt at a smile. "I'm hoping soon to return to playing with my band."

As he turned to face Lara, Henry said, "Thanks for the breakfast. I hate to leave you here with those two invalids, but I got to join the lineup for the insurance men. I heard in the bar, they've started to settle claims. I seen some carpenters already over in the old neighbourhood start to clean up debris."

Lara smiled at him. "It'd be so great for Noreen is she could get out of this house. I'm sure she'd begin to feel better right away." She took the plates to the sink and scraped them clean, while she loaded the dishwasher.

"It's likely to be a while yet. I'll see if I can coax her to come down for breakfast. Getting her dressed and on the move would help." Henry opened the door and began to step through.

"I'll tell her what a sunny day she's about to miss." She touched Henry's arm. "You take care of yourself out there and stay away from that bar where Phillip hangs out."

"If I get my insurance money, I'll be too busy rebuilding to chase Phillip's old crowd."

"What about Phillip? Have you heard anything from him yet?" Jerome asked.

Henry sighed. "No. You know he's my brother and we're the only family left. But it will never be the same between him and me." He stood on the porch and stuck out his arm to check for rain. "Nothing today. With this weather, my hands are itching to saw some new lumber."

Jerome felt all warm inside as he watched the easy interaction between Lara and her uncle. His own father had deserted the family when he was twelve and he'd missed that male companionship. He admired her dark black hair, now straightened and turned under. When she turned toward him, he gazed into her ever changing dark eyes.

"Are you okay to help me work on getting Noreen down for breakfast?" Lara asked. "I'll give you a fresh egg so you can keep her company. It might encourage her to eat."

He nodded. "I'm glad to be out of hospital. Laid up like I was made me feel sicker. Did you know they had to evacuate parts of the hospital during the flood? The bottom floor with the x-ray equipment still reeks from the mould. If you can come over here and help me stand, I'd be glad to assist?"

While Lara put one arm under his shoulder, he raised his body and then pulled her into a close embrace. He leaned toward the heat of her body and familiar scent and she let him for a few minutes then gently disengaged.

She smiled at him. "We can cuddle later. When Noreen goes down for another nap, we'll be alone."

When she was ready, he followed her up the stairs which allowed an ample view of her round, curved buttocks. When they got to Noreen's room, the door was open but she lay still against the pillows and stared at the ceiling. As Lara approached the bed, she flinched and turned away.

"Aunt, I came up to help you dress for breakfast. Jerome will help support you on the stairs. He hasn't eaten yet and could use some company."

Noreen refused to turn around. "Sorry, Lara. I'm not hungry and I ain't leavin this room at all today."

Lara touched her shoulder. "Are you hurt somewhere? I know that woman nicked you on the back of your neck, but you said it didn't bother you." She lifted Noreen's hair to check the wound. "The cut is right here, but it's almost healed."

Noreen rolled over and leaned her head against Lara's arm. "You'll learn child, these scars go much deeper. Sometimes they don't heal."

Lara eased her back onto the pillow. "Did Henry tell you he's on his way to the insurance company so he can fix your house for the two of you?"

He watched as a slow smile spread across Noreen's face. The lines seemed to lessen. "Livin back in my own house would be mighty fine. But, it's more than that. When you lose trust in your people, people who you lived most of your life with, that's hard." The sobs came as if from a deep well, and shook her whole body.

The two of them stood quietly for some time. Finally, the sobbing stopped. Noreen swung both feet over the side of the bed and sat there with her head bowed.

Jerome was fascinated by Lara's ability to slowly and surely encourage her aunt. He decided she could use his help.

"I could sure use some of your nice hot cakes with syrup to get back my strength." He nudged Lara gently with one foot.

"Can you help me with that, Auntie? Mine are still not as good as the ones you make."

Noreen's lips formed the shade of a smile. "Well, I'm told I make the best cakes in lower New Orleans." She struggled to her feet. "From the look of this boy, he needs some nourishment. The two of you go ahead downstairs while I get washed up." She waved at Lara. "Go on now. I'll join you in a few minutes."

He and Lara hurried down the stairs and into the kitchen. He sighed in relief as he realized they had achieved a first few steps on the long road to recovery with Noreen. As he watched, Lara took a bright yellow table cloth out of the drawer and placed two indigo blue cups with matching plates on the table.

She gestured for him to sit while she refilled the coffee pot. "I'll make the strong Spanish coffee she likes. You might find it a little harsh but it's what they drink here in New Orleans."

Lara had joined him at the table when Noreen came in. Noreen went straight to the gas stove and turned on one burner, her hand lingered on the pots and frying pans hanging above as she removed one. "There were times I thought I wouldn't be back here. Lucy was a hard one and would have liked to get rid of me. In her eyes, I was a nuisance."

Lara joined her in front of the stove and put one arm around her waist. "You've had a terrible experience. I was shocked by how the gang members treated you. But, you're free now and we're here to help you get back to normal." She gave Noreen a kiss on one cheek. "Where's the woman I remember who always sang as she cooked?"

Noreen pulled Lara closer. "I've still got you, honey. Henry tells me you'll be with us for a while longer. That's all I need."

Lara turned her head and winked at him.

Jerome responded. "I second the idea. After all, Noreen and I need you to cheer us up, so you'll just have to stay."

"Okay, you two, enough of the blackmail. I told you the choir recital isn't until next month, so I'm not going anywhere until then."

Noreen finished the pancakes and put them on two plates. Jerome had traced a pattern on Lara's bare knee under the table when Noreen turned to bring the plates to the table. He felt Lara's hand surround his as she moved it off her knee. He was grateful for her smile, her eyes deep and dark.

He turned his attention to Noreen. "You've outdone yourself with these. How do you expect me to eat all of them?"

Noreen managed a wide smile as she set down her own plate. She continued to watch Jerome eat and then picked up her own knife and fork. For the first few mouthfuls, she hesitated. After she'd swallowed those, she continued to put larger and larger portions in her mouth; her lips smacked in satisfaction. She followed these with large gulps of the black coffee and then sat back with a smile.

"I sure missed my own cooking. What they feed me down there wasn't real food."

Lara patted her arm. "I always told you, you're the best cook in this city."

Noreen said, "Jerome, now it's your turn to finish your plate." A sudden noise from the hall caused them to turn to the door.

Henry entered and came up behind Noreen's chair. He hesitated and then kissed the back of her head.

"It's mighty good to see you sitting here at the table, honey."

Jerome jumped in. "She's been cooking our breakfast." He studied Henry's face not sure if he should raise the issue. "How did it go with the insurance people? Did you get the settlement you expected?"

Henry's jaw clenched and his eyes hardened. I should have listened to the boys at the bar. They warned me these agents are making excuses not to pay. Opt out clauses which say not covered for water damage and stuff like that."

Noreen's jaw dropped. "You saying we're not about to get anything?"

Henry took a seat beside her. "No, hon. It's not that bad. They'll cover us for the hurricane damage but not the flood. They're saying it was the fault of the local government. The levees should have been higher and officials had received a storm warning for Louisiana but didn't do anything until too late. The flood left eighty percent of this city under water."

Henry ran his hands through his hair. "Some of those officials should go to jail for this. Problem is the flooded areas are mainly the lower and swampy areas. Mainly poor lives there while most well-off white folk live in the north sections. The state government has ignored us. Our huge group of black people who live in this State, we're treated worse that refugees." His eyes were glassy and his shoulders sagged.

Noreen covered his hand with hers. "Don't you worry. We'll get by. But, what about our neighbours? Did you hear about any of them?"

"Many of those living in our section had no insurance and have to wait for the US government to provide trailers. Habitat has started to build homes for a few. The rest will be a long time before they can afford to rebuild. I'm gonna buy my own lumber and supplies to fix our house by myself."

Jerome said. "I'll help you as soon as I'm on my feet. I'd like to pay you back. You've been good to me."

*   *   *

The front door banged closed. The three of them turned to stare at Phillip as he leaned into the door frame. "Sorry, to interrupt this cozy group, but things are about to change around here. No need for my family to leave. However, I don't want Lewis hanging around so Jerome has to go."

Jerome pushed himself up from the table as his hands shook. He watched Lara's tight expression while she glanced over, first at Henry and then back at Phillip.

Henry strode over to Phillip with his jaws clenched in anger. "The boy's recently out of hospital. You could do me a favour if you let him stay for a few days more. Partly he's injured cause you didn't stand up for him with Ray."

Phillip shrugged. "Well, I got debts to cover now. Maybe I want to rent out his room." He glared at Jerome who held his gaze for a few minutes and then lowered his head. "I'll give him to Friday to make other arrangements."

Noreen dropped her knife and fork into the unfinished plate, covered her mouth with her hand and hurried towards the stairs.

Henry glared at Phillip before he followed her. "We pay our way here. The food on the table was put there by me."

Phillip headed towards the back room which left the two of them alone. Jerome pulled Lara into his arms and buried his face into her herb scented hair. But, the weakness came over him again and left his skin hot and sticky.

Lara looked at him with concern. "Hon, do you need to lie down or should we sit outside for a spell? You're beginning to shake."

As he nodded towards the door, she led him out into the fresh air on the porch. He half fell into one of the chairs and clenched his jaw in pain.

"I'll move back to the bus in a few days. The guys are okay and they'll keep an eye on me." He crossed his legs on the coffee table and leaned back into the wicker chair. "Phillip only hates Lewis cause of his rule which forbids drugs for the guys while we're doing a gig."

He relaxed as Lara took his hand and smiled. "I'll take care of you for now. I want my strong man back. The guy who could take these steps in two strides."

Chapter Fifteen

The deep green of the trees and the indigo sky were accentuated by the late afternoon light, when Henry and two men joined them on the porch. Henry probably picked them up in town where labour gathered. The older one was Henry's age with grey streaks through his curly hair and the younger one had muscular arms and dreadlocks.

"This here is my family." He gestured to Jerome and Lara. "They have offered to help us."

He turned back to the two men. "Maurice and Rollie were on jobs with me this spring and are looking for work so I hired them for our place."

Jerome nodded. He saw a shadow of guilt pass over Lara's face.

"I can learn to pound a few nails." She said. "But you know I have to return to my job in Atlanta next month. I'll try to send money. You'll need more cash to do the job right from what you've told us. When do we start?"

The group peered at the drawing Henry pulled out and laid on the table. "We'll need to start in the basement to clean out the stinky water and dry the place out. I checked the kitchen and the wall has a three metre high rusty water line where the water stopped. The paint has peeled on both the walls and the ceiling. The second floor ain't too bad except for the back bedroom where the rain soaked right through the shingles."

Lara asked. "When will you get the money?"

"We can start soon. There'll be no more delays. Once I get the letter of approval from the insurance, I can get credit at the lumber yard for the rest of the supplies. I'd say we start in another week at most."

Jerome grabbed a can of the cold beer which was passed around the table. As the bitter liquid slid down his throat his body felt warm and at ease. He enjoyed the camaraderie of the guys as they discussed plans. He'd worry about Lara's trip back to Atlanta when it happened. Right now he enjoyed her warmth.

Darkness fell over the street as they said goodbye to the two workmen. Lara left to join Noreen in the kitchen to prepare the grilled pork chops he'd seen on the counter for their dinner. He and Henry sat on the steps to watch the men disappear down the road.

Henry explained. "Rollie told me his mother and sister was evacuated to San Antonio, Texas. He stayed back to help with the sandbags. He later heard they were stuck at the airport for three days before they got out."

"What has he heard from them since?"

Henry shook his head. "They still don't know how or when they'll be able to get back home."

"I heard at the hotel, Baton Rouge filled up pretty fast when the city heard the governor would pay for the housing of evacuees. You and Noreen were brave to stay here. Even after you had to leave your house."

"That's where we were headed. Baton Rouge, I mean, but Phillip found us at the airport and brought us to his home. I try to remember that when things get bad."

"Is Phillip back from the hotel yet?"

"No. he's got business there. Still thinks he can find out who mugged him in the back room and took his money belt. But I keep telling him, they're likely long gone."

*   *   *

The next day Jerome stood at the bottom of the porch steps with Lara and held both of her hands tenderly in his as he breathed in a touch of her floral scent. He smiled at her. "It won't be long before you're out of here and back in your own place in Atlanta." A touch of sadness hit him. He'd really enjoyed their long walks and wanted to learn more about the history of the Garden District with her. When he stepped back, he realized her mouth was turned down and her eyes were wide open.

"Why don't you stay? At least until I have to go back. I hate being here in Phillip's house. It was so unreasonable of him to make you leave."

He gave her a warm smile. "Don't you worry. I'll be here right after my breakfast and until I have to leave for the band at six."

The frown lines gradually left her forehead.

"Okay. I understand."

"Anyway, Phillip is just jealous that we have each other. He'd probably like a woman himself, but can't attract one due to his rough attitude. Lewis told me when Phillip's band used to play at the New Orleans Hotel, the manager fired them since they scared all the women away with their rude remarks."

He pulled her back into his arms and gave her a lingering kiss which made her tremble. Then he hurried down to the street and stood by the waiting cab. At the last minute, he turned back to her. "I'll see you when we go over to your old house tomorrow to help."

She nodded and waved. "I'm anxious to see the house again and in the daylight." Lara watched him get into the back seat.

He twisted his body sideways so he could watch out the back window and was thrilled to see Lara's eyes fixed on the cab until they turned into another street.

*   *   *

As Lara headed back towards the house, her shoulders tensed. She knew Henry left this morning right after breakfast for the lumber yard and Noreen had gone back upstairs for a nap. But where was Phillip? Had he gone out and if not, where was he? She glanced towards the parlour door and jumped when she saw him as he stood there and stared at her. She took a deep breath and continued towards the stairs in an attempt to get near Noreen for comfort. She had taken the first step up when her body froze in alarm as she felt his hand clamp across her mouth. Horrified she tried to hook her feet onto something as he dragged her across the floor. They crossed over the threshold into the parlour and she was forced to stand with her body pulled against his thin wiry frame.

Desperate to free herself, she tried to bite his hand. A deep smirk and evil laugh filled the air and his grip only tightened. "I seen you make out with that white boy outside. What's wrong with our kind? With a body like yours, you could have any one of us."

Lara thrashed and struggled as he pulled her further into the room until she felt the back of her legs hit the sofa. Phillip pushed and shifted away which caused her to fall flat on her back. Within a moment, he was lying prone on top of her, as he pinned her with his weight. But her head was free and she screamed as loud as she could. While they struggled, she could feel her denim skirt ride higher and higher up her thigh, while a few buttons on her cotton blouse came undone.

Phillip breathed heavily as his strong arms clenched tighter so she was unable to throw him off her. His grip on her arm felt like a wire band which caused a moan of pain to escape her lips. The grip slackened off and she renewed her efforts to break free.

"You don't want to get hurt, stop struggling. You could enjoy it."

As his head came down to engage her lips, Lara managed to bite him. At the same time, she became aware of someone else in the room moving towards them.

As she reached the sofa Noreen yelled. "Phillip, you get off her now."

Lara breathed out as she felt Phillip's weight move off her body. She struggled to sit up and stared in amazement at the determined look on Noreen's face. She had a gun pointed at Phillip's chest.

"Oh come on, Noreen. You wouldn't even know how to shoot a pistol." Phillip stood up slowly, a look of shock and wariness on his face. He continued to creep backwards towards the door. "We was just having a little fun, the two of us. Nothing for you to get so hot about."

Noreen raised the gun until it was pointed right at his face. "I didn't tell you to leave yet. After what you did to me with your gang, I wouldn't hesitate to shoot you. After all, I learned about guns from them." Her face was frozen in anger, her eyes points of steel. "Self defense, I'd tell the cops."

Phillip stopped where he was.

Noreen held the pistol steady aimed right at him. "You leave my Lara alone, you hear. You been after her since she turned sixteen. No more. I'd enjoy pulling this trigger."

Phillip shrugged and moved to the door. "Just look how she's dressed. Tight skirt around a perfect ass and that blouse exposed two ebony pears. What does she expect?"

Noreen moved closer to him. "Phillip, you hear me or not? I'll say it again. I will shoot you."

His boots echoed on the wooden floor, as he headed to the front door. It slammed with a bang after him.

Lara sat on the edge of the sofa, holding her head in both hands, sobbing quietly. "Thank God you saved me, Auntie. Why do men want to attack me? Is what Phillip said true? Maybe I'm like my mother. Oh, mercy God, I can't be."

Noreen pulled Lara into her arms, and rocked back and forth. "You've done nothing wrong, my luv. You're a beautiful young woman. Any man would be proud to have on his arm. Jerome is a decent man and he respects you."

Lara tugged at her skirt. "Am I dressed like a whore?" She sobbed in anguish.

Noreen pulled a Kleenex from her sleeve and wiped Lara's wet face. "When I was your age, all the young women wore cotton sundresses with short skirts to show off their legs. We were proud of how we looked and wanted men to notice. There's nothing wrong about that. The problem is Phillip and his kind."

Lara leaned her head on Noreen's shoulder. "It's not the first time a man has tried to force me. That's partly why I left this city for Atlanta."

Noreen patted her knee. "I know. Henry told me about the time at the New Orleans Hotel. In this city, it's the drinking and the drugs. I'm glad you're going back to Atlanta where you'll feel safe."

"But, I thought you wanted me to stay here." She sat up straight. "I won't leave you while you're unwell."

Noreen sighed. "You know I'd love to have you stay with us. But not if you're afraid. That's not how I want you to live your life." She stood and gave Lara her hand. "Come on and get changed. I'll make us some hot coffee and we can sit on the veranda. We both could use some sun."

As she climbed the stairs towards her bedroom, Lara cringed. Even though she knew Phillip had left, her skin prickled. How could she continue to live here for the next two weeks with him two doors down the hall?

She lingered in front of the open closet and tried to decide what to wear. It was so hot. As a sigh escaped, she pulled on full denim jeans with a long-sleeved lilac shirt tucked into the waist. She examined her blouse and threw it onto the floor. No way would she wear it again. She'd wanted to look nice for Jerome this morning and look were it had led. Maybe it was good the choir in Atlanta wore navy skirts and starched white cotton blouses. But a uniform wasn't how she wanted to see herself all the time.

With the two women settled into the wicker chairs on the porch, they could watch for Henry to return from his work. "Aunt, let's not tell Henry. We have to continue to live here for now and I don't think he could stand it. The tension between him and Phillip is already so heavy.

Noreen let the rocker stop. "I been thinking about that, too. It's not an easy thing for me to keep secrets from Henry, but I agree with you. It was Henry gave me the gun to protect myself due to my fears from the gang. I'll leave it with you when I'm out. I'll wait to tell him until we're moved back home."

They watched Henry get out of the cab near the house and head their way. His tool bag dragged close to the paved street.

"Well, how nice to see you two relaxed in the sun. Wait until the job is in full tilt. Then I'll need the both of you over at the house to help me." He dropped into the chair next to Lara. "Is there any coffee left for me?"

"I'll go get some right now." Noreen pushed herself off the chair and walked heavily to the door.

Henry opened his toolbox and examined each of the new tools. "What about Jerome? Are you missing him yet, honey?"

Lara sighed. "He'll be over to help us. I really like Jerome. I'll find it hard to leave him when I go back. But, he's got his career with the band. And he may not even stay in New Orleans once this gig is over."

"I know you had some hard times here, Lara. But there are good people in New Orleans. Remember our neighbours are different. You'll see when we go back there."

"Is anyone living in the neighbourhood yet?" Lara asked.

"The electricity has only been back about a week. The water is still unclean. I hear people are there during the day, mostly to clean up, but no one lives in those homes as yet."

Henry's voice turned quiet. "They found a body in one of the houses when the water went down, still in her bed. Neighbours say she was an old woman who refused to leave when the boats got to her."

Noreen came back onto the porch a mug of coffee in her hand which she placed in front of Henry. "You look like you had a busy day and deserve this, hon."

Henry turned to face her. "You're looking pretty cheerful today, yourself. I see more energy and there's good colour in your face."

"I just can't wait to get back to our house." She waved her hand at Henry when he started to say something. "I know it's just for one afternoon. But it's a new start. Are the guys meeting you here?"

"No. We'll take a cab there tomorrow morning after breakfast and meet them at the place. You can bring some cleaning supplies and grub, but that's all. I don't want to be leaving anything there right now. It encourages thieves, I'm told. Some neighbours lost tools already."

Noreen's face broke into a wide smile. "We're going home tomorrow. That's all that matters to me."

Chapter Sixteen

As the taxi got closer and closer to their house in Orleans Parish which was just north of Tulane University, Lara concentrated on her aunt and uncle to assess their reaction. The cab was forced to proceed carefully due the mounds of debris still piled in the streets. Her gaze went from house to house with most of them boarded up and vacant. The yards were full of broken bricks and shingles scattered around the houses. Farther in their journey, she saw houses recently fixed up with For Sale signs stuck into their barren front yards. The silence all around them caused an eerie feeling to fill Lara's chest.

Noreen grabbed her arm. "There's Lolita and Jackson Desalle's place. You remember you went to school with their girl Nicole. At first the brick exterior of the house where she pointed was in good shape with little water damage. However, when they got close enough she could see through the windows the interior had been stripped down to the frame.

Noreen poked Henry's shoulder. "Jackson must be having some repair work done, don't you think?" She turned back to Lara. "Lollie has been one of my best friends. I'd sure hate to lose her."

Henry turned his head to look at the two of them. His face had turned grey and his shoulders were stretched tight. "Don't know. I been telling you all, some of the insurance companies have been slow to settle with folks. Don't forget, we still haven't seen any cash. Just promises."

All three tensed as the cab turned into Orleander Street. All the houses looked the much the same here. Bungalows with aluminium siding, wooden steps and a front porch.

The driver pulled up to number 57 and accepted a handful of bills from Henry. "You sure you want me to leave you here? Most of these houses look deserted and I don't think there's any stores close by."

"We'll be alright." Henry said. "We got our own supplies. I just need you to come for us at six like I asked." He opened the door and got out with his toolbox in one hand.

Noreen climbed out one side with a basket of food and Lara took the pails and sponges with her. The two of them saw their workers already in the yard with their rusty blue Ford truck parked across the street. A large sump pump was visible in the back.

Lara cringed as Noreen stared around her at the closest houses, frozen where she stood with the food basket still in hand. "Where have they all gone? I thought this place would be busy with cleaning and fixing?" Her lips trembled and her face looked puffy.

As she placed her arms around Noreen's shoulders, Lara pulled her into a hug. "Give them time. It's early today. I saw a truck with some men half a block back so we're not alone."

"Let's follow Henry into the house and see what we're faced with." Lara led her up the front steps while Henry pushed open the door. She gagged at the odor of putrid water and mould which overpowered them.

Noreen elbowed her aside, covered her mouth with one hand and stumbled into what had been her kitchen. She ignored the buckled linoleum and made her way to the large GE stove where she opened and closed the oven door. After she moved closer, she hesitated and then reached over to turn on one of the elements. A wide smile covered her face when she saw the burner begin to turn pink and then red.

"Well, it's rusty from the water but it still works." She turned her attention to the cupboards next to it. "The bottom on these cupboards are rotted. Nothin you can do with those." She faced Henry in the doorway. "You up to building me some new ones?"

Henry smiled. "You bet. I can make you some better than what we had. Soon as I can get the lumber."

Over near the fridge, Lara ran her hand over a section of peeling wallpaper as she tried to smooth the red cherries over the butternut yellow background. She jerked it back rapidly when the drywall pressed inward under her touch. "How will we ever dry out these walls?"

Henry gestured towards the basement door while he tied a bandana over his mouth and nose. "We've got to drain out all the water down there or the moisture will continue to spread upwards. That's where the boys and I will start. In the meantime, let's open the windows and doors and hope for a breeze."

He opened the door and started down. "The two of you can start with cleaning the bathroom and kitchen. It'd be mighty nice to be able to use them."

Lara examined Noreen's face for signs of stress. As she'd expected Noreen was already into her cleaning role and had begun to hum a song she had taught Lara when she was young. When Lara felt tears on her own face, she quickly wiped them away and forced a smile.

"Where do you want me to start, Auntie?" She stood in front of the ruined cupboards and waited.

Noreen threw open all the doors and stared at what remained of her large stock of food. "Looks to me like we'll have to throw most of this stuff out. Maybe we can keep some of the canned goods, but my spices are sure gone. Henry and the boys already emptied the fridge into bags. Where did he put those new plastic trash bags?"

After she rummaged through the pail she had carried, Lara pulled out a roll and handed one to Noreen. They both got to work and swept the food off cupboard shelves into the empty bag. "You can pile the dishes on the old table in the corner so Henry can start on the shelves as soon as he has the wood."

Hours later and near finished, they could still hear the rumble of a sump pump from the basement. Henry burst through the front door with two heavy fans, one under each arm. He started them up in the joint living and dining room, one at each end. "It'll take most of the week for the house to dry out, even with the windows open in the daytime. Thank the lord for some sun."

"Uncle, can we save anything from down there?" Lara pointed at the basement stairs.

"Not likely. Most of it will go to the dump just as soon as we can load the truck." He wiped his stained hankie across his sweaty face. "The smell's enough to sicken you. You women stay out of the basement for now."

Lara watched the sudden explosion of tears stream down Noreen's cheeks. "What about the old rocking chair my nanny give me? Those pictures of my family and of yours where in the oak cabinet. Our wedding pictures where on the wall of the den."

Henry put his arms around her and held her against his dirty overalls. "It's only stuff, honey. We're safe and that's all that matters."

He cringed at the wail of sound coming from her open mouth. "Okay, hon. I'll gather up what photos I can find and we'll try to dry them out. I don't promise anything, but we'll try. But, the furniture, it's gone."

He gave her a quick kiss on her wet cheek. "Why don't you and Lara start laying out the lunch in the backyard while we finish up here?" He looked over her head at Lara and gave her a signal.

"What a great idea, Auntie. We're finished with the cupboards. Those men will be hungry when they come up. I'll load these bags into the truck while you set out the blankets. She grabbed the nearest of the full bags and dragged them toward the front door.

From the truck, she watched the three men come down the steps and collapse on the blankets. The fuchsia and bougainvillea bushes they'd planted years ago were in full bloom in their small back yard. A pile of broken live oak branches lined both side of the back steps. When she joined the group, they were seated cross-legged and nosily gulped their cold beer. She could tell Noreen was engrossed in her new task as she dished out plates of potato salad, bean salad and crayfish gumbo. The sweat poured off her face from the sun but she wiped it away with the back of her hand.

Lara took her plate and joined the circle on the blanket enjoying the savoury dishes. "Don't you worry, Auntie? Henry will have your house back in shape for Christmas, won't you?"

He grinned and nodded without raising his head.

She turned back to Noreen. "You know. I've never tasted crayfish as good as this?"

"You always say nice things to me, baby. That's why I love to have you at home with us." Noreen frowned. "But don't you think I'll try to keep you here against your will. Remember, it was me who encouraged you to move to Georgia in the first place. I knew you'd have a better life there."

"Yeah. And I appreciate it. You always think of me first." Lara reached over and gave her a peck on the cheek. "When we're finished eating, how about you and I go for a walk over to Decarrie Street. You used to have friends over there, didn't you?"

"Oh, yeah. That's were Gloria and Lou is living. Or they was living, I should say. I wonder if they got back from wherever they evacuated to. During the storm, it was every man for himself and no time to talk to anyone about their plans. It's only three or four blocks from here. I'm up for it."

Lara collected the empty plates and plastic cups and filled another bag. "Okay. Let's get some air while Henry and the two guys continue to dry out the basement."

As they walked through the northern end of Orleans Parish the flood damage appeared to be lighter and they could see many houses under renovation. The heat and humidity began to weigh heavily on both of them; perspiration soon soaked their light clothing.

Next they approached the area below the Intracoastal Waterway and crossed the border into St. Bernard Parish. Lara proceeded cautiously as she'd heard this section of the city had been heavily damaged. An oppressive silence hung over them and the devastation increased as they approached Decarrie Street.

Lara bit her lip while she and Noreen moved from house to house as they examined the damage. When they stopped in front of what had been a brick bungalow, she begun to wonder if this walk had been a big mistake.

Noreen clenched her hands and began to suck in her breath. "It's Gloria's house and it's ruined." Lara stared at the gutted house. Debris was piled almost to the roofline in the front yard. The For Sale sign had been staked into the brown dirt which had once been the lawn. A permit for electrical work was pasted on the door. On either side, the lots had been cleared to make way for FEMA trailers with newly built steps which led inside. Vacant houses were everywhere, as far as Lara could see. Across the street, stood another house under construction, with a sign marked *Habitat for Humanity At Work.*

Noreen sat down on what was left of the steps of Gloria's house and leaned her forehead on her crossed arms. Between sobs, she said, "They're gone. Probably never coming back."

Lara sat down beside her and put one hand on her arm. "Auntie, they could be anywhere. There are so many people displaced by the storm. Maybe you'll meet up with them again once things are more settled."

Noreen raised her head and became calmer as she got to her feet. "Let's go back to our place. I need to tell Henry what we found out. He'll know how to find them."

Lara placed Noreen's hand in hers as they walked slowly back down the street. Noreen kept her gaze forward with her head down.

When their small bungalow came into view Lara breathed a sigh of relief. The three men sat on the front steps to wait for them and a cab was at the curb. The back of the truck was full, with a tarp tied over the load for safety.

Henry lurched to his feet and moved towards them. "I was worried something happened to you two. Are you all right?"

Noreen raised her head. "We saw Decarrie Street."

Lara nodded her head. "I'm glad we didn't live over there. Looks like the storm hit them full force."

Henry and Lara exchanged glances. He gently took Noreen's arm and led her to the taxi. "Let's head back to the Garden District. The guys can unload the truck themselves. Lara will make you a good strong cup of coffee."

Chapter Seventeen

When the wide and leafy streets of the Garden District came into view, rather than a sense she could relax, Lara felt her whole body tense up. As they nearer Chestnut Street, her heart pounded and her hands clenched and unclenched. She hoped Henry wouldn't notice her fear as she didn't want to explain. Maybe Phillip wouldn't be home.

Beside her in the car, Noreen put her arm around Lara's waist for comfort. Lara stared at the back of Henry's head. "Don't you worry, honey. Henry and I will keep a close watch on Phillip and you won't be left alone with him."

With the question on Lara's face, Noreen nodded. "I had to tell him."

From the front seat, Henry responded. "You're right. I had to know. When's Jerome going to be back I could use him?"

Lara let out her breath. "He had to get settled today since he plays tonight. He'll join us tomorrow at the house. He's anxious to help"

Henry's voice grated. "I don't blame him for wanting to keep clear of Phillip for now." They came to a stop and he paid the driver. "I'll go in first in case Phillip's back. You two can follow when I give the signal."

Noreen and Lara climbed the steps and dropped their tired bodies into the wicker chairs. Lara stared apprehensively at the door which Henry had closed behind him. The minutes dragged.

Finally, the door inched open. Henry motioned for them to come inside. "No sign of him. You're safe."

Henry and Lara sank into the soft cushions of the old sofa in the parlour while they waited for Noreen to arrive back from the kitchen with a cold drink. The icy sweetness of the pineapple juice she poured revived all three of them.

"We've got a heavy day ahead of us tomorrow so I want to get an early start. Are you two up to another round?"

Noreen nodded her head. "You're not going back to the house without me. I need to see what's happenin. And besides, some of the neighbours might come by."

"Count me in every day until I have to leave, said Lara.

The darkness had returned when she heard a car stop on the street. "Where do you think Phillip is? Do you think he'll come back tonight?"

Henry drained his glass and took it to the kitchen. "I sure don't know where he is, but, if he does return he'll answer to me for what he done. You can bet on that."

Lara smiled. "I'm so glad you're here with us."

Henry stopped at the foot of the stairs. "I got to clean up. Until I can get our house fixed up, we have to stay here. I hope he does return tonight. Best we know what he's up to."

Noreen and Lara sat together enjoying the quiet. "This could be a nice house, if someone took the time to clean it and let in some light." Noreen gestured at the dark drapes.

"I could never see myself living here as long as Phillip was alive," said Lara.

Noreen sighed. "The reason these old houses are so large was cause the families all had live-in help. It's too much for one person to keep."

"I got to start the supper, now. You call Henry to join us in about twenty minutes." Soon the three of them were seated around the small table devouring large plates of cold cured ham, fried potatoes and grilled corn."

After she cleaned up, Noreen yawned and rubbed her eyes. "You okay honey if we go up to bed now?" Henry rose to join her.

"With you and Uncle next door, I'll be fine," said Lara. However, she followed the two of them upstairs and noticed how Noreen struggled to climb each step. Tears came to her eyes as she saw the effort. When she placed one hand on Noreen's elbow to steady her, she pushed it away.

"I've got it, hon. Don't you worry about me none."

She was glad to enter her own room and locked the door behind as had become her habit. She peeled off her sticky clothes and slid under the duvet. The softness felt wonderful against her exhausted body.

*   *   *

Only blackness surrounded her when she jolted awake, started by a noise from the hallway. Her mouth was dry with fear and her skin felt clammy. The bathroom door clicked closed. After she crept to the heavy door and pressed her ear against it, she could make out a return of the footsteps and then Noreen's muted voice probably talking to Henry. Since the kidnapping, she had trouble sleeping and often got up at night. Lara made sure the door was locked and crawled back into bed. All attempts to return to sleep failed. Bad dreams drift through her mind. All ended with an image of Phillip's mocking expression and heavy lips only inches from hers. Her heart pounded and apprehension crept up her stomach and ended with an ache in her throat. His grip had been like a steel clamp, exhausting all her efforts to break free.

How would she manage these next two weeks before she left for Atlanta? Guilt hit as she remembered her promise to stay around to help Noreen through her own trauma. The problem was Phillip was bound to return sometime. If only she knew when. She wished Jerome was still here. His smooth hand clasped in hers would relieve the stress. She finally gave up trying to sleep and waited until she could see by the clock in the dim light it was near 6 a.m. Henry would soon get up. Moments later she heard him finish in the bathroom. She decided to get up and help by making their breakfast. Lara stood in front of the bathroom mirror and stared at her strained face. She felt better after splashing hot water on her face and hurried downstairs.

The gurgling noise and strong smell of coffee from the old-fashioned percolator soothed Lara as she layered butter onto slices of toast. The spatter of bacon and eggs as they fried on the grill greeted Noreen as she arrived to join them, humming an old tune as if everything was okay again.

When all were seated and tucked into their meals, Henry laid out the plan for the day. "I'll go with the truck this morning. We got a construction crew coming in to rip out most of the old mildewed drywall. The two of you can follow with a cab like we did yesterday."

"Good. We'll bring the lunch," Noreen chimed in. We'll sit in the back yard again to be out of your way." She put her fork down and looked at Henry. "You got any money to buy supplies?"

"Sure. I kept some from when we paid the ransom. But, I'll sure need the money from the insurance soon." He went back to finishing the last of the bacon and smiled at Lara. "It's good as usual, honey."

Lara had picked at her food and now cleaned off the plate and stacked it in the sink. She returned to the table, sipped her coffee and warmed her hands on the cup. "Jerome said he'd join us around eleven, once he'd had some sleep. You got work for him to do?"

"By that time, we should be onto the floors. He can help us pull up the old floor in the kitchen. He's mainly interested in the rebuilding, but I can't order new drywall until I get extra cash. You'll be wanting all new linoleum, honey. I sure hope the under floor hasn't rotted out."

At the loud knock on the door, Henry jumped to his feet and grabbed his hat from the hook by the door. "Looks like the guys are here. See you all later. I gotta go."

After Henry left, Lara held her head in both hands with her elbows on the table.

"Sweetie, you lookin worried and you didn't finish your eggs. What's wrong? You thinkin you might miss your concert?"

Lara sat back and shook her head. "I'll stay for two weeks more like I promised. That will still give me time to be ready. I miss Jerome, is all."

Noreen placed her hand over Lara's. "I bet it's Phillip that's bothering you, isn't it? I knew you'd not get over his attack this soon. I'm so sorry. He's such a rat?"

Lara forced a smile and squeezed Noreen's hand. "It's great to have you to look after me, but I have to deal with this myself. I didn't sleep well. That's all. Phillip's presence is everywhere in this house."

Noreen waved her towards the door. "You go take your time to get settled and relax. I'll clean up here and make the lunch. When you're ready, get dressed and call the cab for us."

Back in her bedroom, Lara pulled on blue jeans and a high-necked black polo shirt. She fought against drowsiness as she made her way down stairs. Her skin would soon be soaked through in this eighty degree weather. But she didn't care. She couldn't stand any of the workmen to stare at her. She waited by the door. "You almost ready, Auntie?"

Noreen hurried into the hall, a picnic basket on one arm covered with a bright red checkered tablecloth. "Okay, honey. Call the cab now."

Dressed in a red and blue paisley smock which Lara knew she bought at Walmart, her face shiny from her work in the kitchen, she grinned at Lara. "I can't wait to get back to the house. Let's wait for the cab on the front porch."

Lara was grateful to see Noreen's depression had eased a little with a new project underway. But, she knew there would be more days like yesterday when the shadows would return.

*   *   *

When Jerome arrived at the Orleans Parish house, he could tell the serious work was underway. Two huge men from the construction crew rushed past him as he stood on the porch. Sweat glistened on their arms as they carried large pieces of what had been the kitchen wall. When they dumped the plaster into the back of the truck, he heard a loud crash and watched a cloud of dust rise.

He entered the house being careful where he stepped and joined two others hard at work on the living room wall. A few minutes later, Henry came up from the basement to join them. "Glad you could come to help us. You might want one of those face masks. It's a dirty job."

Jerome smiled and wiped sweat and plaster dust off his face. "Thanks, but I'm okay for now." He was glad to see the frown had left Henry's face and he moved around the room like he was ten years younger. He wondered if the two women were here yet. He hoped Lara had missed him yesterday and smiled at the thought.

The next time he carried wallboard out of the house to dump into the truck, he stood at the door and stared at Lara and Noreen who were coming up the walk with a large basket of food. He swiped one hand across his blond curls to shake off some of the dust as he lurched off the porch towards them. A flush of warmth crawled up his arms into his chest as he ran towards Lara, grabbed her into his arms and gave her a quick kiss. He could see she was a little embarrassed but pleased at the same time.

Lara laughed. "The least you can do is help us with the food first. We need to take it to the back yard and Noreen's hot and tired from the trip."

After depositing the basket on the old picnic table the guys had found, he led the way back to the house. He glanced over at Lara, aware of her smooth skin and wide mouth so close, as he wiped at the dust coating on both cheeks. "It's very dirty in the house right now."

Noreen pleaded. "I need to have a look at my floors. Henry said you would remove the linoleum today. Can I come in?"

Jerome bit his lower lip. "Okay but Lara you go with her. The wood is solid on most of them, but there are a few rotten spots in the living room. Water must have come in the broken window. Just be careful."

"Where's Henry?" Lara took Noreen's arm to guide her past Jerome into the front hall. "He said he'd be spending the day here at the house."

"He just left to take the first truck load to the landfill," said Jerome. "The crew members are needed to continue ripping out the old walls. He'll be back in about an hour."

Noreen stood in the hall and stared. "Mercy. Our home is ruined. Will we ever be able to live here again?"

"What do you think, Jerome? From what I can see, the kitchen is mainly exposed two by fours which stand on what's left on our painted blue floor." She studied the wires which lay everywhere, connected to the dangling switches and plugs.

Jerome shook his head. "It doesn't look good right now but it'll get better. We had to remove the stove and fridge but they are useable."

He watched Noreen's face drop and turn grey. He knew it looked like a ghost house and didn't know how to comfort her. At his gesture, Lara put her arms around Noreen and guided her outside back down the steps.

"The new walls will be built next," said Jerome as he followed them to the back yard.

Lara nodded. "That's what Uncle has been telling us. Right, Noreen?"

"Sure, honey. But, I can't imagine it." Her head was still down.

Lara squeezed her hand. "You're right. It's hard to see at this stage. Let's wait until they finish up today. Then we can walk around with Henry and talk about what we can rebuild to make it even better than before."

Noreen sat down heavily in one of the old white plastic chairs from the truck which wavered but held. "Right. I'll have to wait for Henry to arrive. He'll know what to do."

Lara shook her head as they watched Noreen sink into melancholy. Jerome's arms ached as he reached for her and pulled her against his dusty chest. "I've sure missed you, sweetie. Maybe I'm banished cause Phillip wanted to keep us apart and he succeeded."

She kissed his dusty cheek. "Now you mentioned Phillip, I wonder what happened to him. We didn't see him all day yesterday. Did you hear anything?"

"No. I thought he was at the house. I'll speak to Lewis about it when I get back. He knows everyone who comes and goes over at the New Orleans Hotel."

Lara's smile returned and her eyes sparkled. "If you stay until later, you can catch a ride back in the truck with the guys. They go past the hotel on their way home."

Henry came down the steps into the backyard to join them. "He smiled at Jerome. I'm grateful to have you look out for my women." His shoulders drooped. "Those insurance folk got no sympathy for problems of our people. They're saying I still got to wait."

Jerome patted Henry on the shoulder. "You and I need to plan out the layout in the house before lunch. We'll join the women later." His eyes engaged with Henry's and he jerked his head towards the door.

Henry pulled back his shoulders and followed Jerome. He shook his head at Noreen when she tried to follow them. The back door led into the living room and forced them to skirt around the broken floor boards. There was a pile of plaster in one corner directly below a huge hole in the ceiling.

Jerome pointed towards the ceiling. "We knew there was a hole somewhere but it's worse than I expected."

"Yeah. That's where wind and rain got through the damaged shingles. They done more damage than I thought." Henry stared at the floor. "How's Noreen holding up? Has she seen this yet?"

Jerome shook his head in the negative. "So far, it's the kitchen which got to her." Jerome wiped away the sweat once more. "If we could start on one room and get it usable, it would help with the rebuild. Especially in case we get some more rainy weather."

Henry shook his head in weariness. "We got at least another two days to clean out the rotten stuff before we can start building. You sure you've got the time?"

Jerome picked up the crowbar which leaned against the doorframe. He smashed it against the soft wallboard and stood back as chunks cascaded to what was left of the floor. Henry joined him with a second crowbar and pried up the last of the rotten linoleum. He checked the strength of the bare floor as it was uncovered. They two of them worked side by side until Lara poked her head into the room.

"Anyone in here hungry? We got a thermos of hot coffee, beignets and a seafood stew with some of those stuffed peppers you like, Uncle."

With relief, Henry and Jerome dropped their tools and headed out the back door after Lara. Jerome stepped into the clean, crisp air first and took a deep breath. Henry started down the sidewalk towards the front porch. "I'll get Maurice and Rollie from the basement." He chuckled. "They'll be hungry as gators by now."

*   *   *

Moments later, the only sound Jerome could hear was the smack of everyone's lips as they eagerly gouged on spoonfuls of the shrimp and clams. Lara and Noreen were kept busy as they refilled the bowls. When Jerome looked over at Maurice and Rollie, their grey faces were just visible over the large bandanas tied around their necks. He looked down at his own forearms which still glistened with sweat from the heavy work. He recalled Henry had told him how the two men were happy to get any kind of work so they could make some money for food and beer. The two of them now lived with their mother in one of those FEMA trailers in the middle of former swampland.

Back in the house as he tore out more walls, Jerome watched Henry's hair become more and more saturated with grey dust while his face developed deeper lines. It was like he'd aged in the past few days. Still, every once in a while, he'd stop and smile through his fatigue. He must be thinking about the rewards ahead when the work was done.

As they finally headed back to the truck, Jerome caught Rollie's arm. "How about I catch a ride back to the hotel with the two of you when we're finished here." When Rollie nodded, he dropped his tools into the bed of the truck. "Thanks. I got to talk with Lewis before we start our gig tonight."

Henry soon joined them. "I'll join up with you Jerome after I drop the two women at the house. I'd like to have a talk with Lewis myself. We'll leave here as soon as I finish up a couple of chores."

Jerome followed Henry back to the house. He stood in the warm sun and watched how relaxed Lara seemed as the swished her bands back and forth in the basin of soapy water. Noreen's head dropped to her chest as she sat on the old lawn chair where she'd been since lunch was over. He loved the peaceful feeling which fell over him out here in the sunshine. It's what had attracted him to return to New Orleans; the long warm summer days and even the occasional light rains.

Lara had told him about some of the bad storms that had blown through here when she grew up. She'd been thrilled to have the school's closed for the day. But, there was nothing like this devastation. What would it be like if he and Lara lived here in their own small bungalow? He jerked back to reality. She might never return from Atlanta and anyway, he might have to track down his old band if this job didn't work out. That would mean he'd leave New Orleans for good.

Chapter Eighteen

After he swung open the main door into the smoky room, Jerome strode over to Lewis who was seated on a bar stool in the corner. He had been talking to the bartender, a young man dressed in a black turtleneck and skinny black pants. Jerome slouched onto the stool next to him.

Lewis set his shot glass back on the bar where the young man immediately refilled it with whisky. "You been at Henry's old house again. I can still smell the dust in your clothes."

Jerome took a slurp of the beer Lewis had ordered for him. "Yeah, he needs the help. He'll join us shortly. He still hopes to get some news on the whereabouts of his no-good brother. What have you heard about Phillip?"

"I'm told he was after Joel, looking to get his money back. But I haven't seen him here. They're not a group to get involved with, especially his partner, Huberto. He's wanted since he shot a guy while part of a robbery at a liquor store a while back."

Jerome placed his glass back on the bar. "Are they the ones who took the drug pay-off money from Phillip?"

Before he could respond, they both swivelled around at the sound of Henry's voice. "Didn't expect to find you two in the bar." He hurried across the room towards them. The room had filled with the late afternoon crowd.

"It's great you're here, Henry." Jerome patted the stool beside him. "Lewis and I were chatting about the Marrero gang. He says Phillip seems to think it was them who took his money."

Lewis shrugged. "Well, it's what I heard from Phillip. Who knows what really happened? It could have been any of several of the local gangs."

Henry jerked his head towards the near tables. "They in here now?"

Lewis scanned the room. "The white guy with the grey ponytail over there near the windows is Joel. You might have seen him at the Paddock a while back."

Jerome reached for Henry's arm to restrain him, but it was too late.

Henry went straight to the table as Jerome and Lewis trailed behind him. He pushed his way between two beefy men and placed a hand on the table. "I'm looking for Phillip." Henry stared directly into Joel's face. "I hear you might know where he's at."

Joel glared right back, then a forced grin spread across his face. "What's it to you? He a friend of yours?" The smile disappeared and was replaced with an angry, stubborn grimace. "If so, you should find smarter friends."

Henry stood his ground and stared back. "He's my brother. But I got my own score to settle with him."

The man across from Joel relaxed his shoulders. "Rumour has it he was in a fight over on Elysian Fields." Jerome knew the area from some of the guys in the bus. Just over the line from the French Quarter, it was the start of an area of rundown houses and weed covered vacant lots.

Joel's voice drifted off. "Bad bunch hangs around those parts."

Henry balled up both hands into fists by his sides. "You got an address?"

"Huberto lives at 593 Elysian. He's the one who told me about the fight." Joel rose from the table and turned his back on Henry.

He headed towards the men's room at the back. "No business of mine."

When Henry turned to follow him, Jerome grabbed his arm. "You don't want to go there. Phillip will show up at home eventually."

"I know," Henry clamped his teeth shut, pulled free of Jerome's grasp and headed outside to hail a taxi.

Lewis and Jerome stood on the street and watched as Henry got in. Lewis shrugged and jumped into the cab right next to Henry. "Jerome, you stay here. You're still injured from the last time. I'll ride along with Henry."

Jerome hesitated. If he let Henry get hurt, Lara would never forgive him. But the hair stood up all around his collar when he thought about what might happen if they confronted the drug gang. He ran towards the rapidly closing cab door.

"Wait. I'll go with you."

*   *   *

During the ride through the Quarter, all three stared out the windows at the partygoers and later into the devastated streets just beyond. Jerome agreed to stay in the cab to keep watch as Lewis and Henry climbed the front steps of a grey clapboard house and pounded on the door. Through the partly opened entrance, he could make out a slim black woman who pointed to a house across the street. Shortly after, Henry stood by the cab window. "We're headed over there." He pointed. "She said he's in the brown house across the street with a friend. I want to see for myself."

Jerome jumped out. "I'll come with you." He turned to the driver. "Wait here. We'll be right back."

They climbed the steps onto the front porch and knocked. Then they waited aware of two sets of eyes looking at them from behind the half curtain on the window. The door finally opened part way and a smoke-filled voice told them to come in.

The three men were bunched up together in the small pine entrance hall of an old house. The wallpaper in the nearby kitchen was faded, but the room looked clean. The guy who ushered them towards a bedroom in the back was so thin his clothes hung on him and his dreadlocks were tangled and in need of a good wash. As they approached the room, Jerome heard Phillip's voice, "Who's there, Armand? I told you, I want no company."

Henry pushed the door wide open. Jerome could see Phillip lying on a single bed with a thin brown wool blanket draped over him. His exposed right shoulder and chest were covered in white bandages and his face was a greenish grey. Jerome could see his forehead wet with perspiration.

Henry jerked his head towards the man Phillip called Armand. "What's gone on here?"

"I told him not to try to get money off Huberto. We's friends, the three of us, from the Orleans. But, Phillip's too stubborn and he pushed and pushed. He listens to no one. Then Huberto shot him. I was lucky to get him out of there."

Lewis stepped inside the room, his arms crossed, his eyes darted into each corner. Jerome stood uneasily beside him. Henry hesitated and then seemed to make up his mind and went up to the bed. He stood over his brother who stared back at him. "Is that your story, Phillip?"

Phillip shrugged and winced in pain. "I needed the cash to pay you back for the ransom. Don't want quarrels in the family. Besides, no one plays me for a fool. Huberto must have heard at the hotel I had collected cash for a pay-off." His brow tightened again in pain as he tried to sit up. He fell back on the bed and turned to Armand. "You can leave us for a while. I'll call you if I need you."

After Armand left, Henry pushed the door securely closed and Phillip once more pushed himself up, leaning against the pillow. "Listen to me, Henry, cause we don't have much time. I got the money off Huberto's wife before he arrived home and shot me."

He sank back into the bed, his face drained. "I hid it in the bathroom here at Armand's, under the floor boards in the small cupboard.

Henry's eyes softened and he rubbed Phillip's arm. "Why you want to tell me this now?" The pallor in Phillip's face had increased and his eyes were slanted and almost closed.

Grabbing Henry's hand, Phillip rasped. "Cause it's your money. I'm paying you back what you're owed. I'm stuck here. The doctor who Armand brought here to check me out had to leave the bullet in me. That ain't good, he told me."

Henry tried to get Phillip to sit up. "We'll get you out of here. You should be in hospital. Lewis and I can dress and carry you."

Phillip wrenched himself free. "No. I'm not to be moved from this bed right now. The bullet seems lodged close to an artery and I could bleed out. I trust Armand not to tell anyone I'm here. You get the money and take it home. Come back tomorrow and we'll see how I am then."

Phillip's voice faded and his eyes dimmed with the increased pain. Henry finally removed his hand from Phillip's arm and patted his head.

"Till tomorrow then."

Jerome's chest was tight with panic and his throat felt like he'd swallowed a piece of glass. "Lewis, we need to get out of here. Huberto's bound to come to Armand's when he returns home and finds out from his wife what's happened."

Henry came over to join them. He crossed his arms in determination. "You heard him? Give me ten minutes to find the money. If it's where he says it is, then we'll all leave together."

Lewis and Jerome stood on guard in the hall outside the bathroom. They could hear the muffled sound of hammering. Once or twice, Henry flushed the toilet to disguise the noise. After what seemed like hours, the door opened a crack and Henry held up a stuffed duffle bag.

Jerome took a few steps further down the hall, but no one was in sight. "Let's move now. The cab said he'd wait, thank God."

They dashed into the street and ran to the cab and slammed the door behind them with relief. Henry directed the driver. "Drop us on Chestnut Street. I'll show you the house when we get there."

Jerome with Henry right beside him took one final glance out the back window. He saw Armand wave at them to stop. The driver hesitated, but Henry shook his head. "Whatever it is, we're not in a position to help Phillip right now."

Chapter Nineteen

Dusk had started to settle in, when the cab reached the house on Chestnut. Henry opened the door, glanced around with apprehension and then stepped out of the cab and started up the walkway duffle bag in hand. When he followed behind Henry, Jerome saw the heavy drapes in the parlour fall back into place. Lara must have kept watch for them to return.

After they closed the door, Lara met them in the hallway and pulled Henry into a tight hug. "Thank God you're safe, Uncle. Did you find Phillip?"

"Don't worry. He won't be bothering us for a while." His voice was tired and listless. "He got himself shot." He sighed. "I know he's been rotten to all of us lately, but he's still my younger brother and I'm feeling for him."

"He turned to face Jerome. "We'll have to go back tomorrow and get him out of the drug den before Huberto finds out what's missing."

Lara dropped her hands to her sides and looked at Jerome. "Shot? How did it happen?" Her face was drained and her lip twitched but her voice was steady.

Henry stood there his face frozen and wiped the back of his hand across his forehead.

Jerome responded. "Just an argument over the drug deal, I guess."

A frown crossed Lara's face before she led them from the hallway toward the kitchen. "You're both tired. Why don't you join me at the table? I'll brew up some of the some strong black coffee. I know the way you like it, Henry."

Henry hesitated. "I got to clean up first. Where's Noreen at?"

Lara shrugged. "She's gone down already. Worn out from all the stress of the day and worried about you two."

Henry jerked his head at Jerome to signal his intention and backed slowly and carefully out of the kitchen holding the duffle bag behind him. When he was out of sight, Lara confronted Jerome.

"Was Henry injured as well? He seemed so secretive all of a sudden. I know he won't confide in me if there's a problem."

Jerome blushed not comfortable in his reply. "He's probably just tired from all the action and concerned about Phillip."

Lara frowned at him and sighed. "Noreen will be happy to see him anyway. You can help me by setting up the table."

While he found clean mugs and spoons for everyone, Lara hummed out loud as she waited for the percolator to finish.

"You're in a good mood this afternoon."

She smiled at him and put her hand over his as he set mugs on the table. He moved closer to her.

"It's nice here when Phillip's away. I should feel awful for him, I guess but the fact he won't return home for a few days sets my mind as ease."

Jerome felt his spirits sink. "I hope it doesn't mean you're looking forward to leaving for Atlanta in a few weeks?" He would miss her cheerfulness and the closeness the two of them had developed.

Before she could answer, Henry joined them in the kitchen. He had washed his face and wore clean jeans and a fresh plaid shirt. His body relaxed into the chair and he smiled as Lara handed him a mug of coffee.

He downed several mouthfuls before he set the cup back on the table. "Thanks, honey. Sure is good." He paused. "Noreen opened her eyes and touched my hand but she's not likely to come down right now. I worry she won't make it through this attack in sound mind."

Jerome watched Lara cringe as she moved back to the counter. "You know I'll stay with her if she wants and not go back to Atlanta." Her mouth was stretched into a thin line and her eye lids drooped.

Henry smiled at her and gestured for her to sit. "No, honey. New Orleans hasn't been kind to you. We both want you to sing in the concert like you planned. Noreen said it's important for you to be part of the choir with your friend Emma."

A loud knock on the front door caused Henry to jump up and Lara to spill her coffee on the table. Jerome stood beside Henry as he straightened his shoulders and headed for the door. He followed Henry and remained a few steps behind just in case.

When Henry pulled the door open, both men stared at the tall dark officer who stood on the porch. "I've been trying to locate a Phillip Devries. This is the address I was told he was last at. Does he live here?"

Henry moved closer to the officer. "This is Phillip's house and I'm his brother. What is it you want from him?"

"He's been listed as a missing person with us since the storm. The last address we had was on Elysian so I tried there, but no luck. The hotel suggested he'd moved to Chestnut so we're here. Has he been back here?"

"We ain't seen him. But, Phillip is known to travel around the city. I can let you know if he shows up. He being charged with anything?"

The officer shook his head. "I can't talk about that. But, I hear he travels with a crowd always in trouble. He handed over his card. I'd much appreciate your call if he appears."

After the door closed, Jerome followed Henry back to the table. Henry sighed. "They must be seeking him for some drug offence. If he ain't at Elysian, where might he be?"

Seated at the table, Henry clamped his mouth closed and clenched his hands. Jerome was worried by his reaction. He knew Henry still cared about Phillip but he wouldn't want Lara or Noreen dragged into his mess. Jerome knew better than to say anything until Henry decided what to do.

Henry turned towards Lara. "There's something I got to tell you, but you can't tell Noreen about it. I don't want her to take on any more worries."

Lara's eyes widened. "What is it? You know I won't tell her anything you don't want her to know. I wouldn't cause her any more anguish."

Jerome started to get up but relaxed as Henry motioned for him to stay. He was relieved to be included. He didn't want any secrets between him and Lara.

Henry started. "Jerome was with me when we found Phillip today over on Elysian. I don't know how the cops heard about him being there though. I told you some of that but I didn't say Phillip told me how to find the stolen drug money he'd recovered. I got it here hidden upstairs."

He could tell this information had hit Lara hard. She gasped and covered her mouth. "What if the cops come back? For sure, we can't tell Noreen about this."

As he shook his head, Henry said, "You're right about that. We have to keep this a secret from her. Like I said, it would be too much after what she's suffered. I got the bag well hid."

Jerome joined in. "At least you've got the money now to rebuild the house. She'll be happy about it when she sees some progress." He hesitated. "I've got to head back to the hotel, but do I tell Lewis about the cops? They might show up at the bar as well."

Henry shrugged. "He was with us the whole time so I guess it doesn't matter. You tell him what you think. Lewis will keep quiet."

As he walked towards the door to leave, Lara grabbed his hand. "I'm glad Henry told me about the money. I don't want secrets between me and my best friend."

As the door closed behind him, Jerome could still feel the warmth of her hand in his and her soft body so close.

*   *   *

The crew continued to work on renovations almost every day for the next week. Noreen's mood continued to shift from fits of laugher with Lara to long deep silences. She didn't like to be left alone even back at the Chestnut Street house, except when in her own bedroom. Jerome was eager to reach the building site on Thursday morning to see Lara and hear any new developments. The police were eager to trace down Phillip's whereabouts and seemed sure the family was hiding something. Henry had been called to the station this morning to fill out a full report. Henry had his suspicions and had asked his lawyer to go with the three of them.

While he worked in the kitchen, he kept watch out the window for the cab to arrive with Noreen and Lara. As soon as it pulled to a stop, he dropped the crowbar he used to remove plywood and headed for the door. He met them in the middle of the walkway and took one of the baskets from Noreen's hands.

"That's too heavy for you. Let me take it to the backyard."

Noreen managed a smile. "Jerome, you're so kind to us. With you at work here all day, I don't know how you manage to play in the band at night."

Jerome smiled back. "Actually, I enjoy this physical work. I'm also learning a lot about houses in case I have one of my own someday." He gave Lara a meaningful look and watched her face turn a deeper shade.

"You told me you were a traveller. I thought you hadn't made up your mind where you might live."

"Well, this is home for now. Set your stuff on the table and let me show you what I've done so far." He led Lara back around the house and up the front steps. While they stood in the kitchen, he took her hands and gazed into her dark eyes. "I really wanted to get you alone. He started to kiss her lips, but she shook her head and motioned to the other room where the guys were working. "Okay. You're feeling shy right now. I can wait. Tell me what happened with the police?"

Lara dropped his hands and turned serious. "After they grilled Henry for almost an hour, our lawyer intervened. He said unless they planned to charge Henry with something, he'd told them what he knew and he and Henry would be leaving."

The detective said he'd be right back and returned with a more senior officer who confronted Henry. "We're doing our best to secure properties in this uncertain time. People have been displaced or evacuated and squatters just move in and take over."

Henry snapped his head back. "You call me a squatter. This here is my brother you're talking about and we was invited to live in his house."

"Phillip won't be declared dead until all possible areas have been explored. He'll remain a missing person until then. We need to decide what to do with the three of you who live in the house."

The lawyer spoke up. "If Phillip's a missing person, then Henry, as next of kin, would be in charge of the property until he's found. I have here a copy of Phillip's will which makes Henry the beneficiary should anything happen to him. I've done some checking and the taxes on the property are paid up to date. The house can't be sold unless Phillip is declared dead or has been declared missing for over two years."

The detective sighed and seemed to shrink. "Well then you've solved a few things for us. But, we still hope to find Phillip. We'll expect you to call us if you get any word of him." After he stood and the officer opened the door and gestured for them to leave.

"Sounds like a tense meeting for him. Are you frightened by their demands?"

Lara smoothed her hair with her right hand. "Only on Henry's behalf. I guess I was relieved we could stay at Phillip's for now. The renovations here have a long way to go and Noreen and Henry have nowhere else to live until then. When I return to Atlanta for my concert, I need to feel they're safe."

Jerome felt sadness weight on his chest. "You will return to New Orleans, won't you? I can see how much you love your aunt and uncle." He stopped. "I'll miss you. I hope you'll come back."

Lara relaxed as she looked up at him and laughed. "What about you? You don't even know if you'll be staying here in town for long."

Jerome smiled back at her. "Lewis has asked me to stay but I haven't given him an answer. So, nothing definite yet, but I love the spirit of New Orleans. It has possibilities. Especially if you're here."

Chapter Twenty

As she peered out the bus window, the night was black, when they pulled into the terminal and the driver announced Atlanta. The steady hum of the engine and the slight sway of the coach had lulled her into a deep sleep. She yawned and stretched. Emma had insisted she would meet the bus and Lara was excited she would soon see her friend again. She had lots to tell her after the dramatic events she'd been through. She felt a twinge of guilt when she remembered Noreen and Henry as they stood and waved to her. Their house was progressing but it would be several months before they could move back in. When she boarded the bus this morning, she felt bad as she watched Noreen, her mouth turned down in sadness, and appreciated Henry's attempt to look cheerful.

She joined the first group of passengers to clamber off the bus and grabbed her worn suitcase from the pavement where they'd dropped them. She ran into the lounge and searched the crowd until she spotted Emma. The same slender neck and dark oval face with high cheek bones, as the small figure came towards her. Her almond-shaped eyes sparkled over a head of black curls.

Lara grabbed her friend's slender waist and lifted her off the floor. "Emma, it's so good to see you. I'm thrilled you came. I know it's late."

Emma squealed with delight and hugged her back. "I've missed you so. The choir hasn't been the same. All of us will be relieved to have you join us for the concert."

Lara stepped back and gazed at Emma. "You look good. Come on; let's find a cab so we can get to my apartment and talk."

The walkway into the small apartment building was swept clean and the lobby as she remembered smelled fresh. She was glad for the small suitcase as they climbed the three flights of stairs and walked down the hall to her door. It was easy to find with its spray of pink flowers. Once inside, she felt strange as she checked the small rooms. The main area was painted in pale yellow with deep blue accents in pillows and knick knacks. The small kitchen held a square teak table and four chairs. She and Emma settled on the sofa after she found cokes in the fridge and munched on the freshly baked brownies Emma had brought with her.

She relaxed against the cushions. "So, what's happened with you and everyone else since I've been away?"

Emma pushed back against the arm of the sofa, her face serious. "Josie and Owen got themselves in trouble and have left the choir. She's six months pregnant. With you gone, we're short of sopranos and Mrs. Connolly is very worried we won't be ready for our performance at the festival."

She sucked in her breath. "That's much worse than I expected. But, I'm here now. We still have time to catch up with practice, don't you think?" She enjoyed the smooth chocolate while she watched for Emma's reaction.

"Yeah. I think we can do it. If we have enough hours to practice."

Lara hesitated before telling Emma about Jerome. They had shared stories about boyfriends over the years, but this was different. Jerome was just a friend, wasn't he?

"When's our next rehearsal? I can't wait to see the others. I'm sorry to hear about Josie, though. Her strong voice added so much richness to the choir. I'm not sure I can replace her."

Emma pulled her feet under and snuggled into the sofa. "She'll soon have a child to worry about. Imagine that."

Lara pushed back against the pillow and pulled her knees up against her chest. "I would think being in love would make you feel differently about life."

She wondered what it might have been like for her and Jerome. But, he was just a good friend or was it something more? She recalled the night before she left when Jerome came to the house to say goodbye. They're held each other close in the dim light of the parlour while he kissed her deeply his tongue seeking hers. She shivered as she recalled the sensation which ran down the inside of her thighs. She couldn't bear asking him to leave. Feeling brash, she asked him to stay overnight.

Lara smiled to herself. He'd pulled her closer and ran his hands over her shoulders and upper back and whispered he loved her too much. He didn't want to start something so serious while they would soon be apart. They'd wait until she returned.

Emma juggled her arm to pull her out of the trance. "What's with you, Lara? You disappeared somewhere. Are you in love?"

Lara sighed. "I don't know. I met someone. But, I can't tell you about it yet. Give me some time and I will, I promise."

Emma shook her head and then checked her watch. "I've got to go now anyway. I don't want to worry my mom. So, I'll wait to hear about it."

She walked Emma to the door and returned to the sofa. As she pulled up both feet, she placed her head on her knees, and felt a deep pain caused her chest to contract. She never imagined missing Jerome like this.

* * *

The next day as the bus traveled through Vine City, Lara felt she'd come home. Everything was so familiar to her. She had been impressed when Emma told her last night how the city took in at least 100,000 evacuees from Katrina and were able to include several hundred of these new children into the schools. The streets they passed by were clean, lawns on both sides of the street were mowed and what fences existed where in good repair.

As she got off the bus, she could make out the ochre brick front of Mt. Gilead Baptist Church with Pastor Connelly standing on the front steps. After she greeted him, she opened the door and continued towards the Choir Director, Camille Young, whose substantial frame in a navy choir gown stood inside the vestibule.

Camille's face broke into a broad smile as she reached out and pulled Lara into an embrace. Holding Lara at arm's length, she studied her expression.

"I can't believe it's really you. We were afraid you weren't coming back."

Pastor Connelly joined them and took Lara's hands into his own. "Well, child. You've come to our rescue for the festival. We've been searching the community for a new soprano since Josie left us and here you are."

Her eyes dancing, Camille chuckled. "I also need an assistant to help me plan for all these concerts we're expected to perform." She turned to the Pastor. "You're expecting a great deal from what was once a small church choir."

"I know you're up to it Camille. The choir gets better and better each season and we're in demand."

As he turned back to Lara once more, the Pastor asked. "How're your aunt and uncle?"

Lara sighed as she followed them toward the rehearsal room.

"They're managing okay right now. But it's been a very difficult time for them. Thank you for asking."

As she walked through the familiar chapel with its dark oak floors and walls painted gold, she was flooded with a sense of warmth and happiness.

When they entered the choir room, her other friends crowded around her. Wally still looked serious even with his dreadlocks and talk about sports. Shirley was next with her heavy head of curly hair pulled back by a tortoise-shell barrette. Valerie, her former choir partner, was even taller than when she'd left and more beautiful with her deep black eyes in a round dark face. She exclaimed.

"Hey guys. She's back. Lara's returned to join us and just in time." She faced Lara. "I guess you know we perform at the Chastain Park Amphitheatre next week."

She'd always loved the energy and vibration from the group when they were together. She soon joined them in the laughter and jokes as if she'd never left.

"Yeah, I know. Who came up with that name; *Food for the Soul?* It's so corny that I love it."

Camille rolled her eyes. "Wouldn't you guess? It was one of those officials from the City. We'll be singing some gospel, as usual but adding new blues songs. We've increased the practise time to make up for those."

Lara looked around at the group as they continued to fill the choir room and some began to pull on gowns. "Where's Emma this morning? I thought she'd be here by now."

Camille's head drooped as she breathed in. "She'll be late today. Has to take her mother to the doctor for a check on her condition."

Lara froze. "She didn't tell me anything last night. What's happened to her mother?"

As she dropped into a large wooden armchair, Camille continued. "The cancer came on sudden. Emma doesn't like to talk about it much. She seems to hope it will go away if she doesn't accept that it's there. Poor girl. There's just the two of them and no other family."

Lara felt sad but was soon rushed ahead by the group. She pulled the gown over her head and felt it touch her knees. She loved the feel of the pressed cotton. "It's not like Emma not to tell me something this serious. Maybe I talked too much and didn't give her a chance. I'll look for her after practise."

Camille stood. "Let's line up in the choir loft so we can practise for real." She led the group out with Lara in the lead. "Let's not discuss her mother with Emma when all the others are around. She'll just clam up for sure." Her face took on its normal calm expression as she stood in front of the choir. "Right now, I got to concentrate on our performance."

Lara felt her chest tighten and her head lift when the organist played the first bars. Under Camille's direction, she soon joined in with the harmony of the group. She was impressed with the sound she heard. With relief, she realized they were almost ready for the festival. Half way through the second piece, she saw Emma rush through the door to join them. Lara squeezed closer to her friend to make room for her so they would be together.

Emma smiled as she took her place. "I'm so glad you're back with us."

In the choir room after the practise, the noise engulfed the group. It seemed all twelve of them were talking at once. After a while, Lara managed to pull Emma free from the group so they could leave. On the way out, she squeezed Emma's hand.

"Do you have time for a coffee at Peach Café on Spencer?"

Emma gave her a big smile. "Let's do that. It's been so long since we could."

They entered the cheery café with its lime green walls trimmed with white lattice wood and made their way to a booth by a window in the back.

When they were seated, Lara touched Emma's arm.

"I really want to know how you've been. We only seemed to talk about me last night."

Emma stared at the menu on the table while the waitress took their order and brought their coffees. She pulled the hot mug of coffee into her two hands and let out her breath.

"I'm okay, I guess. Still no steady boyfriend for me yet. But, I can tell Wally likes me." She sucked in her breath, her eyes bright with unshed tears. "You've heard about my mom?"

Lara hesitated, her throat tight. "Yes. I found out today from Camille when I asked why you were late." She paused. "How bad is it?"

Emma's voice broke and tears trickled down her cheeks. "It's bad. Breast cancer and it's the invasive kind. She's got no one else but me. I need to look after her."

Lara reached for Emma's hand and held on to it. "You have me now. I'm here and I want you to tell me what I can do to help."

Emma gave a thin smile. "Just to have someone to talk to helps me. I missed you so much, although I know why you had to go. Your aunt has been like a mother to you."

Lara sipped the strong hot brew. Visions of Noreen and Henry at the bus depot filtered into her thoughts. They would miss her for sure. But, they had each other and their mission to rebuild the house would keep them going. For now, she was needed here.

*   *   *

When the sound of clapping stopped, Lara gazed out from the stage at the capacity audience who had started to regain their seats. She could make out at the back a crowd of black men and women. Probably people she knew like firemen, police, bank clerks and a few teachers. You'd find the same crowd back in New Orleans at these concerts.

However, in the front rows nearer the stage, she saw middle class white folk, with the men dressed in navy or black suits and the women in stylish rayon and silk dresses. This was so different from the church concerts they used to play at.

Soon, Camille strode to the podium from the side curtain to introduce each of the performers to the audience. Before the concert, she had instructed each of them to focus on her for their signals. When in her director role, Camille was calm and in control. She had guided them through the first pieces. Lara knew she had put on the best performance of her life. She watched the other members of the choir shift from one foot to the other hardly able to contain their excitement.

By intermission, they had the audience with them and she could relax just a little. Lara realized she had sung better than ever before. Music was in her blood and she would always want to be part of it. Now she could understand what Jerome had told her about his lifestyle. Sometimes he'd been forced to travel across the country, and live in cheap hotel rooms, so he could get to play his saxophone in a really good band. That was why he had come to New Orleans. Lewis's band was that good. She wouldn't want to give up her music for anyone. Her heart jumped. What did this mean for Jerome and her?

They were soon back on stage for the second half and were able to keep up the momentum. At the conclusion of the concert, the audience rose to their feet and the applause came, in wave after wave. The choir finished their encore piece and sighed with relief as they filed back stage to hug each other in triumph. Lara was so hyped she twirled Emma in her arms until they were both dizzy. Then they collapsed onto the hard wooden chairs with laughter.

When Camille joined the choir, she stood on a raised step in the change room and asked for quiet. "You have been wonderful tonight and you all know it. We've reached a higher level and we will continue forward from this evening to even better. I congratulate you and hope to see all of you at practice on Tuesday."

After the laughter, each of them changed into street clothes and Lara and Emma left together. In the bus on the way home, Emma was even more quiet than usual. Lara asked, "What are you thinking about?"

Emma's voice was almost a whisper. "I only wish my mama had been able to see me perform. She wanted to come so badly, but the drugs make her sleep most of the time."

Lara sighed and squeezed her hand. "She'll be proud when the others tell her how good you are." She hesitated. "I'm so sorry about this Emma. How long do they say she has?"

"She might make it to Christmas. That's about it." Tears trickled down her cheeks.

"Then we'll see she'd not left alone. Between you and me and the women's auxiliary from the church, someone will be with her at all times."

Emma smiled in gratitude. "You'd do that for me?"

"Of course I would do that for you. You're my best friend and your mother has been good to me. Do you want me to come home with you now?"

Emma was silent for several minutes. "No. She'll be asleep. But you can tell the others why I can't join them at Danny's for sundaes tonight."

"You mean tell Wally," Lara asked. "He'll look for you. I know."

Emma giggled and dropped her head. "Quiet. He might hear you." She turned her head to check the back of the bus.

When they got to the small brick bungalow where Emma and her mother lived, Lara waved to her until the bus was out of sight.

She joined the group at the ice cream shop. They all understood why Emma had to leave. Most of them had heard about her mother's illness by now. Wally said he missed her but knew how it must feel for her. Lara finished her ice cream and left. She enjoyed the walk in the cool breeze as she strolled down the sidewalk towards her small apartment. Even this late at night, she felt safe on the streets here in Atlanta. So unlike the dark streets in New Orleans that she had left behind. With their sinister darkness which had drifted in lately, they terrified her. Here the streets outside her apartment invited pedestrians.

When she opened the door to her apartment and flicked on the lights, she felt at home. The small blue vase with yellow silk mums, one of her early purchases, brightened up the white cloth on her pine table. Her newspaper was neatly folded on the end table by the sofa. She kicked off her shoes at her bedroom door and dropped onto the bed.

As she gazed at the ceiling, she ached to tell Jerome about tonight. She knew he'd probably be on stage and he didn't have a cell phone so it would have to wait until tomorrow. Maybe she could catch him at the hotel then. She hadn't expected to miss him so much and she wouldn't be going back to New Orleans for a while, at least.

She'd call Noreen and Henry at Phillip's house in a few days. She could ask them about how the building was going and maybe they'd mention Jerome. It was so hot, she pulled off her clothes and decided to sleep naked. Just as she was falling asleep, she wondered what it would be like if Jerome was here, in this bed, with her. She smiled and hugged her body closer.

Chapter Twenty-One

Jerome wiped the sweat off his face, with his old red handkerchief, while he relaxed into a plastic chair in the backyard. He could hardly wait for lunch. This physical work sapped his energy. With a crew of four, they had pulled off all three layers of old shingles and repaired any weak areas. They'd just finished hammering in the last neat rows of new ones, a grey-blue colour which matched the blue siding. He had been assured by Henry, with the inside of the house now clean and dry, he and Henry would soon complete the dry walling. By the end of November, the plan was to have new floors laid and he could then leave Henry to complete the job.

He glanced over to the front porch and saw Henry's slender frame round the corner of the house and head towards him.

"Noreen will be here with the lunch shortly. I sure appreciate all the work you've done for me, Jerome. The boys are okay, but to them it's just another job."

"No problem." Jerome smiled. "The food makes it worth my while." Jerome hesitated for a moment and breathed deeply.

"You hear anything from Lara?"

A whisper of a smile crossed Henry's face and his eyes softened. "She called last night to say their concert was a hit. In fact, she's asked me how to reach you."

Jerome hunched forward in his chair and pressed his elbows into his knees. He rested his head on his upraised fists. "Great to hear. You can tell her to call me at the bar. Lewis lets us take calls when we're not on stage."

"I'll tell her. I think she's missed you."

"Don't tell her, but I'm planning to go up there to Atlanta next month. I hear the jazz is hot right now and I'm always on the alert for something new."

Henry sat back. "What about Lewis? Won't he be needing you in his group?"

Jerome stood and clenched his hands. "The thing is I was hired to fill in for his regular saxophonist. I don't know if he plans to keep me on. I can't count on it."

Henry joined him and gave him a pat on the shoulder. "From the chatter I hear in the bar, you much sweeter than the last one. It's not true only blacks can play jazz."

"It's great to hear it from you. But I got to be ready to move on, just in case. My music is important to me."

Henry gestured for Jerome to sit and pulled up a chair beside him. "Now it wouldn't be you're going up there to check on how Lara's making out, would it? You should know Noreen and I are okay with that, if you are. If the two of you were to keep company, that is."

"Thanks for your vote." He grinned at Henry. "But I don't know what she thinks about it as yet. I just want to see her and then I got some questions to ask her." Jerome turned his head at the sound of a brakes squealing from the street.

Within a few minutes, Noreen, a broad smile on her face, came around the corner of the house. "You all must be starving. The cab was late cause of some kind of traffic jam downtown." She dropped the basket on the table and pulled out containers of shrimp paella and corn bread with coleslaw, as well as some cold beer.

Henry whistled between his two fingers and the two hired hands soon joined them. In no time, silence descended and plates were filled to the brim.

Henry took his place beside Noreen.

"Jerome here has been asking after Lara."

Noreen set her plate back on the table and turned to Jerome. "She's doing what she loves, so it makes her happy. But, her best friend's mother is very sick and that's a concern. But she'd a strong girl, that Lara. She'll be okay."

"Did she ask about me," Jerome said. Then he blushed and looked down.

Noreen grabbed his arm. "Of course, she misses you. I just forgot to tell it to you. I'm so absent minded."

After Henry dropped both plates into the dishpan of hot water, he stood behind Noreen. "Jerome just might see her when he goes up to Atlanta."

Noreen's face broke into a broad smile. "That'd be nice. That'd be very nice."

Henry and Jerome dried their plates and headed back into the house. Jerome knew he'd have at least another two hours before he'd need to head back downtown. The walls were beginning to take shape under the constant dim of the hammer. With the barrage of noise, the two of them worked in silence.

*   *   *

Seated in the dark booth of the hotel, Jerome leaned his elbows on the green Formica table top and directed his gaze at Lewis. What he loved about the Royal George was the way they'd restored the old instead of replacing it with the more honkytonk décor common to some of the newer bars in town.

He's been surprized when Lewis asked him to stay for bourbon after their last number. Jerome was conscious of the intense way Lewis was studying him. Had he messed up somewhere in his routine?

Lewis raised his glass and took a sip. "What are your plans for this winter? You signed up with anyone yet?"

Jerome swallowed hard, as the warm liquor slide down his throat. "No. I'm staying cool to see what comes up. But, I'm not looking to go back to Jackson. Their music is stale."

"I'm thinking about replacing Marcus. He's just not up to the rest of you." Lewis looked him in the eye. "Too much time off with the drink to suit me." He waited. "You interested."

Jerome's mind raced. He sat back against the hard surface of the booth and breathed out. "I wasn't expecting this. Of course, I'm interested. New Orleans is the place to be for a jazz player. You think I'm good enough?"

Lewis's face broke into a wide smile. "I've kept you on haven't I? Besides, I like the way you stuck with Lara even stood up to the gang for her aunt and Henry. You got staying power."

"What's your offer?" Jerome dropped his head. "I got to think about my career and what's ahead."

Lewis nodded. "I thought you was serious about your music. We'll finish your contract first. Then if you sign on in December for a year, I pay the same as now with an additional ten percent after the first three months."

Jerome sucked in his breath. This was more than he had expected. He kept his voice steady. "How about giving me the extra ten percent when I sign up in December? I'll already have done my three months by then."

Lewis reached his hand out to Jerome and they shook. "You got it. Now, there's something else I need to let you know about. I've heard from the guys, Phillip's been seen out at The Paddock. He won't come around here, but he's making noise about his getting shot being all your fault. If he believes it, you'll need to watch out for him. We both know he can be dangerous."

Shock hit Jerome like a pail of cold water. Phillip was alive after all. After what the police said, he and Henry didn't go back to Elysian to look for him. Lewis was right. He'd avoid both Henry and the Royal George since their dispute. But, Jerome might just be considered fair play as a target. He'd need to be cautious.

"I'm sorry to give you such a scare, but better you know about it. Now, I got to get some sleep, so see you same time tomorrow." Lewis rose and ambled towards the door.

Jerome continued to stay where he was. Imagine having his first real job as a musician. In the past, he'd seen plenty of short term assignments, but this was for real. Lara would be excited for him when he told her. He gazed around the crowded bar and felt a sharp pang of loneliness deep in his gut. He'd never had a woman he'd cared about like Lara. He knew it would be at least another two weeks before he could ask Lewis for a leave. Then he could hold her sweet body in his arms. Should he tell her right now? No. It'd be more romantic to arrive in Atlanta unannounced. Maybe even show up at one of her concerts. He hummed under his breath as he headed back to the bus for some much needed rest.

*　　*　　*

Lara grinned as she put down the phone and plugged in the kettle for tea. Noreen had sounded so hopeful about moving back into their house by Christmas. She knew how much her aunt loved that small bungalow with its large kitchen and compact bedrooms. She and Henry had built the home after they got married. Noreen had painted the walls herself and sewed new curtains.

After she poured a cup of the hot liquid, Lara carried it into the living room where she had been reading the music for their next concert. Imagine, their little choir was booked for the next two months. When she agreed to be Camille's assistant, she hadn't realized all the tasks involved to get ready for a concert, besides learning her own pieces. But, she needed the money and it meant she didn't have to work in that fast food place. Back in New Orleans, she'd never have believed how popular the choir had become. It would probably be spring before she could find time to travel back to check on Noreen and Henry. She sighed. Jerome, too, would have to wait. Lara had worked up the courage to ask her aunt if Jerome was okay. She'd been happy to hear, he continued to help them with the house and that he often asked about her.

Lara was supporting Emma by staying with her mother, Mrs. Reed, on Sunday afternoons so Emma could go to lunch with Wally. She knew how important this was to her friend. The latest she had heard from Emma was the doctor had said her mother could be confined to bed by early December. Even with the money her church group had collected for expenses, Emma couldn't afford a full time nurse for her. So Lara, like several of the other girls agreed to help out. Lara grabbed her heavy wool sweater and set out for Emma's house at a brisk walk.

While Lara sat with her in the living room and continued to read her music, Theresa Reed had slept most to the afternoon on the sofa under a quilted comforter. Jealousy had swamped her as she watched Emma and Wally leave, arms linked, absorbed in each other's conversation. She felt the knife cut deep. Why wasn't it her and Jerome so close together? Had she made the right decision when she left him behind? Here in Atlanta she had no fears. But she still had some good memories of high school in New Orleans. What if Jerome wasn't there any longer when she returned? She was suddenly aware Mrs. Reed had sat up and continued to stare at the window. Her voice was so low and feeble; Lara could just make out her words.

"Is Emma okay? I hope Wally will be a good friend for her." She sighed. "Who will look after her when I'm gone?"

Lara sucked in her breath. "You know she'll always have me. I won't leave her alone. And she has other friends in the choir as well as Wally." She helped the woman to arrange the blankets around her knees. "Emma's been like a sister to me."

Mrs. Reed's voice was raspy and just audible. "What about your aunt and uncle in New Orleans? Won't they need you back there?"

"Don't you worry. My aunt and uncle understand my career is here right now with the choir. But, I'll still see them regularly. It was them who wanted me to go to Atlanta to stay with the two of you after I graduated from high school."

While Mrs. Reid waited for Emma to return, Lara tried to continue to read her music but her eyes kept closing. In her mind, she and Jerome were nestled into each other on a wooden bench, as they watched the now calm waters of Lake Pontchartrain. She could see Jerome's long blond hair which rested against her skin, damp with perspiration. She felt the soft glide of his fingers which played up and down her arm like it was a guitar. Tiny needles of pleasure danced up and down her body.

When her eyes blinked open, the sensation faded. What would Jerome be doing now? Sunday was his only day off and he usually spent it with her. What if he had another girlfriend already? She couldn't bear it, but would her aunt even tell her? She'd sounded so positive when she talked about him. Lara shook her head. She wouldn't even think about him right now. Her vivid imagination had caused these pangs of jealousy to eat at the insides of her stomach.

She jerked herself out of her trance and began to wash up the lunch dishes before Emma returned. It had taken great patience to get Mrs. Reed to eat even a small bowl of soup and the crackers were still on the plate. Emma had been so worried; she refused to leave until her mother ate something. Lara smiled. She was glad to do something for Emma. Emma had been Lara's first friend when she was a new girl at their school in New Orleans. *The others had scorned her as the orphan from up north with the crazy mother.*

Chapter Twenty-Two

Brightness had spread across the cobblestone streets, when Jerome paid for his ticket to Atlanta, and climbed into the bus. He'd used all his powers of persuasion to get Lewis's consent for a week off, so he could visit Lara. He smiled as he recalled Lewis's response.

"What ya telling me Jerome? I just hired you and now you're going to leave me so you can chase after your girlfriend?"

"I know this isn't the greatest time, Lewis, but you can keep Marcus on an extra week. He won't mind."

Jerome touched Lewis on the arm. "I just really need to see if Lara is okay. And I need to persuade her to come back here." He stepped back until he sensed Lewis weakening. "Better now than when we're in our busy Christmas season, don't you think."

He walked down the aisle to the middle of the bus seeking a seat next to a heater. His shoulders hunched against the chill of early December, the start of the coldest season in New Orleans. He leaned his head back against the vinyl seat, stuffed his hands into his pockets and closed his eyes ready for the long trip. Within minutes he could see Lara's heart-shaped ebony face and her sensual rosy brown lips, as her arms reached out to welcome him, and hold him close. He immediately felt the heat.

Gradually the warmth of the bus seeped into his body soothing him and he felt himself begin to drift off to sleep. In what seemed like a very short time later, a strong hand gripped his shoulder. He jerked awake and raised his head to see the bus driver standing in front of him.

He yawned. "Where we at?"

The driver smiled. "This here is Mobile, and we're stopping for a short break. You can get out if you want to get some coffee or a bite. Once we're on the State 65, we won't stop again until Atlanta."

Jerome roused himself and stepped out into the cool air. He strode into the small one storey diner, and slid onto a stool at the counter close to the cashier. As he glanced out the streaked window, he saw deserted and dusty streets which stretched between a series of small square buildings in what looked like an industrial park.

He watched two men stump out their cigarettes and pull their jackets tight against the cold before they entered the diner. The leader had shifty eyes which bounced away when Jerome tried to engage him. His partner glared at the line of bus passengers crowded up beside them as they stood in the doorway. When they reached the cashier, Jerome turned toward the closer one and asked.

"Where you headed today? It'll be a cold night, for sure."

"We're headed for Atlanta and are just here to pay for some gas we pumped."

Jerome watched the cashier ring up the transaction and the two men headed back outside. Something about the two of them, he just didn't like. Mobile wasn't likely to be his kind of place. He knew Atlanta would be better from what Lara had told him. He sure hoped she'd listen to his pleas for her to return to her home town.

Back on the bus, Jerome could feel the gentle rhythm of the wheels under him, as they picked up speed on the highway. Out the window, he glimpsed miles and miles of low shrubs on each side of the road against a background of rolling hills.

His hunger abated after he ate the grill chicken sandwich he'd picked up in the diner and washed it down with a root beer. He hoped to find some small café to eat dinner before he showed up at Lara's place in Atlanta later that evening. He felt himself smile when he thought about the surprised look he'd see on Lara's face as she saw him at the door.

A loud grinding noise from somewhere under the bus gave him a start. It jerked to a stop on the shoulder of the road which caused him to slam his head into the back of the seat. All the passengers stirred but no one moved for the first while as the bus driver remained outside. Finally, Jerome, followed by a large man with grey curly hair and dressed in a plaid jacket, climbed out to have a look. The driver stood at the front of the bus and stared at the engine which belched black smoke. He shook his head and spoke into his radio.

"It's Marcel. No. Doesn't look good here. I think you'll have to send a replacement." There was a long silence. "I been telling dispatch for the last two weeks that this bus isn't sounding right."

Marcel looked over at the two men. "We could be here for a couple of hours."

Jerome sighed. He hated the delay when he was so anxious to see Lara. He'd get to her apartment very late tonight.

His companion swore. "Damn. I gotta be in Atlanta for a job interview first thing in the morning. I can't afford to lose this one cause of a broken-down bus."

Marcel shrugged. "The replacement has to come from Montgomery, so we'll wait. Might as well make yourself comfortable." He climbed back into the bus and used the PA system to explain the problem to the other passengers.

Jerome followed him, but dragged his feet on each step. He fell back into his seat but kept shifting and was unable to get comfortable again in the vehicle which was now cold. He stretched out as best he could and tried to get back to sleep.

About an hour later, he was abruptly awakened by the jostling and kicking of the passenger behind him. In the dim light, he could see two youths, arms locked around each other's heads in combat.

"Go find another seat. This one is mine. You're disgusting."

Marcel soon came over to the two boys, who'd wakened several other passengers.

"Calm down you two. The new bus should be here in another hour or so. In the meantime, don't be bothering the others or I'll put you outside."

The cold air now seeped into Jerome's bones and he knew he wouldn't sleep anymore tonight. Should he sit here for another hour and hope the bus would show up?

As he watched out the window, it was deep black with occasional car lights from the road. With no working engine, the heater would continue to be out of service. He couldn't just sit here and wait. With some cars still on the road, he should be able to pick up a ride. He grabbed his knapsack off the top shelf and walked up to the driver.

"Can you let me out? I'm going to hitchhike to Atlanta. I'll get there sooner than sitting in this cold bus."

Marcel shrugged his shoulders. "You're taking a chance. I can't be responsible if anything happens to you once you leave here." He released the door so Jerome come get out.

As he continued to walk down the shoulder of the road, Jerome could feel the chilly air seep into his bones making his teeth chatter. Maybe he'd been too impulsive, taking off like that. He looked back at a long black stretch of road. What had happened to all those headlights he'd watched from his seat? About half an hour later, he spotted two tiny dots of light far in the distance. He stuck his hands in his pockets and continued to move down the road. He'd check back regularly to make sure those lights were getting bigger. Finally, he could make out the front of a white Chevy sedan and he waved frantically to for the car to stop.

He breathed in sharply when the Chevy pulled up right beside him. The window rolled down and Jerome stared at the two unkempt faces of the two men from the diner. He hadn't liked the look of them then and was still suspicious, but what choice did he have. He couldn't walk all the way to Atlanta. He reached out to shake hands with the pale scrawny guy who had his head of unruly red hair stuck out the open window.

Jerome smiled and hoped for the best. "Thanks for stopping. Our bus broke down back down the road and I need to get to Atlanta. What's the chance of getting a ride with the two of you?"

The red haired guy threw his half-empty coffee cup out the window nearly hitting Jerome with it.

"Yeah. We passed that bus. Atlanta is where we is headed. Maybe you can help us out with the gas money. Prices are pretty high right now."

The driver turned to look at them and growled. "I ain't had my say yet. A twenty gets you in the door."

Jerome could feel the red-haired guy's eyes on him as he opened his wallet and took out the money. "Okay. Can I get in now? It's cold out here."

The driver nodded his head and started the car. He pulled away before Jerome had time to fully close the door.

"I told you to get in. We got to keep moving. We got business in Atlanta tomorrow morning, too."

Jerome slammed the door closed and settled back against the seat. Within a short while, the warmth began to penetrate through his jeans and shirt making him sleepy. Only his distrust of the two men in front of him kept him awake. Had he made the right decision to leave the bus? As he stared out the back window of the Chevy, he couldn't make out any sign of traffic behind them. The three of them continued down the dark road in silence. He watched the bright glow of their cigarettes and smelled the smoke as it flowed into the back seat.

The driver punched his partner in the arm. "We better find a station soon. I'm down below an eighth of a tank. I thought you said there was one around here somewhere."

The dim light of dawn lit up the empty road ahead of their car. They must be on a long stretch of deserted highway somewhere between Montgomery and Atlanta, but where. He couldn't tell.

Anxiety flooded over Jerome as he leaned against the back of the bench seat. He couldn't face being stranded twice in one night.

"Don't you know where we are?"

The red-haired guy nodded. "We're about four miles outside Atlanta, but this car burns gas. I remember there's stations near here and most of them open at six."

The driver pointed into the dark at a small building down a side road.

"That's got to be the one you're talking about. We'll head over there and wait for it to open."

Jerome sat back into his seat and watched out the side window while the car pulled into a rusty Mobile station and parked by one of the pumps. By his watch, he could see it was five thirty.

They sat in silence as time dragged by. All three jerked to attention when the lights blinked on and a wiry clean-shaven man with sandy hair opened the door of the station. He must have come in the back door which was why they didn't see him. He approached the car and addressed the driver.

"You guys needing some gas?"

The driver growled. "Yeah. Looks like we do. Fill er up."

Jerome was reassured by the sound as the tank filled. He noticed the driver handing over some bills. Surprised, he saw the two men get out of the car and beckon for him to follow them into the station. He hesitated and stood outside the car door and wondered why they needed him. Fear crept up his spine. He could tell something wasn't right. The red-haired man came back and stood right in front of him. Before he could say anything, the guy slammed Jerome's shoulders against the car door and the driver appeared from the other side and punched him in the jaw.

The pain spread from his nose which was bleeding and down his entire face. He could feel his lip start to bleed as he turned to face the two.

"What was that for? I gave you gas money."

"Shut up and hand over your wallet. You'll be finding your own way to Atlanta from here. We got business which don't include you."

The driver ripped the wallet out of Jerome's hands, emptied out the cash and hurled the empty wallet into the ditch beside them.

The red-haired guy came over to them, shaking his head. "What are we going to do with him?"

Jerome heard the car trunk open, and watched the driver retrieved a rope. Shocked, he felt himself pushed up against one of the gas pumps.

The driver threw the rope to his partner. "Here. You tie this around him. It'll keep him busy until we're clear."

The second man gestured toward the station. "What about the gas jockey?"

"Don't worry," the driver shook his head. "He knows to stay out of our way. You see him come out here to the rescue this guy? Of course not. He won't do nothing."

As he felt the rope tighten, Jerome shook in anger and helplessness. When he struggled to free himself, the guy pulled the rope even tighter. He watched as the two men laughed and slapped their thighs before they got back in the car and drove off with tires squealing on the pavement. He slumped against the gas pump to wait and tasted the salty red blood which continued to drip from the tear in his lip. Surely, the gas jockey would help him now.

Jerome wished now he hadn't been so stupid as to not tell Lara he was coming. She would have been worried when he didn't arrive on time and could have sent some rescuers. He continued to struggle, but it only pulled the rope even tighter. Then he heard the station door open and close with a bang. What did that mean?

Moments later, the sandy-haired man began to untie the rope. "Sorry. There was nothing I could do to stop them. I'd only get hurt as well. Come with me. I got a first aid kit to fix your lip."

Relieved to be able to move his shoulders and arms, Jerome shook himself as if to shake off a bad experience.

"They threw my wallet into that ditch. I'll need my I.D. and my musician license. Can you help me find it?

The two men walked back and forth across the deep sides of the ditch. The light was still dim over the dusty brown surface. Finally, he kicked something solid out of a patch of grass. He cringed as pain stabbed through his ribs while he bent to pick up the brown leather wallet. He checked inside and thumbed through the items left.

"Thank god, they're both here."

"You got any cash?" The sandy haired man gave him a sympathetic look. "I can't give you any out of the register. It's counted every night."

"That's okay. All the cash I had on me was in the wallet, but I can go to the bank in Atlanta." Jerome sighed. "But, that means I'll have to walk the rest of the way."

The guy seemed reluctant to leave him. "You sure you got people in Atlanta?"

"I got a girlfriend. She'll help me out. I just need some cash for the phone. I'll call her when I get closer."

Jerome shook the guy's hand when he handed him four one dollar bills. "Thanks. It means a lot." He followed the man into the station and sat on a chair while he patiently applied an antiseptic to the cut lip.

The sun was beginning to rise, when Jerome started down the shoulder of the road, and stopped to wave towards the station. He felt reassured there were always some good men mixed in with the bad ones in every community. He was light-headed from lack of sleep, but continued to make progress. He faced straight ahead and ignored the traffic which passed beside him. Hitchhiking was out for him. He would walk all the way to Atlanta now.

Chapter Twenty-Three

The next two hours on the road were mind-numbing for Jerome, but it did give him time to think. He'd hadn't totally realized how important Lara had become in his life. As much as he tried to focus on his music, her face floated in every time he played a love song.

Finally, he could see the lighted skyline of Atlanta ahead. He remembered Lara had said she lived in Vine City and he pulled out the scrap of paper she'd given him to check the address. He'd have to get a map from the service station ahead. When he arrived at the door and pulled it open, he saw a large woman with a dark brown face at the cash register and walked up to her.

"Can you give me a City Map? I'm new to Atlanta."

She looked up and smiled. "Atlanta is a big city. What place you trying to get to?"

He pulled out the slip of paper and showed it to her.

"Okay. That's in Vine City? I'll give you this map of the city centre but you'd best walk another two blocks ahead to the nearest bus stop. It's too far to walk all that way."

Jerome looked down. "How do I know when I get there?"

Her espresso eyes lit up and a smile covered her face. "You almost there, honey. When you get on the 6A bus, tell the driver to let you off at the Vine City stop. He'll know. You got a dollar for the fare"

He nodded, took the map and thanked her. He was at the bus stop in no time and one arrived fifteen minutes later. Jerome, relieved to rest his legs, almost missed his stop when the driver called it out. He got off and stared at the wide streets with lush lawns edged by evergreen shrubs. By following the path, he came to a series of four storey white stucco apartment buildings with red clay roofs.

What should he do now? It was almost six but too early to arrive at Lara's place unannounced. He'd probably frighten her. It was so quiet around here. He lay down on one of the garden benches, out of sight from the street to rest. He must have drifted off because when he woke, it was bright daylight. He checked his watch to find it was eight o'clock. Maybe he could catch Lara while she made her breakfast before she had to leave for the day. He smiled as he thought about her reaction when she opened the door.

He watched people come out of their apartments, well-dressed men and women, mainly black but some looked Spanish. He relaxed back against the back of the bench, reluctant to get up. This seemed to be a prosperous town where no one was likely to rip him off.

He took a deep breath and got to his feet. Jerome walked the short distance to the front door and followed someone into the hallway. The smell of fresh scented deodorizer filled the space. He moved down the hall to unit ten and stood there. For the first time since he left New Orleans, doubts about whether Lara would welcome his visit hit him. Many phone lines were still down so they hadn't been able to talk very often since she left. He clenched and unclenched his hands and finally lifted the door knocker. After he let it fall, the door opened quickly.

Lara stood before him, her shapely body dressed in a white cotton blouse and a tight fitted navy skirt. He shifted from one foot to the other, unable to stand still. Jerome wanted to hug her but held back in case he scared her.

Lara's face stared at him and frowned at first but within seconds her eyes grew large against her dark skin and her mouth opened in a gasp.

"Can it really be you, Jerome? What are you doing here and how did you get to Atlanta?" She grabbed one hand and led him into the apartment.

He couldn't help but stare back at her. She was just as he remembered, except for her hair which was smoothly arranged and turned under which set off her large eyes and soft brown lips. He took both her hands and smiled. "You look marvelous, honey. Your career sure agrees with you."

He pulled her closer in a tight embrace and winced only slightly when she kissed him on his split lip.

Lara noticed and studied his face for a long moment. "Jerome, your lip is cut and you have bruises on your cheek. Have you been in a fight?" She touched his cheek gently with two fingers.

He nodded. "The bus broke down and I had to hitchhike here. I picked the wrong car and ended up robbed and beat up. But, I'm okay now I'm here with you." She led him to the sofa and they both sat close together. He leaned his body into hers and snuggled into the warmth.

She kissed him lightly on the cheek. "Why didn't you call me? I could have lent you some money. You didn't have to walk."

Jerome continued to hold her. "I know it was stupid. I wanted so badly to surprise you. I didn't want to give up and call you and thought I could walk here instead."

Lara sighed. "Now, I got concert practice in an hour so I'll have to leave you. But, let me get you some breakfast and then you can sleep until I get back."

He followed her into the kitchen and sat at the table watching as she fussed over the stove and soon set a plate of scrambled eggs, with orange juice and coffee in front of him. The smell was wonderful and made him realize he hadn't eaten anything since lunch.

She stood behind his chair and put her arms around him, kissing the top of his head. "I've got to go now. But, I want to see you rested and with a smile when I return. It sounds like you've been through a bad night." She opened the door and stood there. "I'll be back before long. Tomorrow you can come with me, if you like and meet some of the other singers. How long can you stay?"

"I forgot to tell you, I've got a full time job with Lewis, but he gave me a week off to come to see you. He said to give you his best."

Lara frowned. "I guess that means you aren't about to move here to Atlanta. I hoped it might happen sometime. It's a great town for music and I could help you get settled."

He could tell from her wistful comments, she felt at home in Atlanta and still wasn't thinking about returning to New Orleans. He didn't like to disappoint her but his career with Lewis was doing so well, he couldn't give it up either.

Jerome took another bite of his toast. "We can talk about it later when you get back. New Orleans is right for my kind of music. But, I'm not thrilled about us living in different cities." She smiled and waved goodbye before she closed the door and was gone.

*   *   *

Lara's feet danced down the street as she headed for the local bus. She was so excited to see Jerome; she didn't know how she'd get through the day. She laughed out loud while she climbed the steps into the bus and caused the driver to give her a questioning look. She shrugged and continued on to her seat. Imagine. When she returned home from practice, Jerome would be right there waiting for her. It was so unexpected.

As she arrived, Lara watched Camille ahead of her climb the stairs into the church. She waited for Camille to unlock the door and then followed her into the cool vestibule. Her job as a program assistant with Camille now paid her rent on the apartment leaving her enough money for other things.

Camille turned to face her. "I've started the plan for the music for our Christmas performance. Have you got anything you'd particularly like to sing, Lara? You'll be our lead soprano this season."

Lara cringed inside at her comment. Would she be in Atlanta for Christmas or would she be returning to New Orleans? She was still undecided and wanted to keep her dilemma from Camille for now so as not to worry her. "You know I always love *The Messiah.* Let's wait and see what else you've found for us when we get together." She hoped her voice expressed some enthusiasm since she couldn't afford to lose her job.

Lara glanced over at Emma and Wally in the rehearsal room, their eyes fixated on each other and hands entwined. How wonderful to see them so in love. She didn't feel any envy. She felt smug today with her own man who would be waiting for her when she reached home. Camille gathered the choir at the piano and Lara settled into the serious business of rehearsal. A spasm grabbed her stomach when she thought about what it would be like to leave the fellowship of this group should she return to her own city. She'd have to learn to do without them. Lara took a deep breath and joined the singing. She refused to think any more about her future right now.

Camille's face broke into a broad smile as she kept time with the music. "You were great. Much better than last time. I think we're ready for the concert on Saturday. Lara, will you need a ride?"

Lara blushed. "No. I'll be taking the bus with a friend."

Emma rushed over to her. Her voice teased as she inquired. "Who is this mysterious friend? Anyone we know?"

Lara ducked her head and responded. "You'll see on Saturday." Then she ran down the stairs and headed for the bus.

* * *

Jerome had fallen into a deep sleep on Lara's bed after she left for practice. He got up around noon and made a sandwich. Between the loss of sleep last night and the gash on his head, he was still lethargic. He stretched out on Lara's old grey velveteen sofa to read a magazine until he heard a key in the door. It had to be Lara.

"I'm back, sweetie. Did you have a good morning while I was out?"

Jerome sat up, dropped the magazine on the floor and reached out his hand for hers. "I only woke up an hour ago. I've been reading this magazine about Atlanta. I didn't know it had such a prosperous business centre. It's so different from Mobile over in Alabama where we stopped for lunch yesterday." He patted the seat beside him. "Come and sit by me."

Lara sat and cuddled up to Jerome while he put his arm around her shoulders. He gave her a light kiss. She pulled him tighter and kissed him passionately on the lips. "I've missed you so much."

Jerome kissed her back and pulled her towards him until she lay on top of him. He covered her face with small kisses. She responded by the motion of her body against his as she gave soft moans. He could feel his body yearn to possess her but held back. She might be fearful of men after her bad experiences of the past. He'd need to go slowly. Reluctantly, she sat up, then stood and offered him a hand.

Her voice was shaky. "I almost forgot, I promised to show you the city this afternoon. Did you have some lunch?

He nodded and took her hand in both of his. "I'd like that. We'll have time to explore more of each other later."

Lara blushed and pulled her hands away. "Let's take our time. You're right about Atlanta. It's a great city with a long black history." She went into the kitchen while he followed behind. She poured two tall glasses of lemonade and they sat at the table.

"Lewis told me we should see the old clapboard houses build in the 1900s in Washington Park."

Lara nodded. "They're great. But, you've got to see the historic Ashby Street Theatre, as well. We can take the bus there this afternoon. Would you like to see it?"

Jerome took a long sip and then responded. "It sounds great. What have you planned for this weekend?" He was surprised to see Lara hold her breath and then look into his eyes.

"Would you like to come to my concert on Saturday? I remember in New Orleans, you said you'd really love to hear me perform." She gave him a questioning look.

He set the drink back on the table and put his hand over hers. "You know I'd like that more than anything. I'm thrilled you invited me. I want to know everything about you." He used two fingers to trace a pattern on her arm, his eyes bright.

He watched her body relax. "It'll be great to have you there." She squeezed his hand. "In the meantime, if we leave right now, we'll just have time for a short tour of the theatre before it closes at four."

He sighed. "Okay. Let's go then."

*   *   *

The two of them strolled down the orderly rows of small bungalows with manicured lawns after leaving the bus. Jerome was thrilled when Lara grabbed his hand and held on like he'd become a part of her.

He squeezed her hand back. "This is the kind of house I would want to live in," he said. "Not some big old mansion like what Phillip's got, decaying around him."

Lara's voice rose and became shrill. "I'd never live at Phillip's ever again. I don't like him or the neighbourhood. He's scary. Anyway, it's mainly wealthy whites live there now and not my people. When the original gentlemen from the Old South moved out, the new rich white folk moved in." When she realized what she'd said, Lara bit her lip and gave a quick glance at Jerome to see how he would react.

Jerome swallowed hard. "Lara, whites aren't all bad. In Jacksonville, we lived side by side with black folks with no problem." He felt tightness radiate from his chest down both arms. "What does this mean for the two of us? Would you ever be able to love me?"

Lara looked guilty. She stopped and pulled him closer while she gave him a deep kiss moving her lips across his. "I'm sorry. I didn't mean us, sweetie. It's Phillip and his kind who bring back bad memories. Besides, you wouldn't want to live in the Garden District would you?"

"I don't know. New Orleans is beginning to feel like home to me. What about out where Henry and Noreen have their place? That could be a nice area when fixed up?" He gave her a long slow kiss back. "I'd live anywhere you picked."

Lara pulled him onto a bench in front of the old post office. She nestled into his arms and placed her head on his shoulder. "It's Henry's been talking to me about Phillip's old mansion. He's now the caretaker until we know what happened to Phillip so he'd like me to live there until he can sell it. They plan to continue to fix up their old place and want to move back permanently.

He ran his hand through her hair. "Phillip could still come back you know. Rumours suggest he's out there somewhere. That old house would be a big responsibility for you, hon. What do you want to do?"

She gave a big sigh. "I don't even want to think about it. Right now my career and my friends are in Atlanta. Except for you, of course, and you're important to me." She rose and reached for his hand. "Let's go see the theatre before it closes."

Jerome read the brochure to her as they stood in front of two old red doors to the theatre, now a museum. It had been a family theatre in the early 1950s, one which showed current films. The ornate canopy had been restored to the original emerald green and brick red. Inside, all the seats had been removed, and the slanting floors were covered in an old navy carpet with the stains from many feet still visible. Each wall had columns with the lights restored to working order. Besides the middle aged man selling tickets in the box office, they saw only one other couple who now stood on the shallow stage.

Lara shook her head. "I can't image this as a real operating theatre. It's so different from Chastain Park where we perform. Live entertainment takes up more space on stage and you would need the change rooms, as well."

"It reminds me of the theatre my dad took me to in Jacksonville when I was seven. That was long before he left us." Sadness came over Jerome and his voice trailed off into silence. He realized he still missed his dad.

Lara grabbed his arm and turned him to face her. "You never told me your mama raised you alone. Did she treat you well? Or was she like my mama?"

Jerome remembered Lara telling him about her mother, Cecily, when they lived in Louisville. She'd talked about the string of short term lovers who came and went and of whom Lara was often afraid.

"He forced a smile. "She loved me and my Grandma and Grandpa helped out. I think she really preferred my younger sister, but she always made sure I had food, clothes and a nice place to live. I guess I was sometimes a challenge for her."

They left the theatre and continued down the street towards the bus stop when a cold wind hit. Once inside the shelter, they huddled close to keep warm.

"I'll be glad to get back to my warm apartment," Lara said. "I can't afford to get a cold before our big event on Saturday."

She looked up at him. "I know you must still be tired with no sleep last night."

"I'm okay." Jerome pulled her closer. "Let's stay in tonight and cook. I like being in your home with you."

They ran up the stairs to the bus as soon as it stopped and settled into a seat. Since it was a week night, the bus wasn't full. Both of them were quiet on the way back. Jerome found having Lara near was all he needed to keep him happy.

They made a dinner of chili and garlic toast together and then Lara excused herself and went to the small den to practice for tomorrow's music program. She encouraged Jerome to lie down on her bed for a nap. He soon fell asleep and only woke when she came into the room to get ready for bed. He offered to get up, but instead she covered him with an extra blanket.

She said, "I'll sleep on the sofa for tonight. It's one of those old fashioned models with lots of room." She smiled while she tucked the blanket around him. "With you here, I'll sleep well with no fears or bad dreams. We can change places tomorrow night."

Chapter Twenty-Four

On Saturday night, when they arrived for the concert, Lara pointed out for Jerome the Chastain Amphitheatre where the choir would perform. They left the bus to stand in from of it and he was impressed by the imposing architectural structure. He could tell Lara was almost overwhelmed with excitement when she spied her group of friends, clustered around their choir master, Camille. Jerome stayed close and watched. In a few minutes, Lara turned back to him while her friends stared at him as if he were a foreigner.

As she saw his expression, Lara hurried back to stand beside him. She was followed by a young woman she introduced as Emma.

"So you're the guy Lara been mooning about." Emma smiled at him. "I'm pleased to meet any friend of Lara's. I hope you'll stay for the concert."

Jerome smiled back. "I can't wait to hear your music."

Emma went back to the group and joined a tall black man with dreadlocks. They continued to laugh and joke as they made their way into the auditorium.

Camille came over to walk with him and Lara. She smiled. "Jerome, I hear you're playing sax in New Orleans. You might be interested to know we have a great Jazz Festival at Emery University every fall." She looked at Lara. "Maybe Lara will invite you."

Jerome nodded. "Sounds good if I can get the time off."

The three of them walked over to the stairs which led into the performers back stage room. Camille pointed out two rows in the front of the auditorium which were nearly full.

"These two are for family and friends of the performers. You're welcome to join them."

He slid into an empty seat. "Okay. I'll have a great view from here."

Lara gave Camille a grateful look. He could see her arms tremble when she turned to leave for back stage to change. Later when the curtain rose with the full group in place, he was stunned by the iridescent lavender gown she wore which caused her black hair to gleam. He'd only seen her in the choir uniform, all navy and white, but this performance was the professional level. He was impressed.

*　*　*

As soon as the curtain rose, Lara felt her anxiety return which caused a worrying tightness in her chest. She could see the auditorium was almost full, with a few last minute stragglers making their way to seats. She was glad she could see family and friends close to the front so she could watch Jerome with his gaze fixed on her. Thrilled, she took a deep breath and thought to herself, *if he believes in me, I know I can do this.*

After the first number, the choir members held their breaths and waited until a round of applause gave them reassurance. The applause rolled on and Lara held up her head in realization their audience appreciated what they heard. When silence returned, the choir fixated on Camille who soon signaled it was time for the next number to start. She heard the opening chord and began to sing; Lara's pitch was good and the choir were in perfect timing and rhythm. The practice had paid off.

After several more numbers, she was thrilled when the audience called for an encore. By the end, she knew by the wave of applause, they were a success. Bubbles of joy tinkled through her throat and chest. The Gilead Baptist Church choir had made it big at the Chastain Theatre. Camille had been right about giving them a mix of blues and gospel music. The choir managed to hold themselves together until they exited the stage. When they reached the dressing room, they tumbled over each other, with both laughter and tears.

Lara grabbed Camille around the waist. "Can you believe it? We really did it. The choir was great."

She could see the pride on Camille's face as she faced the group. "You were all wonderful. I couldn't have asked for better. Now you can get changed and join your families. I know they'll want to congratulate you as well."

More subdued, Camille grasped Emma's hand. "I'm sorry your mother couldn't be here. But, I'll drop by tomorrow to tell her how good you were tonight."

*　　*　　*

Jerome waited just outside the dressing room door for Lara. As soon as he saw her, he pulled her into his arms and showered her with kisses on her face, neck and down to her bare shoulders. He was thrilled to see her blush and shiver in excitement. She grabbed him tight and kissed him back. When she finally broke free, he held her hands in his.

"You were wonderful. Why didn't you tell me you were so good? I'm really glad you shared this concert with me."

Lara's face was flushed. "This was the best concert we've ever given. Just knowing you here helped me to do even better than normal."

They made their way down the front stairs and watched the group climb into cars. She grabbed his hand and looked into his eyes.

"Let's go home and make our own dinner, just the two of us. I don't feel like joining the others tonight."

Later, back in the apartment he held her chair back so she could sit at the table. "Relax. I'll cook tonight. You must be tired from your big day."

Her eyes crinkled. "What can you cook?"

"Do you have any crayfish? I know how to make a great Cajun sauce. I'll throw some rice in a pot and then a green salad is easy."

"I've got all those. After all, I lived in the South just like you."

She went to the fridge and took out the ingredients then returned to her chair, content to watch Jerome. Lara seemed impressed as he chopped the vegetables and mixed the fixings for the sauce, then sautéed the fish. Her eyes sparkled as she teased him.

"You have talents I didn't know about. You can stay for an extra week, if you want."

He waved the spatula at her. "Enough rest. You can set the table. I used to cook for my mother and sister on weekends. My mother's food was so bland, it was a nice change."

Lara jumped up to help him when the rice overflowed the pot on the stove. "I'll deal with the rice. Just put the fish onto our plates."

He tasted the food on his plate and then looked up at Lara. "What do you think of it?"

She smiled at him. "The chilies you added give the sauce a nice zing. It's good."

When he finished his plate, Jerome sat back. "A big bowl of strawberry ice cream would be great. Although I think that's more Florida then deep South."

Lara rummaged through the freezer. "How about chocolate crunch? That's all I have right now."

It'll be just fine." Jerome went to the counter to help her scoop ice cream into two dishes. When their shoulders touched, he smiled into her eyes.

They returned to the table to savour the dessert and then cleaned up the kitchen. After she settled onto the sofa, Lara leaned against Jerome's chest and clicked on the TV. Jerome thought back to the scary scene he'd been through on the road and knew it had been worth it. It felt like he and Lara were already living together. He felt safe and content.

When the movie signed off, he pulled Lara to her feet. She held onto his hand and pulled him toward the bedroom.

"Come on. I don't want to sleep alone tonight."

Jerome stopped at the bedroom door behind her. He put his arm around her waist and kissed the back of her neck. "Are you sure? I don't want to rush you after what you've been through."

Lara leaned back against him. "Yes. I'm sure. I want you with me tonight."

He followed her into the bedroom and they stood by the bed while he unbuttoned her blouse and unhooked her bra. She undid his shirt and pushed it back off his arms. He was thrilled when she pressed her bare breasts against his chest; the touch of her bare skin against his own almost overwhelmed him.

His body was ready when she helped him out of his pants and jockey shorts. She wiggled off her skirt and sat on the bed so he could remove her panties before they crawled under the sheets. Lying side by side, he traced the lines of her body with his fingers. He then stroked her neck, chest and continued down to her flat stomach and the sensitive space between her legs. He watched her face and was glad to see her relaxed and breathing softly. He could feel the tension in his own body build and he pulled her closer and closer.

She responded helping to position him on top of her and then held him as they melded into one rhythmic motion. He'd never felt this ecstasy with anyone else.

They lay pressed together until Jerome tenderly murmured into her ear. "My love. Now I know I can't live without out. We have to find a way to be together."

Lara moved her head onto his shoulder. "We'll work things out. It may take some time before we're together, but there won't be anyone else for me."

Jerome groaned. "I don't want to leave you next week. I don't know if I can."

Lara ran her hand across his chest. "We'll talk about how we'll manage that tomorrow. We need to get some sleep. I want to take you to church to meet some of my friends again. You didn't get to talk to them much as yet."

Jerome kissed her on the lips, rolled over and was soon breathing deeply. He could tell Lara was still restless. Probably reaction from the concert and thinking about what lay ahead for the two of them. The last thing he remembered was patting her shoulder for comfort.

*   *   *

Jerome felt some apprehension as they climbed the church stairs on Sunday. True, he'd met some of her friends from the choir at the concert but he didn't really know anyone. Still he'd sensed some hostility from at least one of the men. As a member of the Senior Choir, Lara was given Sunday off after a concert. It also gave the Junior Choir their chance to be on stage.

As he strolled by her side, Jerome felt comfortable and confident. Lara led him to the middle of the church where he could see a young woman in a blue hat sitting with a tall man dressed in a dark suit. He stood back as Lara greeted her two friends.

"Hi, Emma. Wasn't the concert great? I'm sorry we couldn't join you at the diner last night. We were too tired." She gestured at him. "Do you remember my friend Jerome?"

Emma gave him a big smile. "Hi. I'd like you to meet Wally."

He extended his hand to the tall man whom she'd introduced but Wally ignored it.

Embarrassed, Emma took Jerome's hand in hers and gave it a light squeeze.

"Welcome to Atlanta."

When she turned back to face front, he saw her poke Wally in the ribs with her elbow. Then she smiled back at Lara.

"Why don't you join us?"

Wally forced a grimace at Lara and made room for them to pass. Since the program was about to start, they sat quietly and waited for the pastor to enter and take his place at the pulpit.

Lara glanced over at him but he couldn't smile. He'd experienced this racial intolerance a few other times in Florida but didn't know what the issue was in Atlanta. She clasped his hand and he loosened up enough to smile at her.

He hoped she wouldn't follow through in invited the couple for lunch. When the service was over, they followed Emma and Wally out of the church. Lara touched Emma's arm. "I'll sit with your mother next Saturday, Emma. You and Wally need some time together."

Emma's face broke into a huge smile. "It would be great to get away. Then Wally and I can meet with the pastor to discuss our wedding plans for next June. You're welcome to bring Jerome with you."

Wally's face clouded over and he scowled at Lara. "I know you've been a good friend to Emma." He pointed at Jerome. "But, he's a stranger here." The silence stretched out. "I guess, it's up to her who she invites to her house right now."

He watched Lara's face redden. "Forget about it, Emma. Jerome has to return to his band in New Orleans tomorrow morning. At least he's treated well in New Orleans."

She turned and they walked away. During the bus ride home, the two of them held hands in silence until she blurted out.

"I'm sorry about Wally's rude behaviour. He has a problem with mixed race couples."

Jerome nodded. "He caught me by surprize. I sure wish you were going back to Orleans with me tomorrow. Everything could be so wonderful for us there. Black and white couples are part of the scene."

After he blinked his eyes a few times, he pulled her closer. "I hate to leave you here."

Lara leaned her head on his shoulder. "I know how you feel. But, I've got a big Christmas concert to organize. Besides, the doctor says Emma's mother is unlikely to live past Christmas. I need to be here for her."

Jerome felt his face pulled into a tight mask as he struggled with his emotions. "But, tell me you will come back. I'm not losing you."

"Yes. I'll be there for Mardi Gras in February. I promise. Noreen and Henry will be back in their house by then and we can spend the week together."

Jerome helped her off the bus at her stop and they picked up food at a nearby take-out. When they walked back to the apartment, their arms entwined while he carried the bag of food. They spent the afternoon listening to classical jazz on the DVD player and avoided any mention about his trip.

Lara sat nuzzled into his shoulder. "It's your last night here with me. Let's be happy we have each other."

Jerome gave her a slow kiss on the lips for a response. He continued the kiss with his tongue darting between her open lips. "I love you and I'll wait for you, no matter how long it takes."

Once more Lara welcomed him into her bed. After they made love, he found himself lying awake. Although he'd had other girlfriends, Lara was different. He could tell this was a new experience for her. She'd lean on one elbow and watch him breathing when he started to doze. He loved to feel her hand on his stomach and the skin of his chest. He realized what kept him awake was knowing he wouldn't have another night with her for a long time. Was he doing the right thing going back to New Orleans? He rolled over once more. He knew he couldn't leave Lewis short one player for any longer or he'd lose this opportunity. He'd have to go back.

He awoke at the first light of dawn. It was funny how it happened when he had to travel. Even when he didn't get much sleep, he'd wake very alert. Lara came into the room dressed in her same plain navy skirt and white blouse. She'd have to go to choir practice again as soon as his bus left.

"Come on. Time to get up." She pulled the pillow out from behind his head. "I'll make you a good breakfast before you set out on your trip."

When he'd finished dressing and went to the kitchen, she took hot muffins out of the oven. He went over to help me carry food to the table.

"You could have called me earlier. I'd have been more help with breakfast." He kissed her on the cheek and took the plate of muffins from her.

"I liked to watch you sleep. You're so cute with your mouth partly open." She teased. "The coffee is ready and I'm about to start the fried eggs and bacon. You can get strawberries out of the fridge for us and put them into those blue and white bowls with some yoghurt."

She turned back from the frying pan on the stove. "What time does your bus leave?"

Jerome set the bowls on the table and pulled the ticket out of his pocket. "At nine. The bus depot isn't too far."

"Good. I'll be able to see you off before I have to get to practice. Do you want to take a lunch with you?"

"No. The bus will stop somewhere at a diner and it gives me a chance to get off and walk around. Thanks for lending me some money. I'll send it back as soon as I get home."

After breakfast, Jerome helped her clean up. "Your cooking is as good as your aunt's." He held her against his chest and kissed the top of her head.

She had turned to hold him close and sighed. When she finally broke away, she had tears in her eyes. "We'd better leave now before it's too late." She took her straw handbag from the closet beside the door and waited for him to get his back pack from the bedroom.

When they stepped into the hall, it was empty. It was too early for most people to leave for work. He slung the pack over his shoulder while they walked to the elevator. When they left the building, they headed into bright sunlight for their walk to the depot.

The bus terminal was noisy and with the crowd milling in confusion. The two of them stood with their arms around each other as if no one else was there. When the loudspeaker called out New Orleans for the third time, Jerome gave Lara a passionate kiss and forced himself to pull away. "I guess this is it. I have to return to Lewis and the band. You promise I'll see you for the Mardi Gras?"

Lara clutched his hand as he moved toward the bus. "Yes. I'll be there. I'll phone you. And you can call me from the hotel." She struggled with tears. "Please tell Noreen and Henry I'm well."

"I'll do that for you." When Jerome turned back to her, he could feel his eyes sting. "Don't forget about me."

The door of the bus was beginning to close when he reached it. He had to knock to get it open and jumped on seconds before the bus left the terminal.

He could see Lara out the window, frozen where she had stood. He watched as she stood there with one hand still waving. He knew she would miss him but would she miss New Orleans?

He turned back to face the road ahead as he acknowledged to himself, he needed to establish his music career just as Lara was doing with hers. He smiled. Life was good. He now had two precious loves, Lara and his saxophone.

Chapter Twenty-Five

From the bus depot, Jerome travelled through downtown Atlanta with the bus picking up passengers at several hotels. The skyscrapers throughout the banking centre and business core where a surprize to him. He'd arrived in town by foot and Lara lived near the outskirts so hadn't seen this with his own eyes, only read about it. Atlanta was surely one of the new financial centres in the South. At least the distraction had eased his pain for a time from being forced to leave his sweetheart behind.

According to Camille, Atlanta also had one of the most successful jazz festivals in the South, but those things only lasted one or two weeks per year. The big jazz scenes were still in New Orleans and Boston. He'd need something more permanent to support a wife. He felt all warm inside as he thought about starting his own family. Still, Lara's success here in Atlanta was more than he had ever imagined. He'd also realized she was more relaxed this week than she had been their whole time in New Orleans. Could he persuade her to return?

He'd left his saxophone back in the hotel bus for safety, but it meant he hadn't practiced in a week and the band played tonight. Jerome jerked upright in his seat. God, don't let there be any more mishaps with the bus. He expected to arrive in the city at six and they went on at nine.

He shifted the seat back and dozed off to the hum of the motor. He was surprised when he awoke to find over two hours had passed. Out the window, he could make out fields of black soil furrowed with rows of cotton and peanuts. This part of Georgia was much more prosperous than Montgomery.

The driver called out the lunch stop in Opelika, just east of a resort area of lakes and cottages he'd seen on his map. He followed the stream of passengers as they headed for a small fifties-style diner. Every time the door opened to let in a group of passengers, the bell over the door tinkled. He took a seat with several others at a chrome table with red vinyl chairs. Jerome glanced at the menu and choose fish and chips which were said to be local and fresh. When it arrived, he frowned. The battered fish and soggy chips looked like they came right out of a box in the freezer. Since he was hungry, he devoured most of it in short order.

The other guys in his group said they were from either Montgomery or Pensacola. They'd moved to Atlanta to get work. One was selling industrial products and the other sold water purifiers. With their four days off, they were headed home to visit family. Jerome didn't envy them. As a musician, he'd done his share of travelling with bands. He and Lara would want to settle somewhere where they could both work in the same city.

*   *   *

Lara could hardly believe Jerome was on his way back to New Orleans. She wouldn't see him now until February. Where had the week gone? She looked around her apartment. With its sunny kitchen window and cozy living room, it normally kept her satisfied. Now it felt empty. Jerome had promised to call her every night before he went on stage. The phone service had become more reliable over the past few weeks. She stared at the phone jarred by its loud ring. No. It couldn't be Jerome already. Her clock said it was almost two still much too early for him to have arrived. She picked up the receiver.

"Hello. Oh, Camille, it's you." She relaxed and sat down on the sofa with her back leaned against the arm. "I know I promised to give you an answer today. I'd love to help you co-ordinate the Christmas concert this year. It fits in well with my job anyway." Besides, she could use some extra money for the holiday season.

"Great. I was hoping you would agree," said Camille. "Why don't you come to my place around seven this evening and we'll get a start?"

Why not? With Jerome gone she had nothing else to do anyway. "I'll be there. Do you still have copies of last year's program? We can start with those."

"I'll get them out. Considering what Emma is going through with her mother, I thought we could give her a special solo this year."

"We need something to cheer her up. Maybe *The Messiah* would work. She thought to herself that was the one she hoped to sing but Emma needed it more. Camille was so generous in acknowledging her choir members' families circumstances.

"I agree with you."

"I know she'll love it. Emma has been very supportive since I took over as lead soprano. She's never jealous or petty. It'll be good for her to have some recognition."

"Okay. See you around seven."

Lara set the phone down. Good. Emma would earn some extra money from her performance. Lara had already planned to save hers for the trip to Mardi Gras in February.

Lara now found it hard to sit at the kitchen table alone to eat her dinner. What was wrong with her? She'd been perfectly happy to live alone but now she missed Jerome. His silly jokes and sudden grins. She filled the dishwasher and looked at the clock. It was already six thirty. Camille lived in a suburban neighbourhood, not far away so Lara decided to walk. The fresh air might revive her spirits. Before long, she turned up the paved driveway and had a smile on her face when Camille opened the door and embraced her.

"Come on in. Have you had your dinner? We've got lots of leftovers."

Lara replied. "I had leftover chicken paella. It tasted good."

Camille turned toward the tall man with grey wiry hair wearing denim pants who stood beside her. "Have you met my husband, Owen?"

Lara grasped his hand. "Of course. I see him in the audience at most of our concerts." She laughed.

Camille led her into a small den and gestured for her to sit in the large leather chair. Lara admired the flowered oriental carpet which highlighted the dark hardwood floor. Camille sat across from her on the adjoining loveseat. The glass coffee table in front of them was covered with sheet music and old concert programs.

"Let's get started. The organizers want the program by the end of next week so they can begin the printing and advertising. This concert has been one of their best money-makers so far."

For the next hour, Lara was engrossed in the pros and cons of traditional carols as opposed to new favorites. Fully involved in the discussion with Camille, her face felt hot with excitement. She was happy for her friend, Emma. Even her boyfriend, Wally, would be pleased.

At eight o'clock, they'd made good progress. She stood up and advised Camille she needed to get home early. Jerome promised to call her at nine before he went on to let her know he'd arrived back safely. She couldn't afford to miss him. She took the bus back to make sure she'd get there in time. While stretched out on her sofa, she flipped through a magazine, and stared at the phone willing it to ring. What if something had happened to Jerome again? After all, his trip out here was a challenge he hadn't anticipated.

As soon as it rang, she grabbed the receiver. "Jerome."

"Hi, beautiful."

"It's so good to hear your voice. So, you're safely back at the hotel?"

"Yeah. The trip back was great and I arrived at the depot right at six as I'd planned. Lewis was glad to have me back. In fact, he's signaling for me to go on as we speak."

Lara wiped away a tear. "I haven't even heard you play. When I'm visiting for Mardi Gras, I must hear your band. You promise?"

He chuckled. "Of course. I'd love for you to hear me. We're not a brand name as yet, but the audience likes us."

She could hear the modesty in his voice. Unusual for him. "I don't know why I didn't listen to you play while I had the chance. There was so much happening with my family with Noreen being kidnapped."

"The streets seem much safer around here at night now. Even the tourists have started to return. But, the hotel has increased security just in case."

"Good. I want to know you're safe." Lara felt the silence. "I miss you. My apartment feels so empty."

Jerome sighed. "I know it'll be a long three months, but we both have something to look forward to after Christmas. In the meantime, I need to show Lewis how good I can play." Another silence stretched like a heavy fog. "They are calling me to the stage. I've got to go. I love you, honey. I'll play to you the whole night."

*　　*　　*

When choir practice ended on Wednesday night, Emma ran up to Lara and grabbed her hand. "You've got to come to the diner with Wally and me tonight. Please, say you will this time."

Lately, Lara had been reluctant to join them. When Jerome was here, she'd stopped seeing the group. And she was aware Wally preferred to have Emma to himself.

197

"It's not the same as when you and I went out together. We'd blurt out stuff about each other and have some good laughs. I don't feel the same when Wally's with you."

"He does like you, Lara. I know he does." Emma turned to greet Wally who had just joined them. "You want her to come with us. Don't you?"

Wally nodded his head without much enthusiasm. But his smile seemed genuine. Lara hesitated and then decided she'd do it for Emma. She followed them out the church door and down the sidewalk. When they were all seated in the familiar diner, Lara relaxed. The red vinyl booths reminded her of old times being here with the other singers.

Wally brought them each a chocolate sundae from the counter, their favorite dish. She savoured the sweet sticky taste, as she rolled it around on her tongue. Lara glanced up and noticed Wally's expression had turned serious.

"Lara, we wanted to get you by yourself to talk about our concerns for you. Your white boyfriend will only cause you hurt in time. I've seen it many times before with other attractive black women."

Lara glared at Emma. Emma looked down into her lap, frowned and fidgeted with her napkin.

Wally raised his deep voice even higher. "What I'm saying is, we don't want you to get rejected. White boys are attracted to our black sisters, especially ones as beautiful as you are. But once they get what they want, they leave her behind."

Lara jumped to her feet. This wasn't what she expected to hear from friends. "Jerome isn't like that. We were friends since he moved to New Orleans and he helped me when my aunt and uncle were threatened. He loves me and has begged me to move back to the city."

Wally spoke slowly as he bit out each word. "It was the same with my sister Josie. Her boyfriend stayed around for the whole summer and then went off to college in New Jersey. She hasn't heard from him since. Every time I see her she's crying. We just don't want it to happen to you."

Lara moved to stand beside Emma. "Do you believe him? Is this what you think about Jerome and me?" Lara's hands clenched and her lips trembled.

Emma stood up and put her arm around Lara. "You know him best. Just be careful, is all. We didn't expect it to happen to Josie either."

Lara broke away from her. "I just talked to Jerome two nights ago. He's got no plans to leave me. I can tell." She began to walk away. "I'm going home now, Emma. I'll see you when I come over to sit with your mother on Sunday and we can talk. This is the first time, I've felt betrayed by you, my best friend."

As she dragged her feet and stared at the ground on the walk back from the diner, Lara could hear Wally's voice in her head. *White men aren't to be trusted around black women. They're attracted, but they don't stay. Don't trust them.*

Back home, she curled up on the sofa with a blanket over her knees, but in her head she heard the same conversation, over and over. *Once they get what they want, they leave.*

But she knew Jerome wasn't like that. He was her friend. Then she'd remembered his talk about an ex-girlfriend in Jacksonville who was black. What had happened to her? Why hadn't she thought to ask him? Noreen and Henry had accepted and trusted him. They would never want to see Lara hurt. Henry would have warned her if he heard any rumors about him. And Henry was at the Royal George often.

Mixed race couples were quite common in New Orleans. She hadn't really thought about it as an issue. But, they had met at the hotel. Their attraction had been music at first. Lara wished desperately she could call him. She knew he'd still be on stage. Tomorrow wouldn't work since he couldn't afford a cell phone. He'd promised to call her again on Thursday night. It seemed like forever, but she'd have to wait.

She avoided going to bed as long as she could. His familiar scent would make her sad. Lara turned off the lamp on the table beside her, pulled the blanket over her and made the decision to sleep on the sofa where she lay.

Chapter Twenty-Six

The sky had taken on an indigo hue. Wind whipped the rain against the kitchen window, as Lara rinsed the last of the dishes from dinner. She mused about what Jerome was doing back at the Royal George. He was probably still in the tour bus getting dressed since he usually called her around nine before he went on stage. She'd have to wait another hour with her anxiety building. Camille counted on her to pull together the final arrangements for their concert in two weeks, but she couldn't concentrate. Why had she let Wally's dire comments get to her when she had no reason to doubt Jerome?

She shrugged her shoulders in an effort to clear her head. She might as well go over those articles from their last concert to see where they could improve. Most of the reviews had been complimentary, but Thomas Swan from *The Post* had described them as overly sentimental. Lara bent over her notes spread out on the kitchen table and continued to make changes while she nodded her head to the music on the radio. She held her breath when she heard the phone ring. It must be Jerome. She stared at it and waited until it had rung three times before she picked it up.

Jerome's voice was full of longing. "Lara, it's a beautiful warm night here in the city and I wish I had you in my arms right now."

Lara let out her breath and blinked away quick tears. She pushed down the queasy twinge which had built in her stomach. "I miss you too, honey."

"What have you been up to?"

His voice sounded so normal. She relaxed. "I've been at work on our next concert. We've been getting good press from the last one."

"That's good. With Lewis as band leader, we're moving up in the ratings as well. He pushed me to play better and better than I ever had before."

She could hear the pride in his voice. "That's great."

"We go on in a few minutes and I get the first solo."

Lara forgot her earlier apprehension. She felt pleasure in Jerome's success. "I'm still worried about our Christmas concert, but after it, I'll take a break."

"Don't forget about the Mardi Gras. I'm counting on you in person here to join me for it."

"I'll be there for sure." She felt her lips relax. "I'll be able to stay with my aunt and uncle. They'll be back in their own home by then."

"Yes, I know. I promised to help them move just before Christmas. They're planning to take some of the bedroom furniture from Phillip's place since all of theirs was ruined but they'll have to buy the rest."

Lara moved onto the sofa with the phone. "Yeah. Phillip's mansion is still vacant and Henry told me I could stay there if I wanted. But it gives me the creeps."

"We'll talk about it later. I've got to go. I wouldn't want to miss my solo. Lewis has hired this Spanish chic, Jacqueline, a singer from Mississippi and she's something. I don't want to let her upstage me. Bye for now, hon."

"Good luck and goodnight sweetie." The line went dead in her hand. Lara felt the heaviness fill her chest once more. Who was Jacqueline and what was she to Jerome? He seemed to be in quite a hurry to get away. Lara shook her head as if to clear it. I must stop this. Jerome has his career to think about, just like I do. It's all the lies Wally put in my head.

*   *   *

With their success from the last few concerts fresh in their minds, the excitement in preforming at the Chastain had died down for most of them. However, when the curtain opened on a full house on Thursday night in early December, Lara had nervous flutters in her stomach and an ache in her throat. She managed to smile at Emma who stood next to her.

With her mother in the hospital and her condition deteriorating, Emma hadn't known until yesterday whether or not she would make the concert. They had agreed to remain best friends and not to let Wally come between them. Lara relaxed and for the next two hours she focused totally on her own performance. Camille had told Lara, she counted on tonight's performance to be a success and it meant a lot to her. She'd been telling everyone how greatly Lara's musical talent had soared in the past two months and Lara didn't want to disappoint her mentor.

While the choir waited for the applause to die, Lara glanced around the auditorium. The festive décor was more subdued than what she'd been used to in New Orleans. She could see pots of red and white poinsettias set on the four pillars at the sides of the stage each of them tied with white bows. Wreaths of holly and cedar had been tied to the front of the stage. Overall, it gave a quiet sense of celebration.

She remembered what her last Christmas in New Orleans had been like. She'd watched the marching bands in the parade dressed in blue satin followed by a float full of women in full length gold and silver gowns trimmed in white frills and lace. They sat on ornate chairs, surrounded by gold trinkets and stars. Afterwards she'd gone to a local diner with Henry and Noreen, and devoured a festive buffet with piles of seafood; crayfish and other types of shellfish. When she thought back to those times, she missed the spirited crowds of the *Big Easy.*

Her heart filled with gratitude when the concert ended and the crowd stood to give them an ovation. Afterwards, she followed the choir to the dressing room where she embraced Emma and several other girls. She even shook hands with Wally to show she held no hard feelings. Friends were important to her. When the group began to disperse, Camille approached her and took both hands in her warm ones.

"We couldn't have succeeded like we have tonight without you. Do you know how good you are? Not just the solos, but your talent comes out in all the arrangements."

"Music is something I love and I need to have it as part of my life." Lara looked closely at Camille to see how she would react to the next statement. "It could be here or wherever I decide to live my life."

Camille's face drew closed. "Surely, Lara, you wouldn't think of leaving Atlanta. This city needs you. Your music can continue to grow bigger and better in this place." She squeezed Lara's hands.

Fatigue fell over Lara in waves and she withdrew her hands. "I'm not going anywhere right now, except home. We'll see each other on Sunday at the service and can talk more then."

On the long bus ride home, Lara mulled over her dilemma. Her success in Atlanta was far beyond what she had expected. Lara had to admit her talent had expanded under Camille. She was an excellent coach. On the other hand, she loved the spirit and heart of New Orleans even with its menaces. Lara sighed. She had to be honest with herself. She wanted Jerome, but wasn't sure where he would be in her future. As she opened the door to her apartment, she was still deep in thought until she heard the phone.

Jerome's voice brimmed over with excitement. "Congratulations, Lara, honey. I saw a news clip on our TV at the hotel about what a success your concert had been. You're a celebrity."

Lara laughed. "I didn't expect to hear from you this early. Yes, the concert was great. I'm really exhausted, but it's good to hear your voice." She hesitated. "I miss you."

He sounded subdued. "I know what you mean. It's something about the season with families celebrating all around you. I want to have my love close to me. I wish I could hold you and kiss you right now."

Lara blinked back her tears. This was the Jerome she had fallen for. "It seems so long until February. But it's good to have the Mardi Gras to plan towards."

Jerome sounded brighter. "You're right. And we both have lots of performances before Christmas. Let's talk more often. It makes the waiting less painful for me."

*   *   *

This time the sharp ringing of the phone broke into Lara's deep sleep. She pulled herself up in bed. Her alarm clock showed it was just past midnight. She stumbled into the living room to pick up the receiver. It couldn't be Jerome. She had talked to him a few hours ago. She sat down heavily on the sofa. "Hello. Oh, it's you Emma. Is everything alright?"

She heard the panic in Emma's voice. "I'm just leaving for St. Paul's Hospital. The nurse phoned to say my mother won't likely make it through the night. Can you come Lara? I'm really scared to be alone."

"Yes. Of course. What about Wally? Will he join us there?"

Emma sobbed. "He's working the night shift this week for that security company. It would have to happen now. I need you."

"I'll be there. It'll take me about half an hour to dress and get the streetcar to the hospital. Tell your mother for me, God is with her." Lara replaced the receiver and walked into her bathroom. She splashed warm soapy water onto her face, dried it and hurried back into the bedroom to pull on jeans and a sweater. No time for a shower this morning.

*   *   *

The bus was nearly empty with a few nurses in uniform and groggy-eyed students probably coming home from an all-night study session at the college. Lara took deep breaths to calm herself as she thought about Emma's mother. She'd gotten to know her better through the Sundays with just the two of them. Mrs. Reid had been involved in the black civil rights movement in Atlanta in her youth. She'd been in many of the marches. Lara was impressed.

Right up to the time she got sick, Emma's mother volunteered with *Turning Point,* the museum exhibition based on the American civil war where the key issue had been slavery. Oh, God. Sudden panic hit her. Mrs. Reid didn't have long to live.

Lara followed two nurses off the bus and down the street to the hospital. She walked down long corridors full of pale green walls which left her cold. At the front desk, she gave Mrs. Reid's name and was directed to go to Room 401. She continued down the hall to the elevator and rode up to the fourth floor. When she reached the door of Room 401, it was closed. Lara pushed it open and found Emma siting on a chair by her mother's bed. She had leaned across the bed, to hold her mother's hand. Mrs. Reid lay very still with eyes closed.

Emma glanced up at her when Lara reached the bed. Her face was peaceful. "I'm grateful you were able to come. She's gone over to God now. The Reverend just left us."

"It's for the best, Emma." Lara put her arms around Emma's shoulders to give her a hug. "She's suffered with so much pain these last few months."

Emma let the tears flow freely down her face. "I had so hoped she might be here for my wedding this summer."

Lara sat down on the end of the bed next to Emma. "She'll be with you in spirit. And you'll have wonderful memories."

Emma touched Lara's arm. "I told Reverend Joseph the memorial service for her should be quick. It's so close to Christmas season with its special programs and we don't have much family. He said he would make the arrangement with me as soon as I'm able."

Lara smiled at Emma and bit her lip. "I'll help you with that. Your mother's friends from the Gilead community will want to be there. You know they'll all bring their own special food for the reception afterwards."

*　　*　　*

Wally stood next to Emma at the funeral service at the Gilead Church several days later and greeted the guests with her. He was good at knowing what to say to each of them in turn to make them feel comfortable. Lara stood at Emma's other side, nodded and acknowledged people she knew from church services. They were such a close community and she had been privileged to be welcomed into their circle when she arrived in Atlanta. She had established strong roots here.

When the crowds dispersed to the parking lot, Lara said goodbye to Emma and decided to walk to the bus stop alone. Sudden tears flowed freely down her cheeks. Emma would miss her mother. They'd had such a great relationship and shared everything.

Lara cringed. What about her own mother? Her only memories of Cecily where back when Lara was a frightened child, with her Mama standing over her. Cecily's face was crimson and her screams of rage pierced the room.

Chapter Twenty-Seven

The Christmas season had passed for Lara in a happy confusion of concerts and choir performances at the church, especially the two Christmas Eve masses. Camille had been very pleased with her performance and had encouraged her to stay on in the solo role with the choir. Even Wally seemed to have warmed towards her, except when the subject of Jerome came up. Lara had come to understand his behaviour a least a little. His mother, like Emma's, had been part of the American civil rights movement in Atlanta.

Lara worried about the brief phone calls from Jerome over the past two weeks. His band was playing every night and Lewis had come to rely on his solo pieces, but she missed him. Besides, a small suspicion had grown in her mind about the new singer Lewis had hired; Jacqueline, was her name. The shift in Jerome's voice worried her when he talked about Jacqueline, and it was enough to add tension.

*　　*　　*

Jerome knew it was time to get in touch with Lara again tonight. He had to admit to himself his phone calls to her had been short and vague lately. He'd used the excuse about his tight schedule and the practice hours needed for his new solo pieces. But, he knew it wasn't the real reason. Jacqueline, their new singer, was taking more and more of his time. With her dusty brown skin and deep black eyes, he found their attraction had deepened. He enjoyed the fun when she challenged him with her music.

Like last night, when he was tuning up with the rest of the group, she continued to grab his arm.

"Come on, Jerome. Play your new number for me once more so I can experiment with it. The guys are used to harmonizing with you. They don't need you like I do."

Jerome glanced over at Lewis and watched him stare at the two of them. He shook his head at Jerome. With the band due on in five minutes, he'd have to postpone the call to Lara until tomorrow once more.

The remainder of the week, the band played without Jacqueline. Jerome was comfortable back in his old routine with the guys. Lewis patted him on the back after several performances, happy with his progress with the new music. On Friday, after a quick breakfast in the hotel, he remembered his promise to pick up Jacqueline from the airport. She'd been in Mississippi to see her sister who was ill. Lewis had agreed it was important for him to fetch her to make sure she was on stage on time tonight.

Jerome scanned the group which surged through the arrivals gate as he searched for Jacqueline. Had she caught her flight back? When she last called him, she and her brother were stuck in heavy traffic. He felt a strong sense of relief when he spied her mop of wavy black hair. He smiled and she came up to him. His gaze settled on her pixie face, with her dark brown eyes and red lips. She wore skin tight jeans and a slinky stripped top. On Jacqueline, it looked exotic with her bronze skin and deep cleavage. He could tell he wasn't the only one who'd noticed. Jerome stepped towards her just as she turned and grabbed his hand.

"It's so good of you to pick me up, Jerome." Jacqueline smiled up at him, blinking her long eyelashes. "I'd never make it to the hotel in time by taxi. They're so unreliable right now."

Jerome steered her away from the crowd and made a path for them to Lewis's Nissan. He loved the way she fussed over him. Besides, he enjoyed her company, especially during the long periods between sets.

"No problem. But, we'll need to hurry. We don't have much time."

Jacqueline turned towards him, her palms stretched out to illustrate her point. "I just had to comfort my sister after what her husband did to her. He's got a girlfriend, but still wants Suzie to let him live at the house with her and the kids." She grimaced. "I told her, no way."

Jerome kept his concentration on the traffic. "Sounds like she has problems."

"He's a bum. Suzie's got a job at the bank and brings home good money. That's all he's interested in."

His groin tightened when he felt the touch of her slender hand brush his thigh.

"He works when he feels like it as a bartender. I'm sure it's just for the booze." Her eyes smoldered as she looked right at him. "I want a guy who I can trust. Someone who works with me side by side."

Feeling hot and flustered, Jerome maneuvered the car into the small parking space for staff behind the hotel. He hurried to open the door for her and then handed her the case from the trunk.

"Thank god you've got time to change into your stage clothes before we go on. Hurry up. Lewis will be steaming."

When the two of them arrived back at the hotel, Lewis was waiting just inside the door, as he clenched and unclenched both hands in an agitated gesture. He told Jacqueline to get changed and pulled Jerome aside.

"Lara called me a few minutes ago looking for you. Where you supposed to call her? She seemed very disappointed and upset."

Jerome shifted from one feet to the other. "I hope you didn't tell her where I was?"

Lewis shrugged. "Well, yes I did. There wasn't anything wrong with that, was there"? I didn't know you've been forgetting to call her?"

Jerome felt guilt wash over him. "I guess I've been too busy. I promise to call her tonight during our break. I don't want her to worry." He glanced over at the door Jacqueline had entered which was now closed.

"Okay, I don't like women trouble with my boys. But right now, you better join the guys for some last minute practice."

Jerome nodded and left Lewis. He hoped Lewis realized there wasn't anything serious between Jerome and Jacqueline. She was fun to have around. It was her who was always seeking out things for them to do together.

Minutes later on stage, he swayed to the sweet music of his saxophone, lost in his own world. He looked over at Jacqueline, front and centre, dressed in her black and silver sequined dress, microphone in hand, belting out the words to her song. The band was good and he knew Jacqueline's presence had built up the audience. Surely Lara would understand. His connection to Jacqueline was through music and not personal.

After their last set, Jerome was surprised when Lewis gestured for him to come over to the bar alone. Was he still angry about Lara?

Lewis ordered two rum and cokes and set one in front of him. "I'm really pleased with your progress. From last September to now, it's amazing the difference."

Jerome took a sip. "Thanks for noticing. I've practiced hard and I like the new stuff." He watched as Lewis's smile faded and his lips tightened.

"I got a warning for you which I hope you'll take seriously. I been hearing from my boys that Phillip's been seen hanging around the Carousel Bar in Hotel Monteleone. You need to watch out for him downtown since he's still got a grudge against you. He's more dangerous than before. People keep away from him."

Jerome nodded. "I've got no desire to meet up with him."

"Don't tell Henry about Phillip being around. It's best for Henry if the two don't connect. Word has it he's selling drugs again and living with a friend but I didn't hear where."

Jerome nodded his head. "I've stayed away from the Garden District since he disappeared, just in case. He was always so unpredictable."

"I hear it's not where he's living right now. He's too scared the Marrotta boys will pick him up from the old address. The police are looking for him there as well."

*   *   *

After her talk with Lewis, Lara slammed the phone into its cradle and paced back and forth across her small living room. Could he have gone to Mississippi with Jacqueline? A quiet few days, with the two of them. Time to get acquainted. She bit her lower lip in frustration. Maybe Wally was right all along. I shouldn't have trusted Jerome. Lara kicked the sofa leg as she passed it. What to do? She needed Jerome. I don't want to live without him now. How could he do this to me?

After a while, the anger subsided and she wiped the wetness off her face with a tissue. Maybe she was being unreasonable to decide Jerome had cheated on her without hearing it from him. It was her talk with Wally which was making her suspicious. She'd wait until tomorrow to hear what he had to say for himself.

*   *   *

When the applause had died, Jerome disengaged from the band and settled into a corner at the end of the bar near the phone.

Nervousness tickled through his chest before he rang Lara's number. Was he being foolish to worry? She answered on the first ring.

"Hello." Her voice was formal.

"Lara, it's me. Jerome."

There was a short pause. "I'm really glad to hear from you. I've tried several times, but you were never available." Her voice trailed off at the end.

Jerome pushed his back against the wall and twisted both feet into the rungs of the bar stool.

"I know. Lewis told me. He's asked us to work on a new repertoire. Me and the new soloist. It's part of our new contract with the bar to bring in a larger audience."

Lara paused. "I've been hearing about Jacqueline from Lewis. You two seem pretty close." Her silence dragged.

Jerome moved forward to shield the phone with his other hand. "Now, don't get the wrong idea about her, Lara. I've helped her out a few times like Lewis asked me to." Damn. He sounded defensive, even to himself.

"I need to hear from you more often, is all, Jerome."

Pangs of guilt stabbed through his chest as he heard her wistful response.

"We'll be together for Mardi Gras. That's only a month away, baby. I haven't forgotten you're mine." He turned to see Lewis's frantic signal to him. "I've got to go now, Lara. Lewis has given the five minute cue. I'll call you again soon. I promise."

Lara's voice sounded more high pitched than normal. "Don't forget to call me this time. And I want to meet this Jacqueline when I'm in town in February."

Jerome winced. "Bye, love. I'll miss you." He dropped the receiver and sprinted onto the stage and grabbed the sax from its stand. It took a few minutes to settle his nerves, before he could begin to play. Before long, he was concentrating totally on the haunting sound of his saxophone.

*   *   *

Lara stood in the bathroom and stared at herself in the mirror. In keeping with the current style, her hair was now shorter and straightened. She kept it in place with two combs which highlighted her dark complexion. Her normally happy eyes were now downcast and dull. What was she doing to herself with all this worry? Jerome fell in love with her as she was then. Why would he want someone else right now?

But, then why not? How well did she know him anyway? It had been a rapid romance. She remembered what Wally said about men. They're attracted to the woman who's there in front of them, but their attention span is often short. She really knew nothing about this Jacqueline.

What could she do to find out? In the mirror, she could see the determination return to her eyes. When she went back for Mardi Gras, Lara decided to surprize Jerome by arriving at his performance unannounced. She straightened her shoulders. It was the only way she'd see for herself what was going on between him and Jacqueline.

With this plan in her mind, she was able to return to the living room to work on some new concert programs. She'd need the extra money to splurge on a couple of dramatic outfits for the trip back to New Orleans. After all. Marci Gras was all about celebration. She had to look her best.

Chapter Twenty-Eight

Jerome had meant to tell Lara the rumour he'd heard about Phillip being around, but decided it wasn't the right time. He'd decided to wait until they were face to face and besides, she'd probably have to tell Henry which would only complicate their lives. He'd see Noreen and Henry when he went over to help him replace the back steps tomorrow night. Although the house still needed some fixing, the last few times he'd accepted their invitations to dinner, they seemed very pleased with their renovations.

In the last few weeks before they moved back in, he'd been over to help with some finishing touches. He'd stayed late to finish painting the small living room. The sea green paint they'd chosen was just right and he was sure Noreen would be thrilled. He felt a kind of sadness when he finished. He'd set down his paint brush and wiped the sweat off his forehead while he gazed around. His job was almost over so he should be happy. After all, there was something very satisfying about seeing the finished product. Now he could use the extra time to catch up on his practice.

On the bus ride over to Lakeview, he thought again about the information Lewis had confided to him about Phillip. It had been so peaceful for all of them with him gone or at least out of their way. What had Lewis meant by Phillip being more dangerous than ever? As he walked down the short blocks to the Devries' house, the improvements in the neighbourhood although small were noticeable. The worst of the debris had been cleaned from most yards and lay in a pile on one of the vacant lots. Still, he could see many vacant properties, some with *For Sale* signs and others just boarded up. Obviously, many of the evacuees had not returned.

Henry opened the door at his knock, and smiled with genuine pleasure. "Jerome, you never forget about us old folks."

"Who else is going to help build that new set of stairs with you?"

Within a few minutes, Noreen joined them. "I'm glad I got another mouth to feed for dinner. Come on in and drink a little lemonade before you two get started."

Even though he hadn't felt thirsty, the lemonade went down easy. He realized with surprise it felt like home when he visited Lara's aunt and uncle. He followed Henry into the back yard which hadn't changed much from the time they started work here full time. Henry had pencilled out a design of the steps and taped it to the back wall. They stood close together to study it before they began to lay in the support structure. Tomorrow Henry would have cement poured.

"Next flood will go right over these concrete ones. Not tear them out like last time."

Jerome smiled. "Sounds good. Have to always think ahead when it comes to building."

He'd noticed most people who had renovations underway were concerned about strength and used resilient products. He couldn't blame them after what had happened to them with this last flood. They'd almost finished when Noreen called them for their meal.

Henry set down his hammer. "Let's go on in and eat while it's still hot. I can finish up here tomorrow."

Noreen's face opened into a smile and she put plates of hot jambalaya before each of them. "After all that work you done, you're needing something to warm the belly."

She seemed to find the most savoury meats or fresh fish and vegetables around for each of her dishes. Jerome could see why Henry was always happy to eat at home. "It's great, like always. I never find food this good downtown."

Noreen laughed. "I know you're joking with me but I like to hear it anyway."

They finished dinner with her key lime pie which Jerome loved.

"How about I help you clean these dishes before I go?"

Noreen shook her head. "No. That's Henry's job and he enjoys it. You get back to your band. We're planning to come hear you sometime over Christmas."

Jerome found himself humming as he strolled back down the familiar streets on his way to the bus. Did he imagine he heard footsteps behind him? Maybe he was getting paranoid after all the petty crime he'd seen. He turned to see a dark figure half a block down the street. Probably someone was going to the bus as well. He relaxed but picked up speed anyway. The footsteps seemed to get closer and closer. Then he cringed when a hand grabbed his shoulder and spun him around. When he turned to face the figure, he had a flash of recognition.

"Phillip. What do you want from me?"

"What's this? You own this neighbourhood now since I been away?"

Jerome's breath had quickened but he held his ground. "I heard at the hotel you're back into the drug business. This isn't the place for it. You might try the Lower Ninth."

Phillip had planted both feet and stood facing Jerome blocking his way. "I got more business here than you might think. As you know, I got kin who live in one of these houses down here."

Jerome shook his head. "Why don't you leave them alone? You've caused them enough trouble."

"Maybe you're the one who's caused trouble. I hear it was you put the gang on to where I was hiding."

"I keep telling you how wrong you are. Anyway, I'm on my way to meet with Lewis. Let me pass."

Phillip's lips stretched open in a tight smile which didn't reach his eyes. They remained dark points of light. "Maybe it's Lara I come to see. What would you think about that?"

Anger hit Jerome's chest in waves. "You'd better stay away from her. She's well out of your reach anyway."

Phillip shoved him backwards and moved in close. "Why don't you just mind your own business and stay away from mine? The next time I catch you alone you might not make it back to the band at all. And you can tell that to Lewis."

Phillip dropped his arms, turned and walked back the way he came while Jerome stared after him. He felt his whole body shake with fear, his throat felt so tight he could barely breathe. Would Phillip send someone after him? Not willing to take the chance, he hurried forward until he hit a main street and hailed a cab to take him back to the hotel.

Later, in the tour bus, Jerome rushed to pull on his tight black shirt and dark jeans, his performance outfit, before he left for the hotel. Although he'd tried to cool things with Jacqueline these past few weeks, he had found it hard to resist the special attention she gave him. Lara would arrive in town soon for Mardi Gras and he didn't want her to misunderstand the relationship between Jacquie and him.

Chapter Twenty-Nine

Lara perched on the edge of her seat, as excitement surged through her body, when the bus depot on Loyola Avenue came into view. She was back. It was such a great time to visit New Orleans, with the cooler temperatures of February and the bright sunny skies. She turned her head to watch the well-dressed men and women she'd noticed on the bus with brochures in hand get off. They were probably here for their first Mardi Gras. A small Spanish speaking woman with sharp black eyes had shared her seat. She had told Lara she had returned to take up her cleaner's job at the Royal George Hotel where she'd worked before the storm.

After she climbed down the steep stairs with her carry-on, Lara hailed a cab. Henry had convinced her to stay at the house in the Garden District until he and Noreen had a little more furniture. Phillip hadn't been seen by anyone since Henry visited him after he'd been shot by the gang member. She hadn't told Jerome she'd arrive earlier than he expected. She was determined to spy on him and Jacqueline by attending the performance alone.

When she left the cab and climbed the crooked wooden stairs onto the wrap-around porch, everything felt strange. It was hard to imagine she'd lived here all those weeks. This time, there was no warm smile and familiar figure in the wicker chair to greet her. She searched through her large vinyl purse for the key Henry had mailed to her. Then stood there for a moment, before she inserted it into the lock and pushed open the heavy door. Pins and needles crawled up her arms and into her shoulders and neck when she stepped into the silent hallway.

So much had happened in this house, just a short while ago. She found it difficult to put the past behind her like she'd told Noreen. Lara swallowed hard before she ascended the staircase with her suitcase. The quietness of the house felt oppressive. She moved down the hall and entered what had been her bedroom. Everything looked the same, from the white tufted bedspread to the antique oak dresser.

Lara dropped the case on the bed and pulled out her two new dresses so she could hang them. What should she wear tonight? She wanted to look spectacular when she went to listen to the band? She'd give Jacqueline some competition. Hot and sweaty from the bus, she stripped and pulled on her terrycloth robe. Her bare feet felt good as she padded into the familiar bathroom to shower and wash her hair. The warm water caressed her skin and removed the chill from the unheated house.

Back in her bedroom, she struggled with the hairdryer to get her straightened hair back into the new bob cut, short in the back and longer in front. Her face still glowed framed by the long bangs. She unzipped her new silk dress with its princess waist and scalloped sleeves, a soft iridescent lilac with deeper purple highlights. When she checked her image in the mirror, Lara saw how it complimented her new hairdo and berry-red lips. She'd be a significant challenge for her rival. She felt good as she walked down the stairs.

When she noticed the cab out the window, Lara opened the front door, locked it and ran down the steps. She called out to the driver. "Take me to Bacco on Chartres."

She'd have ample time for dinner since the band didn't go on until nine. What would Jerome think when he saw her? Darkness had fallen when they drove down Bourbon Street and circled around to the bistro. As she stepped out of the cab, a momentary twinge of cold fear crawled up her spine. She was forced to walk around a group of drunken men who leaned against a deserted building, plastic cups in hand. Calm washed over her when she followed their gaze. They were transfixed by a local working girl, perched on a stool in the open bar behind her. The woman was dazzling in a black leather dress, with her dark face accented by ruby-red lips and her eyes highlighted with turquoise eye-shadow. Lara felt a moment of sadness to find the woman still locked into her old profession.

She hurried into Bacco's which had a welcome feel with its waxed pine floors and small round tables covered with white tablecloths. The young man who waited on her was as pale as the long-sleeved shirt he wore. It was a nice contrast with his skinny black pants.

"You from around here?" Lara asked.

"No, ma'am." His southern accent was strong. "I'm waiting for Tulane to reopen and need to make some cash."

She ordered the special, creole shrimp stew with French bread and key-lime pie. She gulped mouthfuls of the stew and realized she hadn't eaten anything since a sandwich on the bus. Lara took her time with dessert as she savoured the sharp flavour of the limes. Better than anything she had tasted in Atlanta. As she checked her watch, Lara remembered she had better get over to the Royal George Hotel to get a good seat before the start of the performance. She paid the bill and stepped back into the street which was now crowded. With Mardi Gras to begin next week, the tourists had arrived. She walked past several fashionably dressed couples and her confidence returned.

The marble floors in the lobby of the hotel gleamed and all the old brass railings around the front desk were polished. What a change from when she had last seen it. She strolled into the bar which hummed with the noise of an excited crowd. She was escorted to a table in the section on the left side, about three rows back. From there she could get a good look at every one of the members of the band, but wouldn't be obvious to them. When her rum and coke arrived, she sipped it slowly, as she waited for the band to come on stage.

Lara gripped the glass with both hands and stared. A tall, slim woman with wavy black hair which glinted with red highlights, had walked up to Lewis, gesturing with both hands and talking in rapid manner. She wore a shiny black dress, with a revealing neckline, the entire top covered in silver sequins. That must be Jacqueline. Lara sucked in her breath. How can I compete with her?

She breathed out when Jerome joined the two of them on stage. She was close enough to hear the conversation.

He stood close to Jacqueline. "You ready for our opening number?"

Lara's skin prickled when Jacqueline touched him on the arm and then draped her arm through his. They turned to each other with laughter and then moved to their places on the stage and began to warm up. Lara was still frozen in her seat, her stomach tight and her throat constricted.

Then Jerome began to play. The fluid notes from the saxophone warmed her body and caused a sensation to trace its way down from her chest, over her stomach and into her thighs. Why hadn't she heard Jerome play before? He had played a few short pieces for Phillip at the house, but nothing like these golden notes which now poured from his sax.

Next Jacqueline took centre stage with a hands-free mike, as her body moved to the rhythm, the sensuous sound of her throaty voice drifted over the crowd. Lara cringed. Jacqueline was good. As she glanced around the room, Lara could tell the audience loved every minute of her performance. People who arrived late had leaned against the far wall, drink in hand, as they listened and watched. When Lewis signalled for an intermission, Lara had to make a decision. Should she confront Jerome with her suspicions, and tell him he has to make a choice, or wait and remain silent? He hadn't been expecting to see her until Saturday. She stared back at Jerome and Jacqueline as they chatted with each other while leaving the stage together.

With her stomach tied in knots, Lara rose from her seat and headed to the back room where she knew the band would gather. She couldn't wait any longer. She had to know.

Lara walked through the doorway, head held high, and strode up to Jerome who was still in an animated conversation with Jacqueline. Lara couldn't resist directing a cold glare at Jacqueline.

"Jerome, I wanted to surprise you by arriving early. But, if you are too preoccupied with her, tell me now. I'll take the hint."

When Jerome turned towards that voice, his lower jaw dropped open in shock. He couldn't believe Lara was here in the bar. He took the few steps which separated them and enfolded her into his arms.

"This is a great surprise. When did you get into town and where are you staying?" He turned back to Jacqueline. "This is my fiancée, Lara. I told you about her. And Lara, this is Jacqueline."

Every muscle in Jacqueline's face tightened and her eyes turned to cold slits. "So, this is the girlfriend you told me about. Living up in Atlanta, aren't you? Too bad you came back." She glared at Lara, turned her back and walked away.

Lewis joined the two of them and gave Lara a quick hug. "You're always welcome with my band, honey. But, we've got less than ten minutes to the next session. I'll take you back to your seat and you can join Jerome and me for a drink later." He gestured for Jerome to leave.

*   *   *

Jerome gave Lara a quick kiss on the lips before he let her go with Lewis. As he watched Lara walk away, he realized how much he'd missed her. He breathed out. Then he returned to the stage, picked up his sax and began to run through a few practice notes.

He hoped Jacqueline would cool down in her own dressing room before she joined him on stage.

He gazed out over the crowd until he found Lara in her seat. She smiled back at him and seemed to relax with their connection. Maybe the signs of jealousy from Jacqueline helped Lara realize what he'd been telling her about the two of them. It was Jacqueline who was the aggressor. He had to make her understand Jacqueline meant nothing to him over the next two weeks while she was here.

During the next set, Lara was relieved when the sound from Jerome's sax was even more exquisite and she could tell he was fully into the music. But, as soon as there was a short break on stage between sets, Jacqueline would dominate Jerome's attention while he only tolerated it. Maybe he was right. She could see him look out over the crowd more and more often over the next piece and each time his eyes would rest on her.

At the conclusion of the last piece, Lara walked to Jerome's dressing room and knocked on the door. Lewis opened it. She could tell he and Jerome had been in conversation. She wanted to remind Lewis about his promise.

"I'm ready. Where do you two want to go for our drink?"

Lewis smiled and came over to her. "Jerome tells me you are quite a famous soprano over there in Atlanta. If you ever think about joining one of the local bands, I might be interested."

She relaxed. "I'm just here for Mardi Gras. I'm glad the city is going ahead with it this year. The locals need something to boost their spirits after all they've been through. This time Jerome and I will have a chance to experience it together."

Lewis looked nervous. "It'll take me a few minutes to oversee the clean-up and I'll meet you at the bar."

Jerome grasped her hand and squeezed it. "I can hardly believe it's you. It seems such a long time since I was with you in Atlanta. Where are you staying?"

"I'm at Phillip's old house."

Jerome frowned but held back saying anything. He'd warn her in time. "Where do you want to go for a drink?"

"Let's go to the Carousel Bar. Their 1940s décor will put us in the mood for Mardi Gras." Lara glanced up at him. "Then we can go back to my place later."

When Lewis joined them, the three friends strolled down the crowded street in the warm night air. Lara stopped with a look of shock when they passed an old grey building with a battered bar, open to the street. She could see an aging woman who stood in the open doorway dressed in a red sequin outfit. Her face was distorted with heavy make-up. Beside her leaned a skinny man in silver shirt and black jeans, who scanned the crowd, probably in search of customers for her.

"This is the second one tonight. I'd forgotten this still goes on in this city." Lara sighed. "It didn't used to be so visible."

Jerome took her arm and pulled her away. "It's okay. I know that's not the real New Orleans."

Lewis shrugged his shoulders. "These days, everyone's got to make a living any way they can."

The place they entered had an old world charm with dark oak walls and soft cone lights. They joined the line of couples at the twenty-four seat bar. Lewis ordered his usual bourbon and a rum and coke for Jerome and then turned to Lara. "And what can I get for our visitor to town?" He winked at Lara.

"You're talking to an old timer. All the same, I'll have a vodka martini to celebrate my return."

Jerome proposed a toast. "To Mardi Gras 2006." After they clinked glasses, he turned to Lara. "We'll want to make sure we're on St. Charles Avenue on Fat Tuesday for the Rex Parade. I hear it's the best one to see."

Lara smiled back. "You'll want to be in a good spot to catch the gold and silver beads and doubloons. That's if you can get through the crowds of kids. The guys on the floats love to throw trinkets to them."

After Lewis downed his drink, he excused himself. "I'd better get back to keep an eye on the guys. I guess I'll see you back in the hotel in the morning, Jerome."

Lara touched Jerome's arm. "You're welcome to stay with me for the week. I'll be in the old mansion by myself."

Jerome wanted to be with her tonight. Besides, it was the best thing to do for her protection from Phillip. "Of course I'll be with you. Just give me a few moments to pick up some clean clothes. These are pretty sweaty. I'll pack my bag tomorrow."

With their glasses now empty, Lara and Jerome left the bar and strolled, holding hands, along the street to the tour bus parked in the back of the Royal George. While he went in, Lara waited outside. He rummaged around his bed for some clothes and his kit and shoved them into a bag. When he came out again, he waved down a cab and they tumbled into the back seat.

He pulled her into his arms. "I've missed you so much, honey. These last few months have been long."

She snuggled into him. "I've been so looking forward to being with you."

He kissed her deeply and traced her tongue with his.

Lara pulled him closer and kissed him back. "Now we've got two whole weeks together before I have to return to Atlanta."

When the taxi finally reached the old Georgian mansion, they slowly got out. They held hands until they reached the stairs. Jerome pulled her into another embrace. "This feels like a serious step for us, as we enter this house together. Should I carry you over the threshold?"

Lara breathed softly and gave a giggle. "No. It's not mine. Besides, you might drop me." Then she pulled him close. "It's great to have you stay here with me. Besides, I'm still not very comfortable being here alone."

They opened the door and stood in the front hall. Jerome's suspicions returned. "Well, it looks much the same as before." He knew he'd have to tell her about Phillip soon. It wasn't safe not to.

Lara stopped at the staircase. "Uncle brought a crew over when he finished their house to make some repairs. He had them patch the roof and replaced the front steps. I told you he'd like me to come back and live here. But I couldn't with so many bad memories." She pulled him towards her and started up the stairs.

When they reached her bedroom, Jerome felt shyness flood over him. He dropped his overnight bag on the floor and put his arms around her.

"Lara, I can hardly believe you're really back here with me. It seems like I've waited for us to be together again forever."

Lara unbuttoned his shirt and slid if off his shoulders. She ran her hands over his bare chest. "I want you with me always."

The buttons of her dress came open under his hands and he reached behind her to open her bra and remove it. They stood together clinging to each other. Their two bodies swayed slowly in rhythm, as though engaged in a sensuous dance. Jerome's lips moved gently over hers. He could hear his own deep breaths.

Lara undid his pants and helped him to remove them. Then she guided him backwards towards the bed. She lay across it and he joined her pulling her on top. The two of them wiggled out the rest of their clothing.

Jerome gazed down at her as he stroked her breasts, stomach and thighs. Then Lara pulled him into her and they continued to rock together with growing passion. He could feel the tension build as she pulled him closer and closer while she massaged his buttocks with both hands.

When their bodies reached a climax together, they fell back exhausted. Jerome maneuvered his body to fit against her back and rested one hand on her stomach.

He listened to her contented sighs. This felt so right for them. How could he ever have even thought about Jacqueline?

Chapter Thirty

Over a breakfast of pancakes smothered in sweet syrup and surrounded by savoury browned sausages, Jerome couldn't help a feeling of elation. He was so thrilled to have Lara back where he could touch her. While the two of them cleaned up and washed the dishes, he decided it was time to talk.

"I have something I'd rather not tell you. But, I'm afraid you have to know." He stopped at her alarmed expression. "It's about Phillip."

She stared at him. "Is he dead? I know it's what Henry thinks."

"I only wish it were so simple. He followed me the other night after I left Henry and Noreen and threatened me."

Lara cringed. "Maybe he'll come here. I'd better move to a hotel." She dropped the dish towel and wrung her hands. "Why didn't you tell me before?"

Jerome sighed. "I didn't want to frighten you. Phillip said he can't come around this old mansion since the gang is still after him. And I'm here to make sure you're okay."

"Does Henry know?"

"No. I had to keep it from him because of Noreen. I didn't want to frighten her."

Lara put both hands over her face. "Will we never be free of him?

He pulled her into his arms and kissed her forehead. "He's got more problems than us right now. He'll keep his distance." He waited for calm to return. "Why don't you come with me while I pack up my clothes for the week?"

She straightened her shoulders. "No. I need to get used to being on my own if I do plan to move back to this city. I might as well start now."

They went out to the porch and sat on the two old wicker chairs while they watched the street. Although neighbours were continuing to clean up, there was no longer any major construction in this area. Not like the Lakeview area or the Lower Ninth Ward which had both been hit with storm surges from Lake Pontchartrain. He held Lara's hand as they both relaxed in the afternoon sun.

"I hate leaving but I have to get back to the hotel. Lewis wants to go over a new number with me."

She stood and pulled him to his feet. "It's okay. I'm feeling much better now. The news about Phillip was a shock."

Jerome pulled her to him and gave her a long lingering kiss on the lips and felt her respond.

"I'd like you to come see the performance again tonight. We can talk after about what we want to do at the Mardi Gras parade."

Lara leaned her head on his chest. "It sounds great. I'll see you later, honey."

While Jerome made his way along the sidewalk toward where he'd pick up the bus, his mind raced. He couldn't let Lara leave him again. He couldn't imagine life with her gone.

A chill crept up his spine, like small crawling ants. Did he hear footsteps behind him again? Who was it this time? He turned but could just make out a figure in dark clothes, almost a block away. It was unclear who it might be. He hurried his steps and then turned quickly. The figure was closer and continued to move in his direction. He decided this time he'd take the initiative and wait the phantom out. He made a ninety degree turn and used his body as a block to the sidewalk.

As the man came closer, Jerome's anger rose. The same long curly hair and deep black eyes. He was sure it was Phillip. What could he want?

Phillip continued to stride directly towards him and in time they stood face to face and glared at each other. "You got no business over in this district, Jerome. What are you doing here?"

Anger at Phillip stabbed him in the gut. Jerome gave him a push. "What's it to you? I was told you didn't hang around here anymore."

"I got property here to check on. Just because I can't stay here right now doesn't mean I won't move back some day."

"I told Henry you were around. He'll be after you if you mess with Lara again."

Phillip's fist crunched into his right check knocking him sideways. Pain flooded into his jaw and up to his head.

"You shut your mouth. Henry's my business and not yours. I'll come after you again if you don't mind your own place."

While Jerome stood stunned from the blow, he saw Phillip turn his back and pick up speed as he ran back down the street. He disappeared around a corner.

When Jerome reached the hotel, he found Lewis in the bar. Lewis shook his head at the bruise on his cheek. "What's that from?"

"You were right about Phillip threatening me. He's been following me around town."

Lewis nodded. "I'd watch him closely. He's lived a rough life and survived many fights. Nothing scares him for long." He put his hand on Jerome's shoulder. "Come on. Let's go into the empty room next door and practice what you're playing. You've almost got it."

*   *   *

Phillip's dark mood had cleared after the tussle with Jerome. The kid had better watch out or he'd get worse than a blow to the head. It's too bad he linked up with Lewis who'd be too tough for him to shake. Like most of the old group, he'd had to protect his own for too many years to listen to any threats Phillip might lay on him. All the same, it was time he had a good talk with Lewis face to face. He headed uptown to the bar.

When Phillip entered the bar, several tables cleared quickly. He saw Lewis in conversation with the bartender and went over to join him. "I guess you heard from Jerome what happened this afternoon. Care to hear what I have to say?"

Lewis turned and gestured for him to sit down on the next stool. "What's up? I'm not Jerome's keeper but he's valuable to me in the band. He's bringing in a crowd."

Phillip sat and put his elbows on the bar. "I see no reason for him to interfere with my family. Henry's my brother."

"You got to know Lara's his woman. You leave her alone and Jerome won't bother you."

Phillip's face turned red as he pulled his lips into a straight line. "I had my eyes on her first and she's my niece. Anyway, next time I come across him, I'll break a few bones." He glared at Lewis.

Lewis's stance was relaxed but his eyes glinted. "Like I told you, he's a member of my band. You leave him alone or stay out of this hotel. What's your choice?"

Phillip huffed. "It ain't your fight." He stood and looked at the door. "But, I need to hang out here. So for now, I'll leave him alone. The Marrero gang would like to see him anyway. So, I might not have to get rid of him."

Lewis followed him to the door. "I meant what I said Phillip. I could just as easily clue in the gang as to your whereabouts if you cross me. You hear me. Leave Jerome alone."

Chapter Thirty-One

The next morning when Jerome woke, he could see the slate grey clouds which hung over the live oak trees, from the bedroom's window. As he made his way down the hall to the bathroom, he could smell fried bacon from the kitchen below. He and Lara were to join Henry and Noreen for lunch today, so he'd expected an early breakfast. The late nights performing made it harder and harder to get up. After a warm shower, he stared in the mirror at his mop of blond hair and picked up the brush to wrestle it back into place.

When he reached the bottom of the stairs, Lara walked out of the kitchen to greet him. He felt a thrill when he saw her broad smile which parted her full rosy lips. When he reached her, Jerome grabbed her into a tight embrace and gave her a long sensual kiss.

Lara broke free and leaned her head on his shoulder. "I'd love to spend the day here curled up with you. But, we did promise to see Auntie and Uncle for lunch."

Jerome ran his hands up and down her back before he dropped his arms. "You're right. And Noreen will have cooked up a pot of her Creole stew by now. She'd be disappointed if she couldn't feed us."

Lara turned towards the kitchen. "You can help me by making the toast." She moved over to the stove and began to fry eggs.

Jerome set several pieces of bread on the grill to toast and went over to set the table for two. When the hot plates of food were in front of them, they both ate with vigour.

His stomach satisfied, Jerome cleared all the dishes into the sink and Lara joined him. He loved the domestic chores they shared just like they had their own home. With Phillip gone, the house seemed so normal. The drugs and violence along with the corrupt characters who hung out here from time to time were all gone.

"Are you sure you'd never want to live here again? He asked. "If Phillip doesn't return, I mean."

Lara shook her head. "When I'm here alone, there are too many ghosts. I sometimes see Phillip's mocking face and cringe from those arms of steel."

Jerome hung his head. Then we put his arms around her. "I'm so sorry. I shouldn't ask stupid questions."

With their cleanup complete, Jerome pulled on his worn denim jacket and watched Lara put on a new deep blue cotton jacket she must have bought in Atlanta. A sharp blast of February air hit them when they opened the front door and entered the porch. The wind made it a long walk to the nearest bus stop. When they climbed the steps and found a seat, the crowded bus radiated warmth. Before long, Jerome could feel Lara's head on his shoulder and he put his arm around her.

He kissed her on the top of the head and stroked the smooth black hair. "It's great to have you back. I didn't realize how much I missed you."

Lara sighed. "Me too. I'm glad you were able to help Noreen and Henry move into their place. They're getting older and I know they really appreciated it."

When they reached the Lakeview area, Lara sat up and stared out the window. "I can't believe how much rebuilding there has been since the fall."

As he followed her direction, he noticed many yards now cleaned of debris and other renovated houses with *For Sale* signs on the front lawns. While working here, he hadn't noticed all the progress. He'd taken it for granted.

As they walked up the sidewalk to Noreen and Henry's bungalow, Lara's eyes widened. "The front door and steps have been replaced."

"Henry also had new shingles put on the roof to keep out any moisture."

Lara ran up the stairs and grabbed the new brass knocker giving it a couple of bangs. When the door swung open, she was engulfed in two wide arms and an ample bosom.

"Well child. You're finally back here with your old aunt."

Lara followed her aunt into the house and asked her for a tour. "These new pine floors add style and I love your pale green walls. It's so you."

Noreen's eyes lit up with pleasure. "I'm so happy to be home again."

"Henry has done a great job. I can tell his carpenter skills were very useful."

Noreen's face turned serious. "The neighbourhood is not the same though. Many of our friends haven't returned. They got jobs in other places and settled in. There are lots of empty houses. Still, its home to us."

Jerome nodded. "New people will move in over time."

Noreen led them to the table and poured each a mug of coffee. "What about you Jerome? You settling in New Orleans?"

Jerome glanced over at Lara. "Lewis offered to keep me on as long as I want. My music has improved here. But, I don't know what Lara wants."

Lara set down her cup of coffee. "Well, I have to go back to Atlanta to finish the concert season. It wouldn't be right otherwise. After that, I don't know." Her voice trailed off.

The noise of the front door as it slammed shut caused the three of them to turn to the entrance hall. Henry stood there in the doorway as he dropped his lunch box and brushed sawdust off his denim jacket.

"Lara, girl. Come over here to see your uncle." He held out his arms for a hug.

When she reached him, he pulled her close. She looked up at her uncle. "I can see there's no lack of work for you around town. You sure changed the look of this place."

Henry shrugged. "I was lucky to have the money to start early. The lumberyards are about to run out of supplies now."

When the two of them joined the others at the new oak table, Jerome could see Lara was happy to be home.

"Your seafood tastes better than any of the restaurants, Auntie. I bet you could sell it."

Noreen's face broke into a grin. "Why don't you stay the night, Lara? You can have the small guest room in the back. It's not painted yet but we did get a new bed."

Jerome watched a guilty look cross Lara's face. He hoped she would turn Noreen down so he could have her to himself.

"Not this time. I want to see Jerome play tonight and we'll be very late. I've only got a few more nights to be with him."

Jerome's face broke into a grin. "I'm glad you'll be at the performance. Your presence inspires me to play extra special."

*   *   *

Lewis was sitting at the bar when he and Lara arrived. He'd said he needed Jerome to go over some last minute changes for tonight's program. Lara sat still with a pensive look while he and Lewis argued over the music. When they were finished, Jerome turned to her.

"How did it sound to you in that final set last night? Where the audience engaged?"

Before Lara could respond, he saw Lewis give him an angry look and turned in time to see Jacqueline as she hurried across the room towards them. When she reached the group, she grabbed Jerome's arm.

She slipped her arm around his waist and smiled up at him. "I'm so glad you're here early. I was worried about warming up alone."

Jerome frowned and tried to pull his arm away from her. "Lara and I were visiting her kin over lunch. No need to worry I wouldn't be here in time." He looked over at Lara whose mouth was pulled into a deep scowl.

As he watched, Lara left her stool and walked over to stand directly in front of Jacqueline. She grabbed the woman's arm and tugged. "Let go of him. It's time you realized Jerome and I are a couple. The two of you work together. Nothing more. Did you get that?"

Jacqueline's lower lip pouted and streaks of moisture fell down her cheeks. She still clung to Jerome.

"Jerome, you're the only one to keep me safe. Without you, the other men will be after me like always. I told you what it was like for me in Mississippi."

Jerome shrugged off her arm and stepped back. "You're being overly dramatic as usual. We'll both be on stage in half an hour." He could still feel the hot prongs of anger hit his chest. "This melodrama won't help either of us."

The silence was broken by a loud clap from Lewis. "Jerome's right. It's time for both of you to act like professionals." He shook a finger at Jacqueline. "You can leave the hysterics for later."

Lewis waited for Jacqueline to pull herself together and then put his arm around her shoulder. "I don't want you to ruin your golden voice with all this stress." He moved the two of them towards her dressing room. "I want to see you in the new sexy outfit we bought for you yesterday."

Jerome stood frozen until Lara put her arm around his waist and embraced him. Her lips lingered on his, the intensity and heat built. When she broke free, he touched her lips with one finger. "Now do you see it's not me? I try to be kind to her. She didn't know anyone here and I offered to help out. But, that's all."

Lara responded. "I've left you alone too long, sweetheart. You're a sexy and available man who's about to become a recognized musician. There'll be other women like her who'll seek you out while you're on your own. Before I leave for Atlanta, I'll give you my decision about whether I'll return home for good."

Jerome watched the dressing room door until both Lewis and Jacqueline came out and started toward the stage. He gave Lara a quick kiss. "I'd better join them. We'll talk more tonight."

Lara smiled as she watched the crowd gather. "I'm glad I came back for Mardi Gras. The spirit of the people of New Orleans is still alive if battered. I like that."

Jerome's eyes stayed on Lara as he played. He could tell the band had connected with the audience tonight. All whispering had stopped and all eyes were on him and Jacqueline.

During the break he joined Lara. While they talked, a middle-aged man approached her and stood by their table.

"I hear you performed with the Gilead Baptist Church in Atlanta over the Christmas season? I've been trying to meet up with you." He stopped when Jerome frowned at him. "I'm a promoter. Lewis told me to check out their choir."

Lara touched Jerome's arm. "It's okay." She turned to catch the man's attention again. "I sang the solo. Did you see our concert?

He nodded. "Yes. You have a beautiful voice and a strong stage presence." He handed her a card. "I'm Brad Robinson. I'd love to give you an audition for our symphony choir here in New Orleans. We're looking for new performers. Call me tomorrow, if you're sincerely interested."

Lara gave him a grateful smile. "I'll call." Her whole body twitched in excitement. She hoped Jerome was thrilled with her getting this opportunity."

When the man left, she grabbed Jerome's arm. "Imagine, I'm being asked to a local audition. What does this mean for our future?"

Jerome watched as a look of apprehension crossed her face. He felt an infusion of warmth crawl up his chest. For his sake, he hoped the offer would come true.

"I guess if you get the offer, your decision will determine where you'll live."

She smiled at him. "I guess you're right."

Chapter Thirty-Two

While they shivered in the chill of the February morning, Jerome stood beside Lara on Metairie Street and waited for the King's Parade to start. She was dressed in a black parka and matching chino pants, her brown skin almost covered by a full-face gold mask. As the floats passed, they saw many women wearing the traditional long gowns and white gloves usual for Mardi Gras. Jerome wore a black face mask and his new brown suede jacket with its fake fur collar over blue jeans.

"What I love about this parade is all the families who gather to catch the doubloons," said Lara. "Look at those kids perched on ladders. That's so they can see over the crowd."

Jerome smiled. "Lewis says over on Bourbon Street, we'd be dodging the drunks from last night and stepping over the streams of piss in the streets.

The two stood close together, and held hands, while more floats appeared. The next one set on a flatbed truck which held a dozen men and women dressed in elaborate costumes. The men wore green or gold satin jackets and the women wore long purple gowns with flowing lace trimmed sleeves. A small band strode before them playing *Reunion Blues*. While they sang and waved to the crowd, they continued to throw gold coins and other trinkets.

The next group of floats moved into view with an assortment of characters that followed on foot. Lara pointed at Dracula with his green face and spiked hair, who twirled a necklace of large purple, gold and green balls. Behind him were others dressed as Disney stars, favorites like Donald Duck and Goofy. She dropped her arms and scrunched up her nose when the next group of men and women passed dressed in multi-coloured shirts and accented with Zulu black face. Their hats were covered in feathers and flowers, and their necks weighed down with silver bead necklaces.

"You can bet that group are all black. No white folk would take the chance they might have insulted their black neighbours by wearing that garb. It's from the vaudeville shows."

"Yeah. I must say it surprised me." Jerome nodded his head.

Lara grabbed his arm. "But I do love the mix of people in the crowd from black Americans like me to white folk and then Spanish. They're all having a ball."

Jerome gave her a kiss on the cheek. "Just like us. We can be lovers here in New Orleans and no one cares we're together."

Lara sighed. "Not like Wally back in Atlanta. He's so prejudiced." Her attention turned back to the parade. "Those must be locals." She pointed to a couple on a homemade float. "Look at their signs. They must be protestors from the flood of last summer. I saw them on TV.

Jerome watched as they passed by. One man wore a floating plastic garbage can, labeled, *Lakeview*. Another wore a vest embroidered with *Insurance Adjuster from Hell*. On the hotel balcony across from them another man held up a sign, *Oh FEMA. Where art Thou?*

Jerome sucked in his breath. "The bitterness won't go until more people are back in their own homes. Like Henry said, the government's been too slow to respond to the needs."

Finally the King's float arrived with him resplendent in gold robes and a plastic jeweled crown. He raised one arm to loud cheers from the crowd. His Queen sat beside him in a white gown trimmed in gold, a tiara sparkled on her head. After they passed, groups of people began to break up and wander away. Lara pulled him away from the crowd. "Come on. The parade ends at Riverwalk Marketplace where we can get hot chocolate."

Jerome nodded. "Great. I need something warm in my stomach."

As they wandered through the crowd, Jerome had an eerie sensation someone was trailing them. He turned several times to see a figure dressed in a red, white and black joker costume, face covered by a mask. Whoever it was, they seemed to follow him and Lara. The figure was too small to be Phillip. Regardless, he picked up the pace. "Let's go. We need to beat these hoards if we hope to get a seat."

They forced their way into the *Chocolate Café,* and grabbed a bench seat which soon filled up with others from the crowd. He waved at the nearest waiter. The strong smell of chocolate almost overwhelmed him. When their cups were delivered, Lara wrapped her hands around hers. Jerome straightened up when another body joined them. It was the joker whom he recognized by her accent as soon as she began to speak. Jacqueline didn't try to hide her identity from him.

"Jerome, it was a great parade, don't you think. It's my first one. Yours as well?"

Jerome felt his face burn. "How did you find us in this crowd, Jacqueline?"

She fluttered her hand at him. "Well, when you talked about going with the band last night, I overheard. I asked others where it started and thought you'd be here. I didn't think Lara would mind." She turned and smirked at Lara.

Lara moved closer to him and put one arm around him. She then scowled at Jacqueline. "This is our special day together."

Jerome shifted sideways in his seat and looked down at the table. "Maybe the three of us could share a drink with the crowd at this table. Then Lara and I will head back to the house." He glanced at Lara for confirmation.

Lara smiled up at him and blinked her eyelids in a mocking manner. "Whatever you'd like, honey. This is your time to enjoy Mardi Gras."

He watched Jacqueline's lower lip droop into a pout.

The waiter arrived with their beignets. Jerome and Lara devoured them, hands covered in sweet white sugar. He could feel Lara glare at him when he turned back to Jacqueline.

"I bet it will be a lively concert at our hotel tonight with these large crowds. Are you up for it?"

Jacqueline laughed back at him. *"Eso es lo que tengo que hacer.* I am always ready to entertain."

Jerome responded. "Me too. I couldn't live my life without music."

Jacqueline finished her chocolate, stood up and walked away with her sexy sway.

After a while, he and Lara made their way to Canal Street to catch the streetcar. She asked. "Do you think Jacqueline is still hot for you? She certainly acts like it." Her frown deepened. "It makes me uncomfortable."

Jerome put his arm around her. "Look, as I explained. When she arrived, she didn't know anyone else in the band except Lewis. So she relied on me quite a bit. Now you're here, I don't have the same time for her and she feels it." He buried his nose in her hair to breath in the exotic odor. "You must know, honey. It's you I want to be with."

Her mood remained dark. "What happens when I'm not here? When I return to Atlanta, what happens then?"

"Honestly. She's just lonely so far away from her family." He brushed back her hair from her forehead and kissed it. "I told you I'd wait for you. Jacqueline doesn't mean anything to me."

Her response was petulant. "I bet she can't wait for you to show up for the concert tonight. She'll have you all to herself."

Jerome gave her a hard kiss on the lips and stroked her hair. He held her until they saw the streetcar approaching and made their way to it. They scrambled on and found a seat.

"Come and watch us play tonight, honey. I always like having you there."

She sighed. "I'm still so tired from the trip and would prefer an early night. But then, I'm leaving you to her clutches. Yes, of course, I'll join you. I want to spend all my time with you while I'm still in town."

Jerome felt a thrill when she leaned her head on his shoulder. "I loved spending my first Mardi Gras with you. Any opportunity to share time with you is great. I remember when we toured the Garden District that first time." He gazed into her eyes while hot sparks flooded his chest. She squeezed his hand.

"Once Jacqueline gets used to seeing us together as a couple, she'll soon find her own friends."

"I sure hope so." Lara gave a deep sigh. "I'd rather not have her on my mind while I'm away."

*   *   *

The days flew by while they continued to live in the house in the Garden District. Immediately after breakfast, Lara would go to the market to pick up fresh ingredients for their dinner. He usually napped for an hour, and then practised the music for that evening in the old parlour, until lunch. He noticed Lara, even when he didn't coax her, would show up at his concerts each evening around nine. He'd caught her a few times as she glared at Jacqueline when she found an excuse to move in to rub against him. He was so thrilled she'd been approached with the offer of a contract for the prestigious symphony choir the other night. Since she would leave for Atlanta on Sunday afternoon that was one less issue for him to worry about. She'd have a career here if it was her choice.

On Saturday night, after two hours of practise, he found the dinner table set with good china, silver cutlery and large white napkins.

"Where did you find all this?

Lara grinned. "I was surprised at what you can find in that old mahogany cabinet behind you. You can take the seat across from mine."

She returned from the kitchen with two plates laden with fried grouper covered in a cream sauce sprinkled with herbs.

"You've become a great cook, love. Noreen will be jealous when we invite them over to eat."

"And you've improved your table manners. After months of meals in diners with the guys, some new refinements must be welcome. Would you like to pour the wine?"

"Okay. But only one glass each. We'll save the rest for after the concert." Jerome wrapped the bottle of Baca Noir with a napkin and carefully poured each glass to within two inches from the top.

The wonderful fragrance from the sauce caused them to start on their meals after one sip of wine. Lara stopped after a few mouthfuls, and gave him a serious look.

"You know I'm planning to consider an offer from the symphony for this fall. That is if I return to New Orleans."

Jerome set down his knife and fork and grabbed her hand. "That would be wonderful. I've really worried about your return to Atlanta. I'd go anywhere to be with you, but New Orleans is in my blood and it's where I want us to live."

"It would be a new phase for my career to sing here. When I see how the local people pulled together the Mardi Gras this year, I know there's still hope for New Orleans."

"Have you lost your fear of the streets?"

"I'm still scared, but I've managed to travel around on my own over the past two weeks."

Jerome tensed. Was this the right time for his surprise? He went over to stand beside her, took her hand and got onto one knee. "We've talked from time to time about us getting married someday, but I want a real answer. I love you so I'm asking you now, will you marry me. We can build a life together here or wherever." He looked up at her and held his breath.

Tears filled her eyes and she squeezed his hand. Her lips trembled. "Yes. I've realized this week; I don't want to live my life without you." She stood and pulled him to his feet. Her arms embraced him and he gave her a slow passionate kiss. When Lara broke free, she said. "When I return this fall, we'll have to talk about a place to live."

Jerome picked up her left hand. "I don't have a ring for you yet. I'd like us to choose one together before you leave. Then every time you look at it, you'll remember us."

"How romantic, Jerome. I'd be proud to wear such a ring." She gestured for him to return to his seat. "I know Noreen and Henry will be pleased for us when we tell them. What about your family? I don't know much about them."

Jerome felt his mood darken. "My father left when I was twelve and I haven't seen him since. There's my mother and half-sister whom I visit. I've been on my own since I left high school at eighteen. I didn't get along with my step-father."

Lara offered her hand to him. "Your mother will still want to hear from you. We can tell all of them tomorrow. Right now, let's finish our dinner so you can join the band on time."

As they cleaned up after dinner, Jerome felt very domestic. He dried the china plates slowly and carefully so as not to drop them. The future with Lara felt good to him.

Lara would go with him to the hotel tonight, so they each hurried into jackets and he watched for the taxi to arrive out the front room window. He didn't want to worry Lewis by a late arrival. Since he was so happy, he didn't want to spoil anyone else's evening. He had a sudden hesitation. How would Jacqueline take his engagement? Did he really care? She'd have to get used to it.

Cold gusts of wind hit them when they climbed out of the cab in front of the hotel. When they entered, Jerome was relieved to see the band had started the warm-up. The two of them rushed into the small office near the stage to find Lewis.

When Jerome told him the news, Lewis's face broke into a huge smile. "I'm so happy you two are finally going to be together here. Myself, I never believed in long distance romances. That's why I don't get serious with my women. I've spent my life travelling."

The two of them headed for the stage and he saw Lara relax into a seat near the front. Jerome was pleased. Maybe her presence would keep Jacqueline at bay. He had begun to realize Jacqueline had taken advantage of his friendly intentions. She chose to think it was something entirely different. Lara was right to challenge her.

Jerome felt so wound up after his solo numbers he could see the impact on the audience including Lara. They sat still with rapt faces and clapped with enthusiasm when he finished. He was lucky to have found a partner who also loved music. He imagined Lara would be fussed all the way back to Atlanta about her own coming performance and she was willing to leave that for him.

During the break, Jerome and Lewis wandered off into the bar to talk about the next session. When he returned to the stage, he saw Lara and Jacqueline involved in a quarrel outside Jacqueline's dressing room. Since neither had seen him, he moved closer for a minute to listen.

Lara took the initiative her face pushed near Jacqueline's. "It's time us two women had a little talk."

He saw Jacqueline's lip drop into a petulant pout he'd seen before. "What do you want with me? I've done nothing to you. Jerome has been looking out for me, that's all."

"Well, Jacqueline, you're a big girl now. You've been living in New Orleans for at least a month. It's time you took care of yourself."

Jacqueline began to pull open the dressing room door. She stamped her feet in agitation. "Jerome and I, we love the same music. We will always share that."

Lara slammed the door shut. "You need to know Jerome is now officially my fiancé. We plan to marry in the fall and will live in New Orleans. I'm warning you one last time, to stay away from him. Otherwise, you'll answer to me.

Jerome hung back and watched Lara march back to her seat. He whistled to himself at her gumption standing up to Jacqueline like that. He waited until Jacqueline was back on stage in conversation with one of the other band members before he joined them. When he first met Lara, she'd never have been this assertive. Atlanta had definitely given her new confidence.

Chapter Thirty-Three

Jerome especially loved Saturday mornings in the old mansion with Lara. He hadn't realized how much he'd missed the place. As he passed through the hallway, he watched Lara seated at the large front window, with the drapes pulled back. She liked to see the activity on the street as things returned to normal with the delivery of milk to some homes and boxes of groceries to others. This was life as it should be after weeks of disruption. He stared at the faded curtains, stained floors and lumpy sofa.

"You're right. Even with us getting married, hon, I couldn't see living here."

She nodded. "It's so dark and dusty. But, if it remains in Henry's custody, I know he'll want us to have it."

Jerome shook his head. "A small townhouse or bungalow closer to the main part of downtown would suit us much better. We'll need somewhere I can get back and forth to work more easily."

She stood and walked towards him. In a spontaneous moment, he grabbed her around the waist and kissed her lips.

"Are you ready for our trip downtown? I'm serious about wanting you to have your ring before you go back to Atlanta. I've saved the money for it."

Lara kissed him back. "Don't worry. I'm already engaged in my own mind. A ring would be nice though." She smiled at him. "The girls in the choir will be impressed."

Jerome held her left hand. "How about Macy's" The woman at the jewellery counter has been showing me some, but I wanted you to see them first."

Lara squeezed his hand back and laughed. "Okay. Get your jacket and let's go. I don't want you to change your mind." She pulled her hooded jacket off the rack by the door and buttoned it close to her neck. "Don't forget how cold it is out there."

*   *   *

Macy's was packed with a mix of regulars from town and tourists who had come for Mardi Gras. The local economy still suffered since many former residents, actually over 100,000 hadn't returned. Jerome guided her to the counter along the back wall.

"Hi Mrs. Constantine, I want you to meet my fiancée, Lara. I've told you about her already. We're here to get her a ring."

The sales clerk, a slender black woman dressed in a soft black blouse and tight black pants reached out to take Lara's hand.

"I'm most please to meet you, Lara. You're lucky to have this handsome dude who wants to spend his life with you." She smiled at Jerome. "And I remember which rings you liked." The woman pulled out a tray of diamond rings with gold settings. She selected three of them and arranged them on a velvet cushion. "Now, these are the ones he chose. But, hon, you're the one who will wear it and he said you're free to pick."

He stood beside Lara and watched as she admired all three rings.

Her eyes bright, Lara smiled at him. "They're gorgeous, Jerome." She picked up each one in turn and tried them on. She stopped with the last one on her finger, her smile even wider. "This one's just right for me. What do you think, Jerome?"

He looked at the brilliant diamond in the centre of the ring with small clusters on each side. "It was my favorite as well."

Mrs. Constantine held up Lara's hand. "It surely looks beautiful on your hand."

Lara admired the ring on her hand for a few moments longer. "It's perfect. I'll be thrilled to wear it when I have to leave tomorrow."

Jerome handed the cash to the clerk and waited for the receipt. He gave the box to Lara. "It's yours. Why don't you wear it now?"

I short while later, they left the store hand in hand while they wandered through the mall and smiled at everyone they passed.

*   *   *

Later that afternoon, the two of them snuggled up on the sofa in the parlour to share their good news with family. Noreen and Henry were first.

Noreen responded. "I'm so happy for you baby and Jerome's a good man. Does this mean you'll be staying here? You'll need me to help plan the wedding."

Lara laughed with excitement. "Not right away. I have my work in Atlanta to finish, but I'll be back home after that. Jerome and I will look for a house to rent as soon as I return."

"Jerome is welcome to stay with us until then," Noreen's voice sounded hopeful. "I can see he's looked after."

Lara responded. "Thanks for the offer, Noreen. I'll leave that up to him. Here he is now." She handed him the phone.

Jerome's face turned red but he nodded his head while he listened. "Thanks for all your good wishes, but I need to be close to the hotel for the band. Besides, there are dangers throughout the city after we close around 2 a.m. I can wait until Lara gets back here and we get our own place." He handed the phone back to Lara. "Henry wants to talk to you."

"I hate to give up my little girl, but at least it's to someone I can count on. You tell Jerome he's welcome to join our family. And Lara, don't be too long away. We're already missing you."

Lara set down the receiver and pulled him closer. "Now call your mother. She'll want to hear from you, too."

Jerome bit his lower lip and dialed the phone.

"Hi Mom. Yes, it's Jerome. I want to introduce you to my fiancée, Lara. She's right here with me and we got engaged today." He should have known his mother would be the problem. "Well, of course you haven't met her. She's from New Orleans and has never been to Florida." He shook his head in exasperation. "I promise you can meet her before the wedding."

"What do you mean is Ray invited? Why would he even want to come? He'll probably be away on one of his business trips anyway." Another long silence. "No. I don't think it would be a good idea to include him. You know why. Okay. Let me know if you can come and I'll meet you. Is Janice there? You can leave a message for me at the hotel." He gave her the number and slowly set the phone back on the table. "I told you she wouldn't be happy for me."

Lara grabbed both his hands. "Let's give it some time. The news was probably a shock to her."

He pulled her close. He could tell his mother definitely did not look forward to meeting her new daughter-in-law. He hoped his sister, Janice, would be more welcoming. The future meeting was another barrier they would have to overcome. He sighed and pushed his nose into her hair to smell the jasmine scent. He didn't care. He'd be happy anyway no matter what his mother thought.

*   *   *

The last two weeks had gone far too quickly. On Sunday morning, he and Lara stood at the bus depot as they waited for the dispatcher to call out the departure to Atlanta. He kissed Lara hard on the lips. "I'll miss you even more than before. It seems like we're always living apart."

Lara kissed him back and ran her hands through his hair. "This'll be the last time, I promise. When I return in the fall, it's going to be for good. We'll find our own place and leave Philip's mansion behind."

The passengers who had gathered in a long line-up at the bus door where now seated inside. Lara started to move slowly in the direction of the bus while Jerome followed. He could see the tears in her eyes as she started to climb the steps and he let go of her hand at the last possible moment.

He stood where he was, as though frozen, while the door closed. His face felt tight as he lifted his hand to wave at her. He automatically followed the bus a short way before he dropped his hands at his sides.

Through the window, he could see Lara had both hands over her face and her body shook. The older woman next to her put a gentle hand on her arm and said something to Lara. Whatever it was, Lara sat back, wiped her face and closed her eyes. He heard the motor purr to life and the bus picked up speed. Within minutes it was out of his sight. With sadness in his heart, he walked back to a main street to hail a taxi. He'd be back to his life in the bus until he saw her nexttime.

Chapter Thirty-Four

Exhausted from the long bus ride, Lara pushed open the door to her apartment, stepped inside, and immediately felt at home. Although she had enjoyed the spacious kitchen in the mansion, with the gas range and pine table, it wasn't hers. However, memories of the great breakfasts she and Noreen had cooked together on the stove made her stomach grumble.

That house itself felt too large and had too many dark memories for her to want it in her future. This small sunny apartment had become her home and Lara smiled as she unpacked. She would meet Emma at the wedding show in the convention centre tomorrow. Lara hugged herself as she thought about how to share her special news with her friend. For now, she'd steep herself some tea to have with the beignets she's brought with her and make it an early night.

She rose early the next morning and dressed in a soft white shirt tucked into her blue jeans and suede boots. Right after breakfast she set out. On the bus, Lara mused about how honoured she'd felt when Emma asked her to be maid-on-honour. Today, they would choose the right wedding dress for her big day.

The scene which greeted Lara in the crowded centre, however, made her stop to reassess her commitment. She entered a huge room divided into sections, each one packed with women of all ages and state of undress. Lara stared at the closest group as they pawed through bundles of white. Where would she find Emma?

She stared at a Spanish woman who wore a creamy satin gown while next to her stood a tall woman with peach-cream skin and black hair who looked stunning in a white strapless creation.

She felt a hand on her shoulder. "Lara, you're back. I've missed you so much." She swivelled toward Emma who stood there radiant in a white, floor-length silk gown, the top of the skirt overlaid with seed pearls. "Let's go over to the mirror and you can tell me if you like this one." She saw it had a bodice highlighted by a rhinestone design, and the sheer organza skirt had a few more sparkles down the front.

"It sure is glamorous." Lara gave her friend a hug. "How did you manage to find anything to try on in this crowd? Or is this the first one?"

Emma pointed to a pile of white in one corner next to the mirror. "Not exactly. You sit here, while I try them all on again." Her eyes sparkled. "I know you'll be honest with me. I have to look fantastic for Wally. Her face tightened and she bit her lip. My ma saved the money for it."

Lara ran her hands over several of the dresses pushing them aside. She pulled one out of the pile and examined it more closely. "The one you have on is lovely but what about this one?"

She held up a simple white full-length satin dress, a sleeveless design with a low cut neckline and a v shaped back. The bodice had an overlay of lace and an attached belt made of tiny rosettes was clasped around the skirt.

"This one's so different. It's really you, Emma."

Emma's face broke into a smile. "I love it, too. But, don't you think the neckline is too low for me? Especially for our church. Besides, it might be too cold for the evening without sleeves." She changed into the dress.

Lara asked her to turn in front of the mirror so they could admire all sides. She picked up a matching jacket from the floor. "It's got a jacket. You can wear this inside the church and take it off later for the reception. Remember, it'll be like being on stage.

In the excitement, you soon forget whether or not you're too hot or too cold."

Emma clapped her hands. "You're right. I'll take it." She walked over to a woman at the long sales counter and paid the deposit. The woman came over to their space to pin it for alterations.

"When you've had a chance to change, let's go to the restaurant at the entrance for some tea." Lara could barely hold in her secret. As soon as they were seated, she held out her hand to Emma. "I have a surprize for you as well. Jerome proposed to me before I left."

Emma picked up her hand to admire the ring. "How wonderful. Maybe we could have a double wedding this summer. Wouldn't it be great?"

Lara sat back, her mouth pulled into a straight line. "I don't think Wally would agree with you. He's still not sold on Jerome since he's white."

Emma shook her head. "Wally will get over it when he gets to know him better. Jerome's a great guy." I told you Wally belongs to that civil rights movement crowd. He's a member of the Atlantic History Centre and the African Americans who belong are against any type of discrimination. Some of the younger activists like Wally dream about economic and political independence for their race. My mother told me about it. Because of it, he's fanatical about not mixing the races."

Lara felt tears behind her eyes. "It still leaves me out of his world."

Emma's face looked pinched and her mouth turned down. "With my mamma gone, you're the only close family I have left who'll be at my wedding. You'll still come, won't you?"

Lara pulled Emma's hands into her own. "I'm your Maid of Honour, aren't I? I'll be there. We won't let Wally come between us. You're still my best friend. But, we have to be realistic about him and Jerome. They don't like each other."

Lara waved to the waitress to bring the bill. "I need to get back home soon. Camille is coming over this evening to go over the concert schedule with me. I wouldn't want to disappoint her and I need the money right now."

Emma followed her out the door. "When you and Jerome marry, will he move here?" She hesitated. "Or do you plan to go back to New Orleans for good?"

Lara watched the panic on her friend's face. "We haven't even set the date yet. All those details will come later. In my excitement at his proposal, I didn't think it through."

Emma's face brightened. They chatted about her wedding plans until they reach the bus stop. Then she gave Lara a hug. Emma left on her way to join Wally at his society meeting.

*   *   *

The next night, as he continued down Canal Street on his way to join the band, Jerome came face to face with Phillip who had stopped to block his way.

"So, what's up this time, Phillip? Lewis is waiting for me at the hotel."

"I been hearing some rumours about you. You and Lara, that is."

"I don't think it's any business of yours what Lara and I do."

Phillip's face tightened his eyes as cold as steel darts. "Lara is part of my family and what happens with my family is my business. I don't want you in that family."

"Henry doesn't agree with you. He's given his blessing to us. Now get out of my way."

"Don't you forget, the Marrero gang is still after you? Do you want to put her in danger?"

"How do you know what the Marrero gang is up to? I hear it's you they're after."

"Yeah. That was true a while back. But, we got a new deal going now. I got my own guys. While Mardi Gras is on, we're unloading some of the excess drugs from both gangs. For now, we got a truce."

Jerome shook his head. "I don't care what you do in your drug business. The cops will be onto you once this flood is settled."

Phillip shoved him off the street into traffic. "You take care. I can find you any time and we know who's boss."

His cackle could be heard for the next while as Jerome made his way back onto the street and continued his route.

Jerome went straight to Lewis's office when he arrived at the hotel. "Phillip's still out there and getting in ever deeper, so watch out for him."

"I can handle it. Jerome, calm yourself and get changed. The others are already on stage."

Dressed in his performance gear, Jerome approached the group. While he discussed the routines with two of them, he watched Jacqueline flirt with the bass player. He should have expected it. She's already found someone else to run her errands. He sighed with a sense of relief. Her distance would help resolve any possible conflicts with Lara and that was good for both of them. He'd concentrate his attention on getting ready for when Lara returned.

*   *   *

Lara curled up on the sofa in the living room while she waited for Camille to arrive. They planned to review all the concert programs for the remainder of the season. Should she tell Camille she'd be leaving when it ended? She cringed at the thought. Maybe she'd wait until closer to the date before she confessed to Camille. She knew her Choir Director wouldn't be happy.

Lara sat up straighter when she heard a firm knock on the door. She walked over slowly and opened it. Camille hurried in and pulled Lara into a warm hug.

Lara squeezed her back. "It's so good to have you to work with. You look great, as always."

Camille's face broke into a wide smile. "Now we're the lucky ones to have you in the choir. Have you got New Orleans out of your blood yet? I hear they've got a big jazz festival at the end of April."

Lara concentrated on hanging up Camille's coat and led her into the living room. "It's certainly a city for music." Camille watched her closely and Lara shrugged her shoulders. "Look. I'm here until after the end of our season. I've made no decisions long-term."

She handed Camille a bunch of programs. "What do you think of my comments?"

Camille reached out for the programs and then grabbed Lara's left hand, as she stared at the ring. "This is new. It must have happened while you were away, so is it Jerome?"

Lara felt a sudden shyness and dropped her eyes. "Yes, it's Jerome. We're so in love."

Camille shifted her position. "Congratulations. I'm happy for you." There was a long pause. "Will he move to Atlanta? I'd see what I could find for him. Our jazz festival over at the Emery is getting good recognition. In fact, we had over one hundred artists last year."

Lara struggled with her emotions. "Can we leave this for now? It's all so new and I've a lot of decisions to make over the next few months."

Camille sighed and began to read the concert notes. "Yes. Let's get to work on these program revisions. I'm still worried about the concert in two weeks. It needs more punch. We don't want to lose our momentum now."

For the next hour, Camille and Lara reviewed compositions until they were both satisfied. "Let me get you some tea before you go out into the cold."

Camille shook her head. "I've got to get dinner for the family in an hour. I must be on my way. See you at the rehearsal on Wednesday."

*   *   *

The roasted chicken Lara picked up at the local deli, with some lemonade, tasted great. After she'd cleaned up, Lara sat on the sofa and read while she watched the clock as she waited for nine-thirty when she was supposed to phone Jerome. She now felt more confident in his affection and no longer feared he'd be with Jacqueline. When she did dial, he answered right away.

"Hi. Is it you, Lara?"

"Yes. It seemed like forever before I could call you."

"It's so great to hear your voice and to know you're safe." There was a pause. "I've been lonely since you left."

"I've missed you, too, love." Lara glanced at the ring on her finger. "But, I remind myself we'll be together forever, very soon."

Jerome's voice was clear and amused. "You haven't changed your mind, then. About moving back to New Orleans, that is?"

"No. I really want to be with you. Even if it means I have to leave my family here in Atlanta. However, Emma needs me to see her through her wedding this summer and Camille needs me to get her through this concert season. After that, I'll be free."

"Wonderful. When you return, we can make our wedding plans, and find a small place just for us."

"When you're here for Emma's wedding, we can talk more about our plans." Lara could hear Lewis calling Jerome. "I guess you have to go."

"Yeah." Jerome sighed. "I love you and will play a number just for you tonight."

"I know you'll get rave reviews, no matter what you play." Lara choked back a tear.

"I'll be thinking of you." After that, there was only silence until both said good-bye.

Jerome realized how much he missed Lara. It hurt to talk to her because he knew it was all they had for now.

*   *   *

The next day, she hummed to herself on the way to the pastry shop. The tiny bells on the door jingled when she pulled it open and smelled the odour of fresh beignets and newly baked bread. She stood at the counter and placed her order for twelve iced miniature muffins which she planned to take over to Emma's.

She'd just turned to leave with the parcel when someone bumped into her. She saw it was Wally and his face was pulled into a frown.

"What are you doing here? Emma said you were off to the football game with Simon."

"You're right." But my mamma said for me to pick up something nice for Emma before I go. You got any ideas?"

Lara decided to humour him. Over the wedding, the group of them would be together a good deal. She pointed to a tray in the display case. "Jerome and I love those little cream pastries with the chocolate on top."

Wally ordered a dozen. Then his frown returned. "Emma told me you and Jerome are now engaged. I hate to see you go over to whitey's side. Don't forget what I told you about those white boys."

He continued to follow her out of the shop. His sarcastic comments had stung her. "Why do you have to react like that Wally? Why can't you just congratulate me like everyone else?" She gave him a light punch on the arm and felt better.

He stepped back. "Lara, have you ever tried to date black boys? Simon and Morris are both interested. This mixing of races never works, you know. You can't forget the history."

She felt the skin across her cheeks pull tight as her anger rose. "Why can't you understand Jerome and I love each other? It's no different than what you feel for Emma."

Wally gave the small crowd which had gathered a big smile. "Look, we can talk about this another time. I got to get this stuff over to Emma's house before I go to the game. Come on."

She turned her back and walked towards the bus stop. She could hear Wally's footsteps behind her.

"Look, Lara. I'll give you a ride to the house. Don't be so stubborn."

She refused to look back at him and continued to make her way to the bus.

Chapter Thirty-Five

Jerome was anxious during the ride from the bus depot to feel Lara's arms around him and her soft lips against his.

His heels clunked loudly on the sidewalk as he made his way to front door of her apartment building. Lara must have heard his knock since she pulled the door open and grabbed his hand to lead him inside the entranceway. He put both arms around her waist and covered her shoulders with kisses while her laughter engulfed them.

"Oh, Jerome. I've missed you so much. It's so good to have you here with me. It seems like forever."

Jerome dropped his arms and held both hands while he gazed deep into her eyes. "It won't be long now. Soon we won't have to always be saying goodbye. I keep telling myself, it's just a few more months."

"As she gestured toward the bedroom, she said, "You can help me decide what to wear for the rehearsal dinner." Lara had spread out a soft gold dress with a flared skirt. "I wore this one for the spring concert. Or do you like the other one better?" She pulled a sky blue satin dress with a low neckline and cap sleeves out of the closet.

He stood back while she pulled the blue one over her head. Then he did up the zipper for her and nodded his approval.

She fastened the last strap on her silver sandals and turned a circle in front of him. "What do you think of my dress? Will it work for the dinner tonight?"

Jerome smiled. "You're asking the wrong guy. I confess I've not been to a rehearsal before. But, you look great to me."

He moved over to the sofa and slumped into it. "I'm tired. Do we have to go out so soon?"

Lara followed him and gestured towards the bedroom. "Why don't you have a shower and then get changed? It'll perk you up." She ran her hand down his arm and stopped at his hand which she curled into hers. "Since I'm the maid-of-honour, I've got to be there early for Emma."

Jerome got up and headed into the bedroom. He returned to the doorway naked to the waist and enquired, "Are you sure you don't want to join me in the shower?"

He smiled as Lara grinned back at him. "I'll keep it in mind for later. Right now you'll have to hurry as we're expected at the restaurant for six."

When Jerome emerged from the bedroom she was sitting on the sofa reading a magazine. His blond hair was towel dried and he wore a pearl-grey silk shirt tucked into black dress pants. "Will this do? Lewis helped me buy a few clothes for the wedding. I want to look good for you."

She rose and strolled over to him. Lara reached up and smoothed the collar of his shirt. "I love that colour on you. Tell Lewis for me he has good taste."

On the way to the restaurant, they snuggled in the back seat of the cab. Lara leaned in to the closeness of his body and he hoped she enjoyed the scent of his special cologne. When they reached their destination, she seemed reluctant to leave. However, when she saw the others walk up, she sighed and let Jerome take her hand to help her out of the taxi.

When they entered the dining room, they saw Emma and Wally seated with what was probably his family members. Lara said. I'm glad some of Emma's cousins from Baton Rouge are here. They're fun to be with. Emma waved to her as the hostess led them to the adjoining table. Lara blew her a kiss.

Jerome and Lara were seated at their table; they were soon joined by what Lara told him were some of Emma's friends. Lara explained. "This is Dana and Lee, Morelle and Calvin from the choir. I want you to meet my fiancé, Jerome."

During the evening, he was grateful that Lara managed to divide her time between Emma and Wally and her own table with Jerome and the choir members. Jerome smiled at the other two couples whom he instantly liked. Jerome entertained them with stories about the New Orleans nightlife.

By ten p.m., the two of them had said goodbye to the wedding couple and where back in a cab on their way home. Lara squeezed Jerome's hand. "Well, what did you think? Wally seemed more welcoming than last time. Maybe he's mellowing."

Jerome shrugged. "Don't forget. It's his big day tomorrow. He's probably adrift in a cloud right now. But, Emma's cousins gave me a very strong welcome. They've promised to come to our bar to hear me perform when they're in New Orleans next summer."

Later in bed together, Jerome felt his excitement rise when Lara reached over to run her hand down his chest, flat stomach and over his thighs. He could hardly believe he'd be here with her for four whole days. When he pulled her against him, she relaxed. He'd enjoy her closeness while he could.

*   *   *

The wedding morning started well. Sun streamed in the window while he and Lara drank their last cup of their coffee. He touched her hand.

"I have to be over to Emma's by eight for hairdos and make up. Girl things you know."

Jerome smiled, picked up their dirty dishes and piled them into the sink. "Let me clean up while you finish getting dressed. I'll hang out here until just before it's time to arrive at the church."

"Don't forget to sit on the bride's side of the church. That's the left side."

Jerome chuckled. "I better not get mixed up. Wally wouldn't tolerate me on his side of the house."

Lara shook her head and gave him an amused smile. "I don't know how Emma and I are going to get through this wedding, while we keep you two apart."

He watched as she hurried into the bedroom and returned dressed in jeans and a pastel blue patterned shirt. Her formal dress was in a cotton garment bag under her arm. "I'll see you at the church. We'll be in the vestibule at the back." The cab's here. I've got to go." Lara gave him a quick kiss and closed the door as she left.

*   *   *

Before long, the cab dropped her off at Emma's house where she let herself in. After Lara climbed the stairs, she found Emma seated at her bedroom dressing table. She watched as Emma brushed her hair into a frame of wavy hair on each side of her heart shaped face.

"It took the hair dresser three hours yesterday to straighten my hair for today."

Lara sighed as she admired the wedding dress which was perfect for her slim figure and ebony complexion. She stood behind Emma, ready to assist with the veil.

"You are such a beautiful bride, Emma. Wally will be so proud of you."

A frown crossed Emma's face and her lower lip began to tremble. "I so wish my mother was here to talk to. I know I love

Wally. But, am I ready to get married? Several of our friends from school are already divorced."

Lara put both arms around her friend and kissed the top of her head. "You two are so right for each other. What about your own mother and father? Weren't they happily married for thirty years before he passed on?"

Emma set the brush back on the table and turned to look at Lara with a bright smile. "You've right. I guess I'm going through bride's nerves."

Would she feel like Emma when her wedding day arrived, Lara wondered? Her mother hadn't managed a happy marriage but that was different. She'd been so excited when Jerome arrived last night; they hadn't even talked about the wedding. She'd have to make time to do so before he left.

"Come on. Let's get your veil arranged. It's okay for the bride to be a little late, but we had better be ready to leave soon." Lara laughed. "Otherwise, Wally will think you've changed your mind."

The two women relaxed in the back of the rented limo. Emma clutched Lara's hand all the way to their destination. They walked slowly to the front door of the church. Lara pulled the heavy door of the church open and they entered the vestibule. Lara was relieved to find Jerome where he stood alone next to a small oak side table. Camille and several of the girls rushed towards them to admire Emma's gown and new hairdo. The break gave Lara time to free herself and approach Jerome for a few moments of talk before they went in.

"I love your new suit, love. I've got to go down the aisle with Emma shortly. Her uncle from Baton Rouge will give her away. You can sit next to Camille and Owen and follow us out when it's over."

Jerome grabbed her hand. "You look pretty hot in that pink gown." He lowered his voice. "Someday soon, this will be us."

Lara squeezed his hand and then broke free to rejoin Emma. She watched him as he was taken down the aisle. Moments later, she heard the wedding march start.

At the reception hall, the wedding party assembled near the head table and lined up to greet the guests. Lara stared over at Wally. He looked so different as he stood next to Emma with his dreadlocks tamed into straight corn rows and his black tuxedo hugged his slim frame well. The bride and groom were oblivious to all around them as they gazed into each other's eyes. Lara had to gently tug on Emma's arm to get her attention as the guests approached.

"Okay, you two. You'll have time for kisses when the dinner starts. For now, be prepared to let friends and family greet you as a new couple."

Emma giggled and Wally stood straighter and fixed his tie. They both seemed to enjoy the interaction with guests until Jerome was next in line. He followed Camille and Owen who had hugged both the bride and groom. When Jerome finished hugging Emma, he hesitated then stuck his hand out shake with Wally. Wally glowered at him and took two steps back. Emma bit her lip and her eyes looked down. She tugged Wally's arm.

Emma said. "You remember Jerome, don't you honey? He's Lara's fiancé."

Wally stood where he was and didn't extend a hand. "Yeah. I know who he is."

"Excuse me." Lara brushed past Wally and took Jerome's hand to walk with him over to the small group of other choir members from last night. "I'm sorry about Wally's behaviour. Why don't you join this group until I can break free and then I'll find you a table?" Her gaze went to two of the women in the group.

The two women opened the circle and gestured for Jerome to join them. "We'll be more than happy to entertain him for you Lara."

Jerome smiled at them. Then he grabbed Lara's hand. "Don't worry about me, honey. I've faced worse than Wally."

After a deep sigh, Lara returned to the reception line. She hid her distress from Emma, so as not to spoil her wedding day. But, what would this mean for their friendship? Soon Wally would move into Emma's house when they returned from their honeymoon in Barbados.

The head table looked beautiful, decorated with clear vases holding red roses set against shiny green leaves. After dinner, Emma and Wally had their first dance as a married couple and Lara relaxed knowing it had all gone well.

Next, she and Jerome were to take the lead and invite the other couples in the wedding party to join them. Once in his arms, she pulled him close and rested her head against his shoulder. The scent of his familiar cologne caused excitement to rise up from her toes leaving faint beads of perspiration on her cheeks.

When the music ended, Jerome led her back to his table and gazed into her eyes. I can't even think about getting on the bus tomorrow."

"Let's not think about it. We still have tonight and we can dance until midnight. We don't often have a chance to dance with each other."

"You're right. It's great being able to hold you that close." He kissed her hand. "And I've already forgotten the nasty incident with Wally."

Lara nodded. "Forget about Wally. I know you came here for me and for Emma."

Jerome took her hand and led her back to the floor. The feel of his lean body pressed against hers left her with an electric sensation.

At the end of the evening, they stood arm in arm and watched the new couple leave for their hotel. Lara admired Emma's short yellow silk dress. Even Wally looked good in his grey suit.

"Finally, my duties as Maid-of-Honour are complete. Let's go home and spend our last few hours together." Lara's eyes smouldered under her thick lashes as she grabbed his hand.

"Sounds good to me." He hailed a cab when they got outside. "We don't want to waste any more time."

* * *

When the apartment door closed behind them, he watched Lara kick off her high heel shoes and flex her toes before she headed into the bedroom. Jerome followed, stripped off his jacket and tie and dropped them onto a chair. He helped Lara with the buttons and zipper of her gown which fell to the floor. He continued to remove her bra and panties and stood back to gaze at the shiny skin on her naked body.

"You're so beautiful." Jerome whispered.

Lara pulled him close and unbuttoned his shirt. She then tugged down the zipper of his pants and he helped her remove them. Then he took off his briefs and pressed his muscular body against her warm skin.

They embraced and sat on the bed together, as they covered each other in hungry kisses. He was surprised when Lara pushed him back on the bed and straddled his body with hers. He lay still while she clasped his pelvis with her knees and took him inside as she rocked back and forth. They moved together in a new rhythm until, while he could hear her breath came in gasps. They climaxed together and she collapsed against his chest. Jerome felt his body relax, rolled onto his side, and pulled the sheets over him. Lara rolled against him and cuddled in.

"That was wonderful. I don't want us to have to live so far apart. It's agony."

Lara turned onto her back. "It won't be for much longer. I have one more concert and then I'll be back in New Orleans by late September."

Jerome removed his arm from under her and crossed them both behind his head. "It still seems like such a long time. It's only June now."

Lara sat up on her elbow and traced circles on his chest. "But, I need you to remember, in September I move back for good. I have to wind up things here first so I don't have to return."

Jerome was silent for some time. "Will you move back in with Noreen and Henry?"

Lara smiled. "Yes, I'll stay with them until we get a place. They've already asked me."

Jerome's face turned serious. "Okay. I'll have saved some money by then. Let's get married in October. We'll have a warm day for the event."

Lara sighed. "It'll have to be a small wedding. I'll only have Noreen and Henry and maybe a few of my friends. Emma will probably drive up from Atlanta and perhaps she'll bring some of the other choir members. You said your mother and sister might come from Florida and Lewis and maybe some of the other band members. We won't need a big hall.

"That's fine with me. I get enough crowds with the band. But are you sure? If Emma comes then she'll probably bring Wally. I want you to know I can live with that." He turned sideways so she could lay her head on his chest.

Lara wiggled closer to him. "I don't really want Wally to come with the way he treated you this time. But, you're right. If Wally doesn't come, Emma won't come."

Jerome turned on the bedside lamp. "Wally could change by then. You never know about people.

"I doubt it. I know Wally." Lara gave Jerome a last kiss and curled up on her own side of the bed.

*   *   *

The next day after Jerome's bus pulled out from the station, Lara felt a dark mood come over her. At least this would be the last time they had to say goodbye? She sighed and began to walk back to her streetcar. She had begun to call Noreen almost every Saturday night to keep in touch and had told him to leave a message with them if he needed to talk to her. When she reached home, she pulled out her programs from under the coffee table and began to review them. The next rehearsal was tomorrow night and she'd had no time for any review of her part.

The next concert would be in August at the Amphitheatre and it would be the big one. Camille said it would move the choir into the professional realm and therefore provide some of the members with a good chance to earn real money. It would help her reputation with the classical symphony orchestra she'd join in New Orleans this fall.

The time went quickly with weekly practices with Camille for her solo number. She told Lara the concert hall was sold out already for their performance. Jerome had wished her well last night when they had their regular call. Both Noreen and Henry had expressed regret at missing this special concert for her. Noreen had developed arthritis in her left knee and the long bus ride would aggravate it. Lara suspected they were also reluctant to leave their newly renovated house unattended due to the ongoing crime in their area.

Once on stage, Lara turned her gaze toward Camille's calm face at the podium and knew she'd make it through the evening. The choir reached the right tempo during the first couple of numbers and she could see the audience nodding in approval. That was a good sign. The following number was a bit tricky but she was relieved when Wally as lead baritone led the group through it and the piece went exceptionally well. At least he could sing. She felt for Emma and hoped the relationship would work out. He had treated Emma well, but he made it clear he was the one in their household who would make all important decisions.

As she prepared for her solo, Lara could feel butterflies rumble across her stomach. She took deep breaths and expelled them to warm up as she'd been instructed. Her eyes fixed on Camille and remained there. When Camille gave the signal to begin, she opened her throat and sang. Her eyes remained on Camille to watch for cues and she sailed through her piece. The joy of success tingled through her when the audience stood to give a wave of applause.

Later backstage, she felt envy flood her as she watched the other couples embrace. If only Jerome were here to join in her success. She could imagine being enfolded in his arms while he showered her with kisses. Her blood throbbed at the image in her head.

With so much excited noise in the room, Emma jumped onto a chair and whistled for calm. "Wally and I are glad to invite all of you to a late supper at our house."

After she got down, she went to Lara. "You'll come won't you? I know things haven't been quite the same since the spat between Wally and Jerome. But, we're still friends, aren't we?"

Lara hugged her. "Of course, I'll come. We've all got lots to celebrate. Can I get a ride with you?"

"Come on then. We're going to leave now since I need to set up a food table."

Lara helped Emma set out hot fried chicken wings and some baked goods. She'd made four round pound cakes filled with candied fruit and streaked with a white sugary icing. They set out plenty of coffee and tea.

When the group arrived, they settled themselves in clusters in the combined living room and dining room. Emma insisted Lara take the largest chair in the centre. Camille addressed the group. "Lara's soprano solo was the highpoint of the concert. And

Wally's piece also deserves special recognition. So let's give a hand for both of them."

When quiet returned, Camille came over to sit next to her and placed her hand on Lara's arm. "I'm still waiting for your answer. Have you decided which city will you and Jerome live in when you're married?

Lara's throat felt parched. "You know I love the choir. You've been the best teacher I could wish for Camille. But, I got a really good offer with the symphony in New Orleans and Jerome is already making a name for himself there."

"Listen, sweetie. I'd be the last one to keep you from the man you love. But, I want to let you know scouts where in the audience tonight to consider us for a record deal. You can be recognized here just as well as in New Orleans."

The two women looked at each other for a few moments and then Camille dropped her gaze. "We'll miss you, is all I wanted to say. If you ever want to come back anytime to join us, we'll be waiting."

Chapter Thirty-Six

In the grey dusk, Jerome stood with Henry and Noreen at his side, while excitement caused him to shift from one foot to the other. The three of them were silent while they waited for the bus from Atlanta to arrive. It was late but that wasn't unusual.

Noreen sighed and grabbed his arm. "She's got to be on this next bus. I can't wait any longer."

The next announcement relieved the tension. The bus from Atlanta would arrive in fifteen minutes at sign Number 9. They laughed and rushed through the crowd to make sure they placed themselves in front of the sign to greet her. He recognized her head held high, right away when she stepped onto the roadway. Her dark straightened hairdo, faded denim jacket and tight black capris made him realize how sophisticated she had become.

She waved to them and hurried over. Noreen grabbed her for hugs and kisses. He let Henry go next and then put his arms around her and held her close. Her moist lips against his felt like more.

Noreen gave him a gentle nudge and wrapped Lara in her arms again. "This is almost as exciting as picking you up the first time, girl, when you arrived from Louisville as a child of ten."

Lara laughed and kissed her aunt on the cheek. "I'm a much larger handful for you now, Auntie."

She turned back to Henry. "How have you been making out Uncle? Are you still working too hard on renovations for other people?"

Henry's eyes were soft and tender. "We's all thrilled to have you back." He struggled to hold back the tears. "Yeah, I got more than I can handle right now. Have to pick and choose what I take on. But, it's good to have the work."

Jerome stepped forward and put his arm around her. "I'm glad she'll be staying in your guest room. I'll feel she's safer there."

Noreen smiled. "Stay as long as you want. It's still much too quiet with most of the neighbours still in either Texas or Atlanta."

"That's great. Jerome and I have to look for something to rent so I'll be happy to live with the two of you until then. We've decided on an October wedding."

Noreen's face broke into a big smile. "Well, he can stay, too, until the wedding. October is a good time. Warm enough for an outdoor reception. What do you have in mind?"

Lara looked over at Jerome. "Well, neither Jerome nor I have big families, so something small. You can help us arrange it now that I'm back. You know everyone around here." She put her hand in Jerome's. "Can you stay tonight?"

Jerome smiled. "Yeah. Lewis gave me the night off, bless him."

Henry waved down a cab. "I haven't decided what to do with Phillip's old place? You know I'd give it to you to use, but there's still a time restriction on the title due to his disappearance."

Lara gave him a concerned look. "He was your family. If he doesn't show up, you'll probably want to sell it. That is if you don't want to live in it yourself."

A brief look of pain crossed Henry's face. "That's all over now." He smiled at Noreen. "Noreen and I are happy to be back in our old place and have no use for a big old house like that. We don't fit with those neighbours."

Noreen nodded. "That's right. I still pray for some of the old neighbours to rebuild. But, lots of claims aren't settled yet."

Lara stared out the window until they reached the house. "With the new paint, new sod and that white fence, it looks even better than before the flood."

She squeezed Noreen's hand. "I need you to help me choose an outfit for the wedding. I used to fancy the dresses at Audrey's boutique. Did they reopen?"

"Yeah. Some of the stores in Jackson Square are back and new ones have opened." Noreen got out of the cab and led the way into the house. "It's not the same though."

Jerome noted the house was locked like most people did now with the fear of break-ins from the homeless. He and Lara followed the short hall into the guest bedroom. He was glad Noreen wanted him to stay with Lara for the next few weeks. He'd already started his search for a house for them to rent. When Lara set her things on the bed, he put both arms around her.

"We can start tomorrow to choose our new home. I've lined up two for us to check out in the Faubourg Marigny area."

She kissed him softly on the lips. "Great. It will be our first home together so it has to be just right for us. We'd better join Noreen and Henry for coffee and sweets before we retire." She hesitated. "I've been thinking we should tell Henry about Phillip. Since he's back into crime, Henry needs to know to be on the alert."

"I guess you're right. Not when he's with Noreen though. We don't need to scare her again."

Settled in the living room, Jerome sipped the hot coffee enjoying the aroma. "We'll check out a couple of houses tomorrow, one on Chartres and the other on Royal."

Noreen's eyes widened. "Isn't that too close to Elysian Fields where those drug gangs hang out?"

Jerome took a deep breath. "The area is changing. The Bed and Breakfast crowd has moved in and renovated. He could see Henry's eyes had closed into slits as he reclined in his chair. "I got a big day tomorrow laying new floors so I'll head into bed soon. I guess we should let you two get some rest as well. We can talk more in the morning."

When the older couple had disappeared, Jerome took Lara's hand and they walked down the hall together. He closed the bedroom door and she began to undo some of his shirt buttons.

"It's so good to be back here with you. I've dreamed about this night every day for the last week." She kissed him on the chest.

Jerome groaned and pulled her tightly against him, bending his head to meet her fully on her parted lips. "I can hardly believe you're here with me now. I'm hungry for you." He used one hand to open the zipper on her jeans while she pulled open the snaps on her blouse.

Urgency caused him to pull down his own jeans and discard his briefs while Lara took off her bra and panties. They stood locked together in the moonlight, as they explored each other with hands and lips. As heat rose through his loins, Jerome led her to the bed and they lay on it clutched together. Excitement ran through him as his tongue explored her breasts and continued down to her stomach.

She moaned in pleasure and pulled him on top while she put both hands around his waist and pulled him closer. Jerome heard her moan as his body responded to hers. He soon felt an intense sense of warmth and release. He watched her face relax and felt the warmth of her body before they both lay back on the cotton sheets to rest. Jerome cuddled her against his chest while he stroked her hair.

*   *   *

Sun poured through the bedroom window, while he listened to Noreen calling from the kitchen. Jerome blinked his eyes and kissed Lara on the neck.

"I'll shower first," Lara said. "That way I can help Noreen with breakfast."

"Hmmm." Jerome murmured. He fell back against the pillow to doze.

A short while later, he saw Lara wander back into the bedroom with her hair still wet from the shower.

"Okay, sleepyhead. Your turn." She pulled the sheets back to expose his nude body and ran her fingers across his chest.

Jerome smiled at her before he got to his feet and gave her a quick embrace. "Okay. You go help Noreen and I'll join the three of you in a few minutes." He left for the bathroom.

Seated in their new dining area off the kitchen, Jerome watched Noreen's wide smile as she served a huge breakfast of pancakes and syrup, sausages and hash browns.

"Henry has eaten his first thing and has gone to the jobsite."

Jerome accepted a heaping plate. "Thanks. We're off to check out those two houses this morning."

Lara came to join him with a full pot of fresh coffee. "I'm looking forward to it."

Noreen took her place. "Well, if you get tired of checking out the French Quarter, there are a couple of nice brick bungalows near here for sale or rent."

Lara jumped in. "Since Jerome arrives home so late from the bar, we need to live closer to the hotel. It's too far for him to travel out here, especially if he can't find a cab."

Jerome set down his cup. "Both the properties we're checking out today are small two-storey houses and the rent is a good price. We'll be meeting the landlord over there and I'll ask him about the area."

Lara grabbed his hand. "For me, the important features are at least a small garden in back and a front porch we can sit on together."

A frown crossed Noreen's face. "I'm warning you. Make sure they're not too close to Elysian Fields? I hear bad things about that area."

Jerome shook his head. "No. Marigny has a few small apartment buildings and the bed and breakfast places I told you about. It's different from Elysian."

*   *   *

Jerome followed the landlord, an older black man who lived on Royal Street, as they climbed the steps on the first property on their list. Lara walked close behind him. He hadn't noticed when he pulled up in the cab how close it was located to the street. No flower garden for Lara with this one. The front door creaked and they entered directly into the small living room. They followed him into the kitchen at the back of the house.

Lara turned up her nose. "The linoleum is broken in several places and the green paint has lots of stains. Do you plan to redecorate?"

The landlord narrowed his eyes. "You get what you're paying for. I got nicer places in other areas but they're pricy."

When they returned to the sidewalk, he and Lara both shook their heads negatively. He said to the landlord. "This one doesn't work for us. We'll have to keep looking."

The landlord shrugged. "Suit yourselves. The other one is a two-storey but it's a bit more expensive."

He led them up onto an enclosed front porch with lots of windows. Lara turned to Jerome and grabbed his hand.

"We could put some wicker chairs and a wrought iron table out here. I can imagine Noreen and I relaxing there with our afternoon tea."

They followed him inside. On the main floor they saw a good sized kitchen which led into a breakfast nook with windows along one wall. The living room was large enough for a sofa and two chairs. Jerome liked the bay window which looked out into a side yard.

Jerome smiled at Lara. "Can we see the upstairs?"

They climbed the wooden staircase to find a large bathroom and a master bedroom with two windows.

Jerome said. "What else is up here?"

Lara ran ahead. "There is a small guest bedroom and a sewing room. I like it."

The landlord responded. "Good. I'll show you the back yard."

The back porch opened into a long narrow yard with a cobble stone path and overgrown perennial flower beds. Jerome noted the yard was open to the others on either side which made it appear larger.

Jerome smiled at Lara. "What do you think?"

Lara grabbed his arm. "It's great. This is a house I could live in."

Jerome pulled her close. "Whatever you want, honey, it okay with me. I've been so used to living in hotel rooms and tour buses that this seems large to me."

He nodded to the landlord. "We'll take it if we can have is for October 2. We're getting married then."

The landlord took out his lease form from a canvas bag. "It's yours with a check for $2000 to cover the first and last month's rent. Jerome filled out the form on the window sill and made out a cheque which he handed over. "When you're ready, I operate a second-hand furniture store and can give you a good price."

He couldn't believe how much his life had changed in such a short time. As he looked over at Lara who had a broad smile which almost covered her face. It was worth it. They were ready to begin their life together.

*   *   *

Jerome arrived early at City Hall the morning of their wedding and felt a flood of anxiety as he climbed the stone stairs which led to the large oak front doors. He was glad Lewis had agreed to meet him here an hour before the ceremony. His mother and sister would also be here but he wasn't sure when they'd get into town. After he entered the office of the Justice of Peace, he was directed into the chapel set aside for weddings. He sat in the waiting area and breathed out a deep sigh.

Before long, Lewis joined him. "How're you feeling? I hope you're not ready to escape?" He chuckled.

Jerome relaxed, his stomach beginning to settle. "I really appreciate you doing this for me. I don't have too many friends in New Orleans with the band hours."

Lewis said. "I've become close to the both of you and I'm glad to see this day."

They turned their heads when the door burst open and a noisy group wandered through. Noreen and Henry both had big smiles and each had an arm around Lara. "Now, honey, you just stay calm. Your groom is here already so you don't need worry he won't show up." She gave a hearty laugh.

Jerome stood up and stared at Lara in wonder. She looked gorgeous in a white strapless dress cinched at the waist with a beaded belt. Her shiny black hair was tucked under and covered with a short lace veil. While he gazed at her, the three of them moved into the room and made their way to the seats on the other side.

Noreen said. "Don't you two look very formal in your slate-grey tuxedos? Jerome, I'll never get used to you in your shiny shirts at the bar after this. I know you're not supposed to see the bride but since we're doing an informal ceremony it should be okay."

Lara gave him a shy smile, her eyes glinted with moisture. He smiled back but couldn't bring himself to say anything in front of all of them. He'd tell her how beautiful she was in private when they reached the altar.

His mother was the next to arrive. She came over right away and gave him a big hug. Mom had died her hair red and appeared much thinner than when he last saw her. She wore a mauve satin dress and matching jacket which must be new. His sister, Janice, looked pretty sexy in a tight red dress with narrow straps across her shoulders. She gave him a kiss on the cheek, wished him well and then the two of them moved over to the other side to greet Lara and her family.

Janice said. "Lara, you're so beautiful in that strapless silk dress. It's so original." She took Noreen and Henry's outstretched hands and shook them. "So pleased to meet you. This is Jerome's and my mother, Ellen." Ellen gave Lara a stiff hug and managed a smile at the other two.

Janice turned back to Lara. "Where's your maid-of honour?"

He watched Lara's mouth turn down as she dropped her head. Then the door swung open and Emma and Wally rushed in. Emma's face was stretched tight in anxiety. Camille and her husband, Owen, followed them in and he recognized three or four others from the choir.

Emma rushed over to Lara and took both her hands in hers. "I'm so sorry we're late. I meant to be here to greet you when you arrived." She glared over at Wally who shuffled his feet and stayed silent.

Lara smiled and squeezed Emma's hands. "You're here now and that's all that matters. Wally, can you usher my guests to the left hand side and, Lewis, can you take Jerome's mother and sister to the right side."

Lewis crossed the floor to stand beside Lara. "The Justice of the Peace tells me we're next. After I get Janice and her mother seated, then Jerome and I will go in first and wait at the altar for you and Henry. Emma can follow behind you." He held up a black velvet cushion. "Don't worry. I've got the ring."

Even though this was a civil ceremony, City Hall had spent time to make the room look like the inside of a church with an altar. The Justice was friendly and knew his job. Neither Jerome nor Lara was members of a local church. She told him Wally was shocked about it but Emma had finally coaxed him to attend. He hoped Lara wouldn't have regrets since she more comfortable in a formal church and would miss the music.

Before he realized what had happened, they'd exchanged vows and rings. When he gazed into Lara's shining brown eyes, so full of love, he smiled and told her what he'd held back. "I can't believe this beautiful woman is now my wife." What did it matter where they had the ceremony? They were beginning a new life as a married couple.

Back on the steps, bathed in sunlight, the two of them greeted their guests. Janice had made friends with the girls from the choir who would make sure they got to the reception. Lewis, who had insisted on driving the married couple there, moved them towards his car. They drove the short distance in silence. While the couple entered the private dining room, he went back out to park the car.

Happiness flooded through Jerome when he saw how thrilled Lara was with the decorations Noreen had chosen for them. Long tables covered with white linen had been arranged in a horseshoe shape. A gorgeous centrepiece of white roses with small blue flax accented the head table where Lewis led them. Jerome gave her a long kiss before she relaxed into her chair. Lara smiled at Emma and Wally who took the seats to her left. On his side were Lewis and Janice. His mother had a place on the long section next to Janice.

His appetite had disappeared this morning with all the excitement but now his stomach grumbled from lack of nourishment. The main course of grilled quail with pear soon arrived and he let Lara start and then dug in. They glanced at each other over glasses of chardonnay. He'd chosen it from the local Pontchartrain Vineyards for the occasion. Lewis called for quiet as Henry stood to give the toast to the bride.

"Noreen and I have been blessed since a young girl stepped off the bus and into our arms all those years ago. Lara, we're not giving you away since you'll be living right here in our city of New Orleans. And I've come to know this young man of yours who is already like a member of our family. You'll all join me in toasting these two wonderful people."

Jerome grabbed Lara to him and kissed her tenderly on the lips.

Lewis rose and turned to Jerome. "I've got admit I've only know Jerome for about a year since he's joined our band. But, I consider him to be like a brother to me. I'm proud to know his new wife, Lara, a warm and generous young woman who holds her family close to her heart. Please join with me in toasting this newly married couple."

Jerome placed his arms around Lara for a long passionate kiss. The guests cheered. As Lara pulled back and began to take her seat, Jerome remained and watched Wally's reaction. He stood rigidly beside Emma with no glass in hand. Had he refused to toast them? The shocked look on Emma's face told him the story. He'd never be able to forgive Wally for slighting Lara with that gesture.

After the last guests had departed, Lewis had dropped them off at their new house. Jerome picked Lara up into his arms and carried her onto the porch. Lewis found the keys and let then in the front door so he could set her down inside. "We've done it, sweetheart. From now on we're Mr. and Mrs. Decarie."

Lara kept her arms around his waist. "It's so wonderful. We're safe in our own home in this city we've chosen to make ours."

Chapter Thirty-Seven

They'd been living in their new home for two months, when Jerome told Lara he wanted to plant a privet hedge in the backyard. It would someday be a separation line with the house next door. The couple who lived there were loud and had a tendency to walk into Jerome and Lara's yard at any time with no invitation.

With the porch door open, he could hear Lara in the kitchen fussing over the roast chicken dinner and fried peppers she was planning for their dinner. As he put one of the last small shrubs into the hole he'd dug, he heard her steps on the porch.

"Dinner's ready, hon."

He waved at her. "I'll be right there. Just two more plants to go."

He entered the small 2 piece bathroom off the back porch and washed the dirt off his hands before he joined Lara in the kitchen.

"Something sure smells good." He put both arms around her as she stood at the stove and kissed her on the neck. "I knew I was smart to choose you as my bride."

Lara laughed and pointed towards the table. "We'd better eat since you have to leave at eight. Will you be late getting back tonight again? Fridays used to be your late nights. Now it's Saturdays as well."

Jerome sighed. "We're into the pre-Christmas season with lots of tourists in town. Lewis says the hotel is full and we can expect to be on until at least two."

Lara frowned. "I worry about you coming home so late from that place. I bet you didn't tell Lewis about the break-ins neighbours told us about, just two streets over."

Jerome shook his head. "It wouldn't do any good. What can he do?" He paused. "Are you scared to be alone?"

She hesitated. "I loved this neighbourhood when we first moved in. Remember how I used to sit on the front porch at night to watch for you?"

Jerome felt guilt wash over him. He knew since the break-ins, Lara never left the house after dark, even to sit on the porch. He took her hand and squeezed it.

She continued. "I miss you, that's all. The symphony will be busy with our own concerts later this month as well, but for now its afternoon practices only."

"How are you getting along with the other singers in your new choir? Have you made any friends yet?"

Lara smiled in gratitude. "Thanks for your worry about me. No real friends as yet. The role of a classical soloist is different from what I did in Atlanta. During practice, I work with Jenna and Franklin, the other two soloists. The conductor is marvelous, so talented and willing to share. But mostly, I work alone. But the pay is great."

"We can both use the extra cash to get this place in shape. We still need lots of furniture even after what we bought and what Noreen leant us." He carried some of the dishes to the sink. "Let's clean up so I can play some warm up pieces before I have to leave. It's so hectic when I get there I don't have the time. I have some good news though. Lewis has promised me another raise in January."

Lara joined him at the sink, the remainder of the dishes in her hands, and dried them as he washed. "Great. Maybe later when the mansion on Chestnut sells, there's something we can use. But until Phillip gives permission to sell, it will just sit there."

"Henry told me houses aren't selling well anyway due to the crime which has been out of control since the storm. The lack of jobs also keeps people from returning home." Jerome emptied the water from the sink. "Apparently the Mayor asked the government for help since the police who are left can't handle it, but nothing has happened so far. The police are outnumbered by the criminals."

Lara gave him a troubled look. "You be careful, honey. Take a cab home and don't take any chances. I want you safe."

He pulled her close and kissed her on the lips. "I didn't mean to scare you, love. Lewis always insists on a cab for all the players at that hour, if they're not staying in the bus. Don't you worry."

Jerome hurried upstairs to the spare bedroom for practice. He was sorry, he'd concerned Lara. Actually, this was a quiet street where young couples, both gay and straight mixed at the local supermarket and argued over the few fresh fruits and vegetables which were now in supply. In what seemed like a short time, he heard Lara call to him.

"Cab is here."

He quickly changed into black chino pants and a slate grey shirt. Then he ran down the stairs, his sax under his arm and kissed her full lips before he rushed to open the door.

"Don't wait up for me, love. We'll have all day tomorrow to ourselves. Maybe we could go for a picnic. Or even better, we could stay in bed all day."

Lara laughed and followed him to the door. She stood there until he got in the cab and then closed it. He was glad he'd invited her to a few late night dinners with his band. Now that she knew them better, she hadn't worried about him so much until these recent break-ins.

*   *   *

Jerome crept silently up the stairs and opened the bedroom door so he wouldn't wake Lara. After he dropped his clothes in a pile by the bed, he pulled the covers aside and slid under the sheets. He couldn't resist pressing his body against hers for warmth. To his surprize, she turned and pulled him into her arms as she covered his face with small kisses.

"You're home safe with me," Lara whispered in a sleepy voice.

Jerome enjoyed her warmth while he kissed her on the mouth. "I'm here with you love as I always will be. Now, let's get some sleep. It's two-thirty."

"Don't forget you promised me a picnic tomorrow." She snuggled back under the covers.

Jerome stroked her hair. "A picnic, it is then. How about the Botanical Gardens? We can sit on one of the benches and admire the new flowers."

When Jerome arrived in their kitchen on Sunday morning, Lara already had the picnic basket filled with shrimp salad, smoked salmon and French bread. They enjoyed a quick breakfast of hash browns and scrambled eggs with steaming black coffee and then headed for the bus.

The bus dropped them right outside the well-designed grounds of the gardens inside the huge area of City Park. They choose one of the many elaborate stone benches and enjoyed their lunch. When they were finished, Lara filled the basket with their dirty dishes and closed the lid. "Let's explore the Tropical Forest Room in the conservatory. I haven't seen it since they reopened in 2002."

Jerome gave her a gentle smile. "Whatever you would like. This is your day." He followed her into the large building filled with tropical flora and huge greenery. The sun had begun to set when they finished their tour and headed for the entrance to the park. He heard a sudden shuffle of feet behind them, and held his breath as he turned. He then breathed out in relief. It was two guys he'd seen earlier in the day strolling through the greenhouse.

"It was a wonderful day for me," sighed Lara. "The last time I was here was with my high school class."

"I had a great time, too. We should explore New Orleans more often." He held her hand as they waited for the bus. "We've lots of gardens in Florida, but I needed someone like you to share them with."

Lara sighed. "Well, tomorrow I'm back to practice with the orchestra from one to four. What about you, Jerome? Is Monday a slow day?"

"We'll be back to winding up the band at midnight, at least until Friday and Saturday night. Then it will depend on the crowds."

"Okay, I'll wait up if I don't get too sleepy. For dinner tonight, we'll have some cold fried chicken and potato salad which is in the fridge so I don't have to cook."

"It sounds great. Let's go to bed early tonight. I have a busy day tomorrow. Lewis wants me to help him with some stuff at the hotel around six."

As usual, Lara had let him sleep in while she made the breakfast and he joined her around ten. He was glad to see her good spirits from yesterday were still with her. He filled his plate and sat at the table waiting for her to join him.

"Are you looking forward to practice today?"

Lara smiled. "As we get closer to a real concert, the practices seem more meaningful. I can tell from the Choir Director's comments that my voice has improved. It's just the nights."

Jerome saw her mouth turn down and her shoulders droop. "What's wrong? Are you still glad we choose this house?"

She nodded in the affirmative. "It's just a little spooky around here at night when you're away at work. One night last week, I needed eggs and milk for breakfast but I couldn't make myself go to the store until the next morning."

Jerome sighed. "Are you okay to take the bus back and forth to practice?"

Lara smiled. "I don't want you to worry about me. I'm good coming back from practice as long as it's early in the afternoon when the streets are quiet."

After breakfast, Jerome went out to the backyard to finish some work. He now wished it was more enclosed. The hedge he'd planted wouldn't provide a barrier for at least another two years. He wondered if he should plant one on the opposite side as well. When he finished, he returned to the house to do some practicing.

While he was in the middle of a piece, he heard Lara call him for lunch and went downstairs.

She had placed large glasses of lemonade on the table for each of them beside plates of tuna salad with green eyed peas and crusty French bread.

"We're eating early since I have to leave around 12:30 for my practice. I hope that's okay for you."

"Of course. Lunch looks great. You always come up with something different." He took a mouthful. "This is very good." They ate in a comfortable silence and he helped her to clean up.

With lunch out of the way, he watched Lara hurry up the stairs to change and waited for her to return. He'd walk her to the bus stop so she'd be more relaxed when she arrived.

Back at the house, he returned to his practice. They would be doing a new number this week-end and he would need to know how to manage the notes seamlessly. Around 4:30 p.m., he heard the door open and went downstairs to see if Lara had returned.

As soon as Jerome saw Lara, shoulders rigid and jaw clenched, just inside the door, he knew it wasn't going to be good. He rushed over to her.

"What happened, honey? You look awful."

She fell into his arms and clutched him, her body shaking. "I saw Phillip. He followed me."

Anger crawled up Jerome's neck. He kept his arm around her and led her into the living room where she sat on the sofa and leaned against him. "Okay. Tell me exactly what happened."

"I was on my way home from practice as usual. About a block from the house, I heard footsteps behind me. I tried to walk faster, but shortly after a hand grabbed my arm. Although I was frightened, I gathered my courage and turned to face the intruder. I found myself staring right at Phillip. "What—you don't talk to me no more?" I continued to stare at him and he finally dropped his hand."

"God. Not Phillip again. I ran into him over near Henry and Noreen's some time ago but haven't seen him around here. How did he look? What did he do?"

"His hair was long, tangled and almost grey and he's very gaunt. His eyes looked haunted like two black beads in a shrunken face. He grunted something about where's Jerome at? He threatened to make you pay for what you got him into. He seems to think you caused all his problems."

"That's what he accused me of when I saw him as well. Something to do with me sending the gang after him. It's all in his head."

"Well, he glared at me for a while and then ran off through one of the side paths between two houses. I yelled at him that I would tell Henry and you I'd seen him, but he paid no attention."

"You're right Lara. We need to tell Henry what happened. Noreen could be in danger if he turns on them instead."

She nodded. "We'd better tell him in person. It'll be less of a shock. I'll distract Noreen and get her out of the room. That will give you time to bring him up to date and maybe come up with a plan."

"Okay. We're invited there for dinner on Wednesday night. Although, I hate to tell Henry about how Phillip is deteriorating. After all he is Henry's brother. But we need to keep the two of them safe. Phillip's not in a good place."

Chapter Thirty-Eight

On Wednesday night, as soon as Lara returned from her practice session, Jerome suggested they leave for Henry and Noreen's. He needed to get this ugly business over with after being awake most of the night. They exchanged a warm greeting when Noreen opened the door for them. He could smell the wonderful odour of pork roast from the kitchen as she led them into the living room.

Lara asked Noreen to show her the master bedroom they had finally painted in a coral shade. He watched the two women disappear down the hall and then sucked in his breath and turned to Henry.

"I don't like having to tell you this, Henry, but Phillip is very much alive. I've run into him around town a couple of times. I thought I could handle it but last week he confronted Lara on her way home from practice."

Henry jumped to his feet. "He's still alive and here in town." He curled his hands into fists and punched them against his thighs. "I'll find that brother of mine and when I do, he won't bother Lara no more. That's for sure."

Jerome struggled to stay calm. "Now sit down and listen to me a little longer. Phillip's eyes are wild and he's scrawny, his face grey looking. We figure he's on cocaine again. He also told me the Marrero gang are still after him and are getting close."

Henry set his jaw. "I don't want to hear any excuses about him. He knows better than how he's been acting."

Jerome gazed directly at Henry. "We're telling you because we want to make sure he doesn't bother Noreen. But, maybe it would work for you to talk to him. It might bring him into the reality of his own situation."

Henry sat back. "I know where some of his old buddies used to hang out. I'll talk to them and see if I can get a meet up with him. Just maybe he'll still listen to me. You're right. It's worth a try."

They sat quietly and waited for the two women to return. During dinner, they talked about new cafes and shops which had opened downtown. Noreen shared the news several former neighbours had returned and had hired construction crews to clean up their places. Henry would have work on one of the reconstructions.

On the way back home, Jerome held Lara's hand.

"Henry will seek out Phillip and hopefully that will be the end of his tracking you and me."

Lara put her head of his shoulder.

"I sure hope so. I don't want to keep worrying about you while I wait at home every night. After they arrived home, both of them felt exhausted from the stress and they turned in early."

*   *   *

Hours later, Jerome jerked awake and sat up in bed. In the dim light, he glanced at the clock to find it was only 3 a.m. There. What was that noise? It came again. Loud crashes which sounded from somewhere near their backyard. Within minutes, Lara sat up as well.

"What's that noise? Could Phillip be after us again?"

Jerome swung his feet over the side of the bed and stood up to search his jeans for his cellphone.

"I better call the police, in case it is. You stay here."

He went out into the hall with the phone and crossed over to the spare room to check out the window.

After the dispatcher said the police would be on their way, he crossed the hall towards the bedroom. He could make out Lara's figure creeping slowly down the stairs, her back against the wall. What was she doing? Fear crept up the back of his neck and he moved towards her. He forced himself to stay quiet, in case the intruders heard them.

He was in the middle of the stairs when he heard her pull open the door onto the porch. Why was she putting herself in such danger? Whoever was down there wouldn't stop for a woman. When his feet hit the floor in the hallway, he heard a loud bang followed by yelling and more shots. There was no sound from Lara.

As he entered the porch in the darkness, Jerome grabbed his gun from the shelf where he'd hidden it and rushed outside. In the dim light, he could make out three men running away across the backyard. One shape was very familiar. The man turned and started towards him. He held his breath as anger seeped through him and then he pulled the trigger. The closest man fell while the other two ran away out of sight.

Jerome ran back to the porch and pulled on the light switch. A yellow glow flooded the inside porch as he made out a small figure lying on the floor in a pool of blood. His chest felt like it was pierced by a knife as he ran to Lara and cradled her in his arms.

"Please, please, open your eyes, my love." Her body remained limp but he felt a slight pulse at her neck.

Moments later, two policemen ran up the back stairs to join him. The first one felt Lara's pulse and turned to look out the door. "She's alive. The ambulance will be here soon."

Jerome clutched her to him. "But, there's so much blood."

He could make out a third policeman who knelt by the fallen man in the yard. When he joined them, he said, "I don't think that one will make it. He keeps saying he wants to talk to Jerome. Is that you?"

Jerome nodded and continued to hold Lara. "I don't know him and I'm not going anywhere. My wife needs me."

He stayed with her until the ambulance arrived and loaded Lara onto a stretcher. "Where are you taking her?"

"We've got to get her to the hospital. She's still losing blood."

The policeman from the yard yelled at him, "Look will you talk to the guy outside? Then I'll give you a ride to the hospital on my way back to the station. I have to wait for a second ambulance to arrive."

Jerome walked over to the stairs and slowly descended into the back yard towards the fallen man. Guilt overwhelmed him. He'd shot a man and that man was likely to die. He kneeled beside the man and pulled back in shock. It was Phillip. He'd shot Phillip. It was even worse than he'd expected.

Phillip rolled his head and opened his eyes as he stared right at Jerome. "Henry. I need to talk to Henry." His face turned even greyer and he lay still. "Tell Henry he's still my brother." His body became quite still.

The officer checked for a pulse. "I think it's too late for him." He stood up as the ambulance attendants arrived with their stretcher and loaded the man into the back. He gestured at Jerome. "Come with me and we'll leave for the hospital right away. You can come to give a statement tomorrow."

*   *   *

Jerome felt himself begin to drift off asleep where he sat on the hard vinyl couch outside Lara's room. He jerked awake when her stretcher returned from the operating room and followed her and the attendants into the room where she was placed in bed. After a short wait, the doctor joined them.

Jerome confronted him. "Tell me how she's doing? Will she be okay?"

The doctor looked him over. "Are you the spouse?"

When Jerome nodded, the doctor gestured for the two attendants to leave and pulled the curtains around the bed which enclosed them from the hallway. "We've been able to remove the bullet and stop the bleeding. She's a healthy young woman and should pull through with no long term effects. However, she needs lots of rest right now. I suggest you go home and come back tomorrow. If there are other relatives, let them know the same."

He decided to tell Henry and Noreen in person about what occurred and took the bus back to their house. He didn't want to scare them anymore than he had to. What should he do about Phillip? Should he tell Henry what Phillip said? Was it possible that Phillip was even alive?"

He called the police station while still on the bus. The policeman who'd given him a ride to the hospital had given him his card. He waited in suspense until the man answered.

"It's Jerome. Can you tell me about that guy they took in by ambulance?"

"You're asking about Phillip Decaries, I imagine. He didn't make it. But don't worry. It was obviously self-defence when he broke into your house and shot your wife. We'll all testify to that fact."

"Thanks. I hope you'll keep in touch. I need to know what's happening."

Jerome held his head in his hands. God. He'd actually killed a man. Phillip had become a criminal over the last few years, but he was someone Jerome had known. He shuddered.

When Henry opened the door, Jerome staggered through and headed for the easy chair in the living room. He fell into it and gave a deep sigh before he lifted his head to look at Noreen who'd joined Henry.

Noreen patted his hand. "What's going on, Jerome? Where's Lara? You look awful."

In jerking sentences, he told them what had occurred at their house during the early morning hours. They both looked relieved when he told them Lara would be okay and that they could visit her tomorrow. He stuttered over the next part.

"There's worse." He squeezed Noreen's hand. "I shot a man in our backyard." He stared at Henry. "It was Phillip and the cops told me he didn't make it." He dropped his head and stared at his hands. "Before he lost consciousness, Phillip asked me to tell you he still wants to be your brother."

Henry dropped to the seat across from Jerome, his eyes closed. After a few minutes, he shook his head and grabbed Jerome's hand. "Phillip's gone. I can't believe it. I always wanted to protect him as my younger brother. But, he'd been going downhill for a long time. No longer the young man I remembered." He sat up a small smile on his lips. "He could be so generous and such a comic when he was younger. He helped me out of bad spots so many times. "He dropped his hands to his sides.

Noreen moved to sit beside Henry and took his head into her arms. "There, it'll be alright. It was the drugs. He changed so we hardly recognized him. There wasn't anything we could do to change him back."

*   *   *

When Jerome walked into Lara's hospital room the next morning, she had her head propped up against two large pillows. Her grey face had more creases under the eyes, which were dull from medication. She tried to smile for him and reached out her arms.

"Give me a hug. I'm so glad you're okay."

He rushed over and took her into his arms as he kissed her on the lips. She tried to respond but winced in pain and pulled her arms across her chest before she dropped back against the pillows.

"I'm sorry, hon. I should remember you're not well yet."

She took a deep breath. "It felt good anyway. Did you find out what happened? Was it Phillip and his gang? I couldn't see much from the porch."

Jerome shook his head in the affirmative. "I'm so sorry you got injured. I should have made sure I was down there first. You're so brave."

Lara shook her head. "It wasn't the fault of either of us. Phillip lived in a different world and as family; we got caught up in it."

He took one hand in his. "I promise you'll never be at risk from anyone again. I've thought about this all night. We'll move back to Atlanta where you'll be safe as soon as you're better. Henry and Noreen will understand."

Lara shook her head against the pillow. "Phillip is gone now. He can't hurt us anymore. There's no need for us to move. New Orleans wasn't the threat after all."

Jerome smiled. "Whatever you want is good with me."

"I'm committed to building my career as a singer right here. I like my Director and the orchestra and I'm learning more every day. Pull the chair up to the bed and keep me company for a while before they take me away for more tests."

Jerome relaxed into the chair. In his own mind, he was relieved not to move on to somewhere new. He'd learned a good deal from Lewis and his career would develop more in time. He wanted to settle with Lara and he wanted to make New Orleans their home. He could relate to the other long-term New Orleans residents who'd moved back to the city from their evacuation spots. He wanted to join with them in their work on rebuilding the community, preserving the culture and uniqueness of this very special place. Over the past few months, it had become their home, his and Lara's. They'd raise their own family right here.

About the Author

New to fiction writing after a nineteen year career in government concentrating on non-fiction and business writing, I discovered a deep attraction to creating a range of new characters and following them on their journeys. As a writer, I'm very compelled by the ever evolving nature and abilities of humans to embrace change and build that into my stories.

This novel, *Differences Between Us,* is psychological suspense which combines drama with intricate relationships. A mixed race couple, Jerome and Lara, find love while surviving in a city which is still coping with a hurricane.

I have had a short story, *Canal of Destiny,* published in an online newspaper, *Quick Brown Fox,* in 2010. Other publications include articles published in The Globe and Mail and a number in community newspapers. I am a Board Member of the Canadian Authors Association and Past President of the Niagara Branch. I enjoy travelling, photography and gardening and treasure my previous years of downhill skiing.

Acknowledgements

Special thanks for my friends at the Fiction Guild Writers Group in Oakville, Ontario for the many hours of feedback and critique: especially Sheila Gale, Barbara Fraser Winter (Wood), Donna Kirk, Kimberley Scutt and Liz Hegge Bryant for their dedication and detailed critiques which helped to shape this novel in the early days.

I cannot forget all the support and encouragement I received from fellow members of the Niagara Branch of the Canadian Authors Association Fiction Writers Group. You are too numerous to mention each one by name, however, over the years Samantha Craggs provided clear advice and suggestions for improvements that were right on, Janice Barrett and Heather Sanders for their ability to pick up on tone, Chris Paxton who was a master on grammar and more recently Pamela Nomina who convinced me I had what it takes to be published and Sharon Frayne for her deep understanding of the craft of writing and what works.

Thanks to my husband, Ken Gansel who was supportive about my potential career as a writer right from the beginning. Ken suffered through many hours of missing me when I was glued to the computer in my home office. Thanks to my daughter, Sherry Meehan who was a reader for an earlier novel and has offered support to me over my career as a writer.

Thank you to my professional mentor, Brian Henry, of Quick Brown Fox online newsletter who taught me how to put a story together so it intrigues and entertains your readers.

To purchase your own copy go to:
www.amazon.com

For further information about the author, go to my website at:
www.newfictionwriter.com